Love, Rebooted

C. ROSE DAHL

"Well, is there an opening for me in your schedule?"

A tiny smile peeked through her otherwise stony
façade. She possessed beautiful lips, full and lush and
she'd painted them fire engine red. They were the type
of lips he'd like to kiss and continue kissing until she
was breathless.

"Yes. I'll stay. Just for a little while."

"Wonderful." He gestured toward an elevator that
would take them to the law firm's suite of offices on
the eighth floor. He and Jazmin waited patiently while
a large group disembarked. When it was their turn, he
allowed her to enter first. The black and white wedge
sneakers she wore lengthened her shapely legs and
drew his eyes to her round, perky butt. Micah closed
the heavy outer door, then pulled the metal gate
across. He pushed the button for the eighth floor and
the elevator groaned. It slowly lifted.

Alone together, the space felt intimate. Jazmin
watched the numbers overhead while Micah watched
her. Under his examination, her left foot started to tap.
The heat between them cracked and sizzled like wood
on a fire.

Dedicated to Liz & Crystal G, along with the many other friends, mentors, and coworkers who believed in Jazmin and Micah's story.

LOVE, REBOOTED

Chapter One

Droplets of cold water slid down the side of the frosted metal and onto Jazmin's fingers. She crossed the showroom with a champagne ice bucket pressed against her chest, her whole body aware of, and hypersensitive to, the drafty interior of the store. She shivered.

Jazmin had begun working at 5th Street Hosiery and Lingerie Boutique while attending Temple University as an undergraduate. Over the years, she'd done everything from restocking and assisting customers to measuring clients for costumes. Tonight, she'd agreed to host a private fitting for several dancers.

She breathed a sigh of relief when she reached the sideboard. She set the bucket on the mahogany tabletop and then shook her arms to stop their trembling.

Although she'd graduated two years ago, and had since started her own company, she didn't mind helping out. Victoria Fontenot was like a second mother.

"It's beautiful," Jazmin told her three-year-old cousin, Destiny, who waved her latest masterpiece in the air: a Monarch butterfly coloring sheet.

The pint-sized Picasso lay on a nearby Victorian era-inspired chaise. The little girl's burgundy corduroys blended in with the dated, floral print. On more than one occasion Jazmin had told Vicki, the owner of 5th Street Hosiery and Lingerie Boutique, she needed to retire the well-loved piece. Jazmin was met with one excuse and then another. The sofa was one of the few possessions Vicki had salvaged from her mother's New Orleans home and shipped to Philadelphia after Hurricane Katrina.

Jazmin wiped her hands on her slacks and removed several cloth napkins from the bottom drawer of the buffet server. She expertly folded the red and black fabric into rosebuds and then placed the blooms beside a bowl of chocolate-covered strawberries. Afterward, she turned to face her younger cousin.

"I need you to scoot to the back."

The little girl's face fell. "But—"

The bells above the front door jingled, cutting short Destiny's protest. A blast of cold air entered and rustled the window drapes at the same time it freed miniature Christmas ornaments from the front window's display. Vicki had dressed a mannequin in a ballgown made to look like an evergreen tree. The satin ribbon around the mannequin's waist danced in the breeze while bright-colored balls skittered over the hardwood and settled on the area rug at Jazmin's feet.

"Miss Brenda!" Destiny scrambled off the settee.

Two fluffy cotton candy puffs of hair bobbed up and down as the preschooler raced across the room.

Jazmin's best friend propped her suitcase against the wall and set her purse on top. She stooped, opening her arms.

"Hey, munchkin. How's my favorite girl?" Brenda asked. She hugged Destiny tightly before standing to her full height of six feet.

Brenda sashayed forward with the three-year-old clinging to one reedy leg. Though outside winter was settling in, and, as a result, the night's temperatures would reach the low thirties, Brenda wore peep-toe booties. Always the fashionista. She must've come straight from the airport after choreographing a show in Baltimore, or Boston, or Baton Rouge. These days Jazmin couldn't keep up with her best friend's traveling schedule. Jazmin glanced at the clock above the door. She hadn't expected Brenda to arrive until after Destiny's bedtime.

"Perfect timing. Some of your students are stopping by to try on costumes."

Brenda had started out as a dance instructor while still in college and many of her protégées continued to shop at the store.

"First, I need to get this princess to bed." Jazmin gave her little cousin what she hoped was a *no-nonsense, this is not up for debate*, look.

"Please, just a little longer?" Poking out her bottom lip, Destiny untangled herself from Brenda's leg. "Please?"

Jazmin counted down from five to herself and braced for a tantrum, knowing one would follow her refusal to bend. The terrible twos had been nothing compared to the six months Destiny had been a three-year-old.

Brenda winked at Jazmin and then dramatically announced, "I almost forgot"—she slapped her palm against her forehead— "I picked out some souvenirs just for you, Destiny."

Destiny followed Brenda who strolled to the store's entrance where her luggage rested against the wall. After rummaging through her oversized purse, she pulled out a large plastic shopping bag.

Destiny clapped her hands and hopped up and down. "What is it?"

Brenda produced a delicate straw handbag embroidered with the word "Bahamas." She also handed Destiny a paper fan with swirls of red lace painted along the edges. The handle bore the name of a cabaret. Destiny owned a fan from all Brenda's shows.

"Thank you!"

"You're welcome, sweet pea." Brenda tickled Destiny on her neck and behind her ear. "Why don't you head to the back office and put all your treasures inside your new pocketbook?"

As Destiny skipped across the showroom, her tiny fingers wandered over bustier ribbons, through crinoline tutus, and between feather boas. The sales area resembled more of a parlor than a store. Vintage French show bills and framed art prints decorated the walls. 5th Street Hosiery and Lingerie Boutique specialized in custom-made brassieres along with professional cabaret and burlesque costumes.

"Don't forget your backpack," Jazmin reminded her.

Destiny twirled. She fluttered the fan in front of her face like a Spanish flamenco dancer. The women smiled while they watched her put small toys and a few crayons into her glittery pink bookbag. Jazmin softly whispered her thanks to Brenda.

After Destiny disappeared, the two friends walked side-by-side to the main display case. Brenda was a good friend. Vicki also. The small village had proven helpful over the years after Jazmin's cousin, Destiny's mother, left town, leaving Jazmin to step in as the girl's guardian. Being a single parent hadn't been easy. Nevertheless, Jazmin was determined to make sure Destiny knew she was wanted, that her little cousin never again experienced the pain of a parent leaving and, as a result, taking their love with them. "I missed her," Brenda said, interrupting Jazmin's thoughts.

"She missed you too."

Jazmin's eyes mirrored the sisterly affection in Brenda's gaze. When they reached the display case, however, Jazmin smirked. She arched an eyebrow, challengingly.

"Don't think you're getting out of helping."

With her mouth agape, Brenda pointed a perfectly manicured finger at herself.

"Yes, *you*." Jazmin placed a gentle yet firm hand on her

friend's back and steered her around the counter. "Unpack the costumes and hang them. It's like riding a bike; it'll all come back to you."

Feigning astonishment, Brenda's eyes widened. "You must have me confused with a damn maid. I just got off a plane." Using a box cutter, she opened one of several large packages resting on the floor. "You wouldn't even be here if it wasn't for me, *Miss Thang*." Her voice laced with false indignation. She pointed the blade in Jazmin's direction.

"Yeah. Yeah. I know you're the reason Vicki hired me," Jazmin replied. A smile tugged at the corner of her lips.

Brenda followed orders but not without more grousing.

They'd both attended Temple University. They were computer science majors and even had freshman seminar together. Back then Brenda had gone by Brandon. One rainy Saturday afternoon during sophomore year,

Jazmin spotted her classmate leaving Miss Vicki's arm-in-arm with a drag queen who was a dead ringer for Cher. Brenda opened up more after that chance encounter. Jazmin had no idea she choreographed everything from children's dance recitals to drag performances all over Philadelphia. While probably more gifted at coding than Jazmin, Brenda preferred studying dance over technology. The decision was the first of many rifts between her and her traditional, Chinese-immigrant parents.

With Brenda left to her assignment, Jazmin made her way to the rear of the store. She scooped up the blue and white Christmas balls from the floor and stuffed them into her pockets. Pushing aside the velvet curtain that separated the storeroom from the sales area, she stepped out of sight only to return a few moments later with a pair of scissors and a bouquet of roses. She made quick work of disrobing the flowers from their delicate tissue paper covering. Careful not to prick herself, she sheared off the tops. The blush pink and wine-red rosebuds added an elegant touch.

Without warning, Brenda's shrill, cat-call whistle sliced through the quiet. "Girl! Girl!"

Jazmin spun around.

"Sorry about screaming but when did you order this?" Brenda reached over the counter and grabbed a black brocade leather faux corset with a sweetheart neckline. Zigzag leather straps crisscrossed the front while chain metal draped along the side.

Jazmin's eyes flashed with humor. "Who said that's mine?" A tiny grin peeked out from behind the innocent mask she wore.

"D'ya think I don't know you after all these years?" Lifting a bustier from the box, Brenda angled her head. "This peacock feather satin one is clearly for a burlesque magic show or a raunchy parody of Swan Lake." She went through the contents of the other boxes before stopping at the last. "Don't get me started on this basic pink and black lace corset dress. It looks like it fell off the proverbial Moulin Rouge truck."

Jazmin laughed. "Enough. Sasha, Phoebe, and June will be here any minute. Go. Put the closed sign on the door and then help me hang everything."

"No. No. No." Brenda pinned Jazmin with a *no-nonsense* look of her own. "You've got to try this on." "You're kidding? We don't have—"

"You can waste more time arguing and still put it on, or you can just humor me."

Their silent standoff lasted less than a minute before Jazmin's shoulders dropped. Defeated, she took the outfit from her friend's outstretched hand. "Fine."

"You won't need knee-highs or garters because I know you've got on a pair of black, granny stockings underneath those librarian slacks," Brenda teased.

Jazmin mumbled irritably as she walked behind a dressing screen. She had given up a lot of her humdrum habits over the years, but her cold weather survival skills were not among them. Unlike Brenda, Jazmin was from the Midwest. Her mother had raised her to be prepared in case she wound up stranded out in the open during a blizzard. As Jazmin kicked off her brown work flats and shimmied out of her trousers, the first notes of "Lady Marmalade" played.

"Seriously?" Jazmin shouted while pulling her sweater over her head.

"It seemed fitting," Brenda fired back. She had played this song in college whenever they got ready for a girls' night out.

Jazmin stepped from behind the screen and reluctantly turned in a circle. "Happy?"

The two women made an awkward pair. Brenda dwarfed Jazmin's five feet five inches and was as thin as a rail. Jazmin, on the other hand, had a slight pooch belly and plenty of butt and boobs for them both.

"Bitch, you look fierce! Oh, do the dance I taught you." "No way."

Brenda set her phone on the countertop, amplifying the song. She tugged off her suede stiletto boots and hurried to Jazmin's side.

Bumping her lightly with her hip, Brenda said, "I'll do it with you."

No longer able to hide her amusement, Jazmin's smile expanded. "Let's get this over with." She twisted her neck from side to side to loosen the muscles.

As horns trumpeted, the friends sauntered forward on the balls of their feet. Brenda mussed her neat bob while Jazmin rubbed her palms along the sides of her auburn, afro mohawk. When the song reached its crescendo, they spread their knees apart with their hands at the same time they lowered to a seated, squat position. Jazmin and Brenda wiggled their hips in a circular motion while they mouthed the French lyrics.

Jazmin giggled. Her barely contained breasts bounced up and down. She was having fun despite her earlier objections.

"Excuse me," a baritone voice cut through the noise.

A man stepped from behind the waist-trainers and corsets with removable snap skirts. Jazmin lost her balance and fell on her ass. Brenda, meanwhile, darted toward the display counter to shut off the commotion coming from her phone. The man seemed just as shocked to see them as they were to see him because he tripped over an open steamer trunk stuffed with cheap bachelorette and Halloween costumes. Covering her body, Jazmin scrambled to her feet and ran behind the dressing screen.

"We're closed!" she hollered once out of sight. Her fingers fumbled over the hook and eye clasps on the back of the corset. She peeked around the barrier in time to witness the stranger's full lips curve into a smile.

Chapter Two

Holy shit!

The image of the beautiful woman and her round ass in a pair of cheeky panties replayed in Micah's mind. He blinked unable to tear his eyes away from the dressing screen she'd ducked behind. He wanted to make sure he hadn't imagined her. Bound in leather. Shimmying and wiggling her hips. A crescent moon-shaped birthmark on her inner right thigh. Earlier, when he'd agreed to drop off contract papers on his way home from the office, he had thought the errand would be routine. Instead, he stepped into the shop and interrupted a pair of barely-dressed employees twisting and shaking to "Lady Marmalade." He'd stumbled. Hell, his breath had literally been taken away and a bruise on his shin the size of a golf ball could attest to it.

Micah gazed down at the contents spilling out of the overturned trunk laying open at his feet. Tacky Mardi Gras necklaces with miniature plastic penises in place of beads glittered on the floor, the only sign of the provocative show that had just ended.

"Can I help you, Hunny?" the saleswoman behind the counter asked.

Reluctantly, his gaze shifted. He didn't want to miss seeing the petite dark-skinned beauty with the killer curves if she chose to come out of hiding.

"Excuse me?" Micah replied, trying to focus.

"Looking for a Christmas gift or an anniversary present?" she asked, more persistent.

"No... is Victoria Fontenot available? I'm from Stein, Martin, Randolph and Associates?"

The woman's eyes narrowed. Her heavy mascara and eyeliner made her pinched face appear even thinner. Perhaps, she was the store owner's daughter or niece. Micah hadn't worked on Victoria Fontenot's paperwork and, accordingly, didn't know much other than Fontenot planned to franchise her business, first in South Jersey and then Baltimore.

"I have some contracts for her to sign."

Seconds dragged by and still the young woman's unpleasant expression remained. Micah chuckled to himself. She couldn't be more than twenty-four or twenty-five. She had no idea that he wasn't easily intimidated. He'd endured worse appraisals from bailiffs, judges, and even fellow attorneys. At last, her face finally relaxed, and Micah's gaze followed hers as she looked past him. The alluring leather-clad dancer emerged from behind the dressing screen.

She wore pants and a sweater with a starched white collar underneath; she crossed the room with her hand outstretched. As Micah strolled forward to meet her, he caught the subtle floral notes of her perfume. His nostrils flared. Although she'd changed out of her sexy lingerie, he still found her mesmerizing.She wore her hair in a short, tapered afro. The Grace Jones-esque haircut suited her. She wasn't tall like her coworker, or as slim. Even so, Micah knew there were luscious curves beneath the frumpy sweater and baggy pants. Their hands connected and he instantly felt a jolt. They locked gazes and his heartrate quickened. The woman snatched her hand away. Not wanting to come across like some Lothario, Micah fixed his face. His traitorous body, however, continued to respond as if it had a mind of its own. He would have to start reciting professional basketball players' stats in his head if things continued. Anything to calm down his growing desire that currently pressed against the front of his pants.

"I can take those papers. Ms. Fontenot is gone for the day," the woman said, not quite looking him in the eyes.

"Micah Clarion. Nice to meet you..." His eyes lowered to her name tag. "Jazmin."

"You too." She inclined her head toward her statuesque co-worker who nodded curtly. "You already met Brenda."

"Pleased to meet you," he said to Brenda who was still looking him up and down. Unbothered, Micah returned his attention to Jazmin. "Sorry to intrude earlier. I did call out
when I entered."

Though she waved off his words, Micah noticed she made sure not to touch him again when he handed her the paperwork.

"Well, if that's all"— she gestured toward the door — "we have a private fitting this evening."

Micah moistened his lips. He hated the next question he had to ask.

What he really wanted was to ask her out on a date, not grill her about the tech entrepreneur who had revamped the store's website, driving a record-breaking number of new customers to the lingerie boutique. Another win for the mysterious Tech Philly—and Micah's promotion at work depended on him tracking down that company's elusive creator. He'd promised his father and bosses that he could convince the city's hottest digital brand whisperer to take on their law firm as a client—and the senior partners, Stein, Martin, and Randolph desperately needed an image makeover, especially since the rise of the #MeToo Movement. Several former employees' grievances had gained traction on Twitter and, although the firm settled out of court, the reputation damage was considerable.

Not for the first time, Micah questioned his dad's insistence that working for a top dog firm would ultimately benefit Micah in the long run. Micah hoped Jazmin didn't take his inquiry the wrong way or, worse, lump him into the same category as his employers. He really needed this lead to pan out. Tracking down Tech Philly's designer was proving to be a trickier proposition than he'd imagined.

Luckily, his cell phone beeped, delaying the request he'd rehearsed on the way over.

"Excuse me for a moment."

He pivoted slightly and then removed his cell from his inside coat pocket. It was his ex-girlfriend checking in to find out whether or not he'd left the office. This evening, he'd made plans to have dinner with her. A sigh of exasperation escaped Micah's lips as he thumbed a reply. When he turned around both saleswomen's heads swiveled. He'd picked up on their silent exchange. He had even noticed Jazmin's head shake slightly in response to whatever comment her friend had mouthed behind him.

"One more thing..." Micah toyed with the gold sports ring on his right hand. "You may or may not be familiar with Tech Philly. It's a fairly new company. My firm has tried to get in contact with the start-up's creator but hasn't had much luck."

While both women tried to keep their expressions neutral, the lawyer in Micah was certain they'd at least heard of Tech Philly.

"I read somewhere that the company worked on Ms. Fontenot's website."

Silence settled around them. After a few beats Brenda broke ranks. "Go on," she encouraged. She no longer stared at Micah as if her eyes could burrow a hole in the side of his head.

"My firm's senior partners would love it if Ms. Fontenot could put in a good word. Maybe she'd be willing to share J.J.'s contact information with us. A cell number?"

"I'll talk to Vicki," Jazmin blurted out. She gestured toward the door.

Micah's stomach dropped. She'd dismissed him again. He turned to go but, despite her blunt words, he wanted to ask her if she'd like to grab coffee sometime. Instead, he turned back and blathered about his job.

"My firm needs an updated website. I don't even think we have a social media presence."

He chuckled uncomfortably. His laughter bounced off the walls and sounded forced even to his ears. He cleared his throat. What was going on? He wasn't usually this nervous or tongue-tied around women. His gaze skimmed over Jazmin. She was beautiful. And he heard a soft hum just before her eyes fled from his. Had she really moaned? The idea that she might feel the same instant chemistry as he did made Micah want to beat his fists against his chest.

"Ta-dah!"

A little girl materialized from behind velvet theater curtains that Micah could only assume concealed the store's "employees only" section. The girl's big brown eyes twinkled. She spun in a circle with her arms out-stretched and then dropped to one knee. She finished the impromptu performance with one hand on her bouncing hip, the other hand in the air, and a trium-phant smile. Her lips and part of her chin were stained with red lipstick.

Brenda dashed around the counter. "I got her." She scooped the child into her toned arms and carried the little girl back behind the room's makeshift dividing wall.

Jazmin's brown skin tinted an embarrassing dark rosé. "I'll walk you out, Mr. Clarion."

"Please, call me Micah."

She offered him a tight-lipped smile. He admired how she straightened her spine and marched forward professionally. He glanced at the lacy bras and match-ing panties on the shelving behind the main counter, by far the most tasteful display in the store. 5th Street Hosiery and Lingerie Boutique was no place for a child.

What kind of example is she setting?

He looked over his shoulder. The velvet curtains still swayed. It was apparent the child had gotten into Jazmin's purse and makeup.

Maybe she couldn't find a sitter and had no other choice.

Micah's feet dragged as he and Jazmin neared the store's entrance. "That little one's got a lot of spunk."

"You've no idea," she replied.

They stopped. She rotated her shoulders and tilted her neck from side to side. If she were his woman, he'd knead the tension from her body each evening.

"She has good taste in lipstick. Fire engine red?"

A glimmer of mirth shined in Jazmin's eyes. She'd painted her lips the same color. Her small response set fireworks off in Micah's chest. She had let her guard down a little. In view of that, he made sure to keep his expression casual. The task was difficult. He removed his business card from his wallet and handed it to her. Arousal, like goose flesh, spread up his arm, making the hairs stand on end.

Beneath Jazmin's long lashes he saw a desire that mirrored his own. Once more, he felt a caveman-like urge. Part of him wanted to throw her over his shoulder and carry her out into the night.

"All of my contact information is there, work, cell, and email. If Ms. Fontenot has any questions please have her contact me," he said evenly.

He imagined taking Jazmin back to his condo. There, he'd indulge her every wish. He opened his mouth to speak but quickly closed it when the bells above the front door jingled. An icy bluster accompanied three young women into the store. The chilled night air whipped against Micah's face. He backed away from Jazmin like a teenager caught making out under a porchlight, abandoning whatever thoughts he had about pursuing her as a potential partner for a one-night stand.

He glanced around and again scanned the storeroom. His eyes caught a wall display to his right dedicated to pasties. There was also the fishnet bodysuit on the mannequin across the room. Micah was certain he'd never seen that kind of thing being worn by anyone other than an exotic dancer. He remembered his first look at Jazmin, how her large breasts had spilled over her corseted top while she danced and sang about taking a lover to bed. His lips pressed together, forming a thin line. He nodded in her direction and then squeezed by the ladies who stomped slush from the soles of their thigh-high boots. Beneath their short faux-fur puffer jackets, they wore bandage dresses, one of them featuring cutouts at the waist.

Outside, Micah joined the bustling flow of pedestrian traffic. He stuffed his hands in his pockets. He headed toward the Bank and Bourbon Restaurant on Market Street. He hoped the dinner date with his ex-girlfriend ended quickly. His head was a jumble of emotions, and he couldn't get images of the dark-skinned salesclerk dressed in leather and lace out of his head. A twinge of something Micah couldn't quite put a name to had sparked between them before it quickly flickered and died. He was sure her friend had picked up on it, also. He raked a hand over his face. He'd known guys who'd fallen for strippers, but he'd never thought he would one day count himself among them.

Chapter Three

Temptation.

As far as Jazmin was concerned, Micah Clarion was sexy as sin and far too tempting. He wore a professional haircut, a short Caesar, which showed off natural waves. His neatly trimmed moustache and goatee added a rugged and dangerous quality to his appearance. Jazmin could tell Brenda's former students were attracted to him, also Forgetting all about the private fitting that brought them into the shop, they had giggled loudly and flipped their hair. Jazmin envied their lithe bodies, complete with long muscular legs and flat stomachs. Their actions reminded her of the leading ladies in the romantic comedies she liked to watch. Yet, Micah had ignored them, even Sasha who had bent at the waist while she removed her boots, effectively putting her derrière in his path. Of course, Jazmin's inner voice had cheered at Micah's disinterest.

Once the door banged shut behind him, her excitement deflated. He was one of the good guys. If only she'd met him under different circumstances. Usually, she wasn't attracted to serious business types. Nonetheless, her nerve endings had sparked to life when their hands connected. The electricity, like pinpricks when a sleeping foot awakens, had traveled up her spine and settled at the points of her breasts. Shocked and confused by her body's reaction, she had instinctively pulled her hand away. As she looked up to meet his gaze, a hint of surprise flickered then disappeared so quickly that Jazmin questioned whether she'd seen anything at all. She made sure not to touch him again when he handed her Vicki's paperwork. In fact, now that she thought about it, she couldn't remember the last time she'd had sex. Maybe that's why her body was behaving like a horny teenager's.

She could still smell his cologne. The scent of spice and cedarwood lingered in the doorway. Staring at the empty space he'd occupied, Jazmin rolled his business card over her fingers. Geesh, she really needed to pull herself together. She'd been lusting after someone who probably wore a suit and tie daily. Also, by the creases at the corners of his eyes, he was six or seven years her senior. She rarely dated older men because the ones she'd met were looking for long-term commitments, and she didn't do relationships.

The velvet curtains rustled behind her. She held her breath, expecting to see a preschooler run out. Instead, Brenda strutted forward like a model on a Paris runway during fashion week. Sasha, Phoebe, and June shrieked with delight and bounded in her direction. They peppered her with questions. They didn't bother to take turns or wait for a complete answer.

"When did you get here?" Phoebe asked.

"Why didn't you call and let one of us know you were coming?" Sasha's gesturing hands emphasized each word. Her blonde ponytail flopped back and forth.

"You cut your hair!" June cried out.

Not wanting to be a part of the reunion and needing to check on Destiny, Jazmin maneuvered around them. Brenda lightly took hold of her arm as she passed.

"Destiny's sleeping. I cleaned her up and laid her down in Vicki's office," she whispered in Jazmin's ear.

"Thank you."

Jazmin massaged her neck. She was exhausted. She'd worked all day before coming to the store. Brenda patted Jazmin on the shoulder and then returned her attention to her friends. Jazmin, on the other hand, excused herself. The last of the costumes needed to be hung and steamed. In truth, she was jealous of her best friend. Brenda talked about her latest show in the Bahamas and how much fun she and the cast had on their days off. They'd gambled at Atlantis Hotel and Casino on Paradise Island, stuffed their bellies with fried red snapper and plantains, shopped on Bay Street, and napped in the sun on the beach. Jazmin couldn't remember the last time she'd taken a solo vacation.

Occasionally, she'd leave Destiny with Vicki if she had to travel for work; but, even then, she'd only stay away for one night, and definitely no more than a weekend.

She kept busy sorting the costumes and accessories and hanging them on the rolling garment rack. Next, she broke down the cardboard boxes, emptied the trash, and wiped off the counter and the display case. Twice. She was out of things to do, out of tasks that justified her antisocial behavior. Taking a steadying breath, Jazmin rejoined the small gathering. She smiled politely and encouraged the women to sample the chocolate-covered strawberries and other hors d'oeuvres she'd laid out. Brenda also shooed Sasha, Phoebe, and June toward the small buffet of food and drinks.

"Did he ask for your number?" Brenda asked as soon as the others were out of earshot.

"No. He gave me his card, but I don't plan on calling him."

Brenda put a hand on her hip like a disapproving schoolteacher.

"What?" Jazmin asked.

"Did you see the way that man was checking you out?

"Of course, he was. I barely had any clothes on."

Brenda tsked. "Later too, after you got dressed. And I know you were getting all hot and bothered. Don't try denying it."

"I'm not saying I wasn't."

It had been a long time since Jazmin had been attracted to a man from the onset. To think, this one had practically seen her nude. If she could turn back time and erase the embarrassing dance performance, she would.

"I'm too busy with work to date right now," she added.

"Who said anything about dating. It's overrated. Getting some D..." Brenda's voice trailed off at the same time Jazmin raised her hand, signaling stop.

"He's not my type."

Brenda sucked her teeth. "You mean he's not a bad boy and doesn't still have Similac on his breath?"

Jazmin shook her head and expelled a snorty chuckle. "His shirt was wrinkle-free, and, at eight o'clock at night, his slacks still had a starched crease. He may not be a senior citizen, but he's way too uptight."

"She wouldn't know what to do with all that milk chocolate," Sasha said, strolling over. She handed Brenda a champagne flute. "It melts in your mouth and in your hand."

Brenda covered her mouth, but she wasn't quick enough to stop the laughs that escaped. She playfully swatted at Sasha, hitting her lightly on the shoulder. The sweet floral notes of the champagne tickled Jazmin's nose.

Sasha turned her attention to Jazmin and smiled falsely. "Did you want some? I figured you were on the clock." She shrugged her shoulders as if that were explanation enough.

Without another word, she turned and rejoined the other dancers. They didn't bother muffling their giggles as they gossiped about what Sasha had obviously overheard. Jazmin ignored the women. She and Sasha had never gotten along. Although one of Brenda's more talented dancers, Sasha had a competitive streak a mile wide and was always trying to one-up someone.

"Sounds to me like you're making excuses," Brenda told Jazmin. She took another sip of the bubbly, amber-colored liquid. "Even if you're right about him being uptight, that doesn't explain why you didn't tell him Tech Philly is your company or that you're J.J."

"I'm not in the market for new clients," Jazmin said. "Plus, it's a bad idea to mix business with pleasure." Especially based on the intensity of her and Micah Clarion's attraction toward each other.

Jazmin puffed out an exasperated breath and then motioned to the back room where Destiny slept. The little girl wasn't her biological daughter, but Jazmin had assumed responsibility for her cousin Cicely's baby before the child could walk. She and Cicely were more like sisters than cousins. When they were in high school, Cicely's mom lost her battle with breast cancer and the girls vowed to always be there for each other. No matter what. So, Jazmin stepped in when Cicely flunked out of college her senior year, more concerned with getting her singing career off the ground than going to class or being a mother. Cicely thought it was more profitable to make "money moves," her term for hanging out all night with wannabe producers and rappers, drinking and getting high.

"You know the situation," Jazmin said to Brenda. "If I want to start the process of officially adopting Destiny, I need to focus on presenting myself as a stable single parent to the adoption agency, not a twenty-four-year-old whose priorities can be put on hold because a hot guy crossed my path."

Especially one whose eyes are deep mahogany with flecks of gold.

Jazmin frowned, her annoyance at her traitorous thoughts growing by the second.

Chapter Four

Micah could kick himself for not asking Jazmin for her phone number. He had been instantly attracted to her. Excitement had filled his chest like nervous jitters just before a big game, as if he were squaring up against an opponent at center court and waiting for the referee's whistle to blow for tip-off.

"And then the girl just fell off the runway," his ex-girlfriend said, swirling the olive in her martini.

Micah stared blankly. Eleanor Deerfield sat across from him in the fancy hotel restaurant. She babbled on about attending a couture fashion trade show last week in New York City. He'd dated the debutante for two years. Tonight, he was reminded why their relationship would never have lasted. She was pretentious at her best. At her worst, she was rude and bossy. A lot of the women Micah had dated over the years were only interested in having him on their arms at social gatherings. Eleanor was just like the others, parading him around a room like a prized pooch at the Westminster Kennel Club Dog Show.

While he believed he'd eventually settle down and have a happy marriage like the one his parents shared, he wasn't in a hurry to enter matrimony. Eleanor hadn't taken him at his word. She was on the hunt for a husband and had insisted Micah take their relationship to the next level. She'd called him ugly names when he'd ended their association and she'd even managed to conjure up a few tears. Since the night of their breakup, they'd run into each other occasionally. He was always polite but kept his distance. She could be hot-tempered. Her fiery personality was something that had fueled their sex life. Still, the spark had faded and soon her antics had grated on Micah's nerves.

This was the first time Eleanor had captured Micah alone. Earlier in the day, she'd called to invite him to dinner under the pretense of business. Something to do with her family's foundation. The waiter was due to return shortly with dessert, but Eleanor had yet to reveal any details regarding their need to meet. Micah didn't like manipulative women. He drained his whiskey and raised a finger to stop her jabbering.

Bristling, Eleanor pursed her painted lips in a pout. She wore a tailored, white tuxedo suit with a blue rhinestone corset that drew attention to her breasts. Her hair flowed in loose waves to her shoulders. Although she'd modeled when she was younger, Micah recognized she couldn't hold a candle to Jazmin who, in addition to possessing natural beauty and setting his pulse racing, seemed fun. Hell, she'd been lip-syncing to "Lady Marmalade" when he'd entered the store.

Micah outlined his mouth with his forefinger and thumb. Frowning with agitation, he was reminded just how long it had been since he shared a fun, easy-going relationship with a woman.

"Why am I here, Eleanor?""Always business. You haven't changed."— Her fingers tightened around the stem of her glass— "Deerfield Foundation has nominated Tech Philly as this year's Millennial Titan recipient." She batted her eyes demurely.

That look had worked on him in the past, especially during disagreements. She had played the role of femme fatale well. Seeing her embody the trope now, however, raised Micah's suspicions.

She continued, "Daddy and Nathaniel Stein have a standing tee time at the club. Daddy is pushing hard for you to make junior partner. He always liked you."

Micah was happy to hear he hadn't lost favor with the old tycoon after the fiasco that became of his relationship with the man's daughter. The last thing he wanted or needed was to piss off her dad who was known for his Midas touch. It was common knowledge that any company or individual Daniel Deerfield vouched for would ultimately go the distance and make those who had the foresight to get onboard at the ground level very wealthy.

Curious as to how many more meals he would have to endure with Eleanor seated across from him, Micah asked, "I take it Stein mentioned that I have to track down the tech guru and convince her to take on the firm as a client to be considered for the promotion?"

He was more than a little irritated that his bosses thought they could pull his strings. Although he was not as irritated with them as he was at his father, who was always telling Micah to show more initiative. His dad often bragged about the high-profile cases his older brother Paul had landed. Just once, Micah would like to move out of his brother's shadow and for his dad to stop comparing his two lawyer sons.

"Let's talk about us." Eleanor drained the rest of her martini.

They were interrupted by the arrival of dessert. Eleanor tossed her napkin on the table when Micah asked for the check at the same time he handed the waiter his credit card.

"Micah!"

Thankfully, there weren't many guests dining in the restaurant, just an elderly couple who'd been seated across the room. There were no eyes or ears to witness Eleanor's performance.

Micah wasn't fooled by her show of outrage. She'd selected the Bank and Bourbon Restaurant in the prestigious Loews Hotel because they'd dined there several times while dating. Originally a savings bank and the country's first skyscraper, the upscale hotel, located in the heart of the city, was just a short walk from the historic Liberty Bell. Micah knew Eleanor had an ulterior motive, specifically to bed him in one of the suites upstairs. At his continued silence, her brow creased, and her nose scrunched. She looked thoroughly put out by his disinterest. Still, he had no intentions of giving in to her tricks. Micah forked a piece of six-layer German chocolate cake. The coconut and pecan bourbon sauce tasted delicious. He sighed with pleasure. Eleanor, on the other hand, shot daggers across the table at him from beneath long faux lashes.

"Please. Spare me the dramatics. There is no us, Ellie. I will not sit here and debate fiction."

The only indication his words had gotten under her skin was the sound of her acrylic nails tapping against the glass tabletop.

"J.J. is elusive but also Black. That's why Stein and Martin put you on her trail. As far as I know, she's not a part of any committees, sororities, or organizations. I thought you'd like to be my date to the gala." Eleanor smiled sweetly. "Daddy can introduce you."

Dammit!

It seemed that everyone else was better suited to plan his life. He'd run into another dead end this evening. He'd been certain that someone at the lingerie sex shop would have information on J.J. since the store had hired her to upgrade their website. An old email address. A cell number. Victoria Fontenot had been one of J.J.'s first customers. Micah sipped his drink. Maybe too much time had passed. The store's website had been redone almost two years ago, after all.

"I'll escort you to the gala," Micah told Eleanor. His left eye twitched involuntarily. He pushed aside the glass containing the last of his drink and sipped his ice water, hoping to extinguish his rising anger. "That's all."

He took another bite of cake and then immediately decided he'd have to put in some time at the gym after tonight's meal. The Loews never disappointed. Yet another reason Eleanor had suggested they eat at the hotel restaurant. She was fully aware of his sweet tooth. "Why don't we go upstairs and discuss?" she asked.

"No."

When Micah offered no further response she stood, though not before pausing to gauge his reaction. He continued to eat.

"Good night!"

Eleanor released an unladylike noise that sounded an awful lot like a snort. She snatched her purse off the table and rushed from the room. He could hear her all the way from the lobby, demanding that someone call her a cab.

Micah set down his fork. His mother had read him the riot act after she learned about his and Eleanor's breakup. She couldn't understand how he could walk away from someone so beautiful. Micah was certain his mother would never speak to him again if he brought Jazmin home. The salesclerk represented everything in a partner his mother didn't like. She wasn't a debutante and definitely didn't come from the right family or background if she worked in a boutique lingerie store. None of that crap mattered to Micah, though. He dated women of all races and ethnicities and from all walks of life. He had never brought one home, however. A fact that weighed on his conscience tonight.

The waiter brought the check and Micah signed his name glad to be rid of his ex-girlfriend and to have the sham of a date over with. He exited the hotel onto Market Street and headed in the direction of the Delaware River. Ahead stood the Ben Franklin Bridge. It connected Philadelphia, Pennsylvania to Camden, New Jersey. He loved Philly at night. Several throughways and buildings, including City Hall, the Cira Center across from 30th Street Train Station, and the Loews Hotel, were often draped in colorful neon lights. The bright colors always made him feel as if the city was pulsating. At Eleventh Street, Micah decided to head south, too wound up to go home.

He dialed his longtime friend, Adam Goldberg but disconnected the call when it went directly to voicemail. They had graduated Temple Law together. Adam had asked Micah to think about leaving Stein, Martin, Randolph and Associates so they could start their own firm. Both men were more driven by helping the community than by contract law. Micah knew exactly how the idea would go over with his father. George Clarion envisioned his son making partner by thirty-five and Micah stepping out on his own was not part of the plan.

His brothers were successful in their respective fields and a promotion would help Micah get closer to the figures they brought in. If he made junior partner perhaps, between puffs from smoking a celebratory cigar, his father would say, "Good job. I'm proud of you, son." The last time Micah heard his dad utter those words he and his friends had won the under ten, division three-on-three Gus Macker basketball tournament. That was over twenty years ago.

Micah turned up the collar of his coat. The temperature had dropped since he left the office. Smells of hot grease and fried onions now filled the air. A line wrapped around the corner of 4th Street. Although it was well after dinner time, people waited outside Jim's for cheesesteaks. Micah looked in the big front window as he passed by. Autographed celebrity photos and news articles decorated the walls. The cooks chatted up customers and boisterously poked fun at out-of-towners. He continued walking. He saw Ishkabibble's to the left and chuckled softly. While in law school, he and Adam had often traveled to the South Street eatery. They'd purchased chicken cheesesteaks and Gremlins from the takeout window. The grape and lemonade drink contained more than enough sugar to propel them through endless hours of mock trial preparation. It was better than any energy drink on the market. Under its influence, they'd thought up their best defenses.

Micah's mind drifted back to the uneasy feeling he got when discussing Tech Philly with the sales associates at 5th Street Hosiery and Lingerie Boutique. His gut told him the store was still a good lead. He believed Jazmin definitely knew more than she'd let on. Maybe he'd lean on her a little. He'd dealt with skittish and close-mouthed witnesses before. Charming Jazmin was a far better plan than relying on a favor from his meddlesome ex-girlfriend. He'd possibly get one step closer to J.J., and maybe he and Jazmin could explore each other physically.

Cheering erupted behind Micah. Glancing over his shoulder, he noticed a party in full swing down the block. An upper deck bar provided a lively soundtrack for Micah and others who'd decided to bear the cold. He laughed out loud when he heard a rowdy group of women sing the familiar Patti Labelle refrain. As the lyrics stated, Micah welcomed Jazmin creeping into his dreams. He would touch her mocha chocolate skin, silky and smooth. In his mind, he could see their bodies intertwined between satin sheets. Hell, if given a chance, yes, he'd give Jazmin a go. They'd fuck until her savage beast cried, "More. More. More!"

Running his fingers over his hair, Micah wondered if he had indeed drunk too much Magnolia wine. Or in his case, bourbon.

Chapter Five

Jazmin's cell phone buzzed. Pulling the device from her back pocket, she saw she'd received a message from Ms. Vicki. A package had arrived for her at the store. Jazmin rubbed her eyes. She'd spent over three hours entering code last night after Destiny fell asleep. At least, she'd tried to. Micah Clarion had snuck his way into her thoughts while she had worked, and, as a result, she'd been left sexually frustrated for the second night in a row.

She'd pictured him whispering naughty promises in her ear. Felt the heat of his breath on her neck along with the touch of his fingers between her thighs. She shuddered from the imaginary contact. Shaking her head from side to side, she attempted to loosen the pull of her imagination. She also hoped to quiet Brenda's nagging voice in her head.

"So, why didn't you tell him you're J.J.?"

Of course, her best friend hadn't seen a problem, not even after Jazmin explained Micah probably thought she was a stripper. She'd left little to the imagination dancing the way she'd been dancing while dressed in a corset. Plus, how would it look? Jazmin Johnson, half-naked CEO.

The fragrant smell of fabric softener filled Jazmin's nose as she plucked a sweatshirt from a nearby hamper and brought it to her face. She hadn't gotten around to putting away the clean clothes. The sweatshirt, with its collar cut at an impractical angle to show off one bare shoulder and unable to ward off a chill from the softest whistle of wind due to its thinness, was her favorite keepsake. Its faded letters spelled out Mackinaw Island. She along with her mother, older sister, and cousin, Cicely, had vacationed there the summer before she'd left for college. Jazmin sighed. That was the last time they'd all been together.

Having already dropped Destiny off at preschool, Jazmin walked the short distance to 5th Street rather than look for a parking spot in front of Vicki's boutique. Crowds of people were already bunched up at intersections even though it was only a little after nine in the morning. Traffic horns blared as angry drivers bullied pedestrians, urging them to walk faster. She scratched at the peeling temporary tattoo of *The Hungry Caterpillar* on her wrist. Destiny had put it on her last night after she'd read the picture book for the one-hundredth time.

Jazmin pulled the halves of her leather jacket together. Her fingers nimbly pushed the buttons into their holes. Though the sun was shining, there was still a chill in the air. She ignored her reflection in the foggy, dew-covered store windows she passed by. Her face was clean but free of makeup. Fifteen minutes later, she arrived at 5th Street Hosiery and Lingerie Boutique and found Vicki in her office.

"You've got to stop getting your mail delivered to the store," Vicki fussed. "A certified letter came this morning."

Standing behind her, Jazmin wrapped her arms around the older woman's neck. She ignored Vicki's chastising tone.

"Morning," she cooed while smoothing down the riotous flyaway hairs on Vicki's wig. Vicki's sweet-smelling floral perfume was soothing in its familiarity. Jazmin's mother also wore Chanel No 5.

"Alright, enough already. It's on the settee." Vicki sipped her coffee, black, no cream, a little sugar.

She was pricklier than usual this morning. Pops, Jazmin's neighbor and the self-appointed block captain of La Avenida, probably had ended their date early last night when Vicki rebuffed his marriage proposal. Again. The two seventy-somethings were sweet on each other and had been from the moment they were introduced. Whenever Jazmin commented on Vicki getting married, the older woman always said the same thing.

"I've been down that road and I don't care to go back. I'm too old to be saddled."

Jazmin left the office so as not to be on the receiving end of Vicki's ire. She had no idea who sent the letter, but curiosity had her tearing open the envelope. Her jaw dropped as she read.

We're pleased to inform you that your company, Tech Philly, has won New Business of the Year for its innovative achievements and commitment to the Philadelphia community.

Deerfield Foundation would present her with The Millennial Titan Award at a New Year's Eve gala in four weeks. Jazmin skimmed through the names of past winners. All were major players in the Philadelphia business world.

Plopping down on the settee, she covered her mouth with one trembling hand and continued reading. The winner received two hundred and fifty thousand dollars. It wasn't nearly the dividends Jobs or Gates saw when they'd started out, but to Jazmin two hundred and fifty thousand dollars was life-changing money. She and Destiny could live comfortably without worrying how'd they'd survive if her client pool dried up. In the world of internet start-ups, it didn't matter how successful Tech Philly was now. Her company could fade away overnight. She had to constantly reinvent herself and cell phone apps were her lifeblood and her failsafe. At present, they paid for little luxuries like Destiny's gymnastic classes and maintenance on Jazmin's car. She dreaded the day she would have to sell her baby or trade it in for something cheaper and more practical.

With the prize money, she would be able to afford to send Destiny to the best kindergarten program in the city. She'd be able to pay off bills, including a significant portion of her student loans. Most importantly, less debt increased her desirability as an adoption candidate. Jazmin had a good chance of being approved because she was a relative. All the same, she didn't want any hiccups. She was determined to give Destiny the loving home she deserved.

Jazmin's cousin and Destiny's mother, Cicely, hadn't contacted them in almost five months. The last time they'd spoken she was headed south. Brenda had tried to locate Cicely when she was in Atlanta for the grand opening of the Tyler Perry Studios, but was unsuccessful.

Out of the corner of her eye, Jazmin saw the paperwork Micah Clarion had dropped off earlier in the week. Vicki must've signed the contracts this morning because a pen bearing the law firm's name and logo rested nearby. An image of him handsomely dressed in a tuxedo sporting a congratulatory smile flashed across Jazmin's mind. She quickly dismissed the thought. No way could she ask him to accompany her to the New Year's Eve gala. The last time he'd seen her she'd been dropping it like it was hot. How embarrassing! Jazmin laughed to herself at the irony of the situation. She made a living revamping websites and reshaping other people's digital reputations.

Feeling lighter, she bounced off the sofa. Her tennis shoes squeaked as she crossed the wood laminate flooring. She rushed through the showroom and into the back office.

"Good news?" Vicki asked, looking up from her papers as soon as Jazmin entered.

"Yes ma'am." She thrust the letter into her mentor's hands.

While reading, a smile slowly spread across Vicki's face, making prominent the age lines that the seventy-something-year-old had worked hard to camouflage.

"Congratulations!" Vicki opened her arms wide, and Jazmin stepped forward into her embrace. "You did it, sweetie. You're living the dream!"

Jazmin welcomed the hug though she had to bite down on her lip to stifle a sniffle. She missed the Midwest, missed southwestern Michigan, but, most of all, missed her mama. Vicki had filled in. She'd provided advice and offered encouragement over the years. Still, there was nothing like being cradled in Geraldine Johnson's arms.

Vicki pulled back and affectionately pinched Jazmin's flushed cheek. "Chin up," she instructed. "Letter says you'll be doing a photo shoot in two weeks. It'll take you that long to decide which wig to wear."

Smiling, Jazmin wiped away the tears that rolled down her cheek. At twenty-one, she'd been the youngest tech mogul since Zuckerberg. At twenty-four years old, she would be the first African American female to receive the coveted Millennial Titan. To maintain a little anonymity, as well as to separate her professional life from her personal one, she wore false lashes, heavy makeup, and weave to interviews and press conferences. Even journalists had a hard time recognizing her without all the bells and whistles.

Jazmin allowed Vicki to slowly spin her around and push her in the direction of the storage closet. She needed to find a hairdo worthy of two hundred and fifty thousand dollars. The task was not as simple as she had hoped, however. The shop's organization system was non-existent. She was likely to find nipple tassels and pasties in the same storage bin as Saint Patrick's Day top hats and Mardi Gras beads. She knew there was a tub of wigs somewhere in the closet. She'd even checked the online inventory database. According to the records there were over a dozen wigs in stock in various colors, lengths, and styles. If only she could find them. After thirty minutes of bending and stooping, all Jazmin had to show for her efforts was one shoulder-length wavy jet black wig.

Letting out an exasperated huff, she decided to take a break. She headed to Vicki's office. Jazmin's cell binged just as she flopped down on a tufted burgundy office chair. She'd received a message from her older sister, Rose Mary.

I got another letter from Reggie.

"Burn it," Jazmin replied aloud as she typed her feelings on the matter to her sister.

When would Rose Mary let up? The last thing Jazmin needed right now was to get entangled in Reggie's crap. While she waited for her sister to respond, Jazmin stretched her torso, turning left and then right. She'd acquired knots in her back during her fruitless wig search.

Since June, Destiny's father, Reggie, had sent letters to their mother's home in Michigan. Jazmin typically had her packages delivered to the shop so they wouldn't disappear from her front step. She had her mother's house in Michigan listed as her permanent residence. Rose Mary intercepted Reggie's missives and relayed their contents. The last letter had revealed Reggie's upcoming release date and his desire to meet Destiny. He was serving a two-year prison sentence for accidental discharge of a firearm that had resulted in the injury of another person.

Rose Mary was the only person in the world who knew she had dated Reggie prior to Cicely hooking up with him. The summer after freshman year, Jazmin had earned a prestigious internship at one of the leading tech companies in Philadelphia. Reggie had provided the music for the welcome reception. The two hit it off from the start. She had talked about her cousin, the talented singer, and he had seemed captivated by Jazmin's midwestern drawl along with her knowledge of all things tech-related. Both she and Cicely liked bad boys and Reggie had bad boy swagger dripping from the top of his fitted cap to his unlaced sneakers. He'd known all the club bouncers and bartenders, and, accompanied by Cicely, the three of them had spent the summer party-hopping all over Philadelphia.

By August, things soured. Reggie didn't want to compete for Jazmin's attention. Apparently, she spent too many nights networking with other interns and clients. To ease his mind about where her loyalty lay, she decided to give him her virginity. Despite his promises of happily-ever-after, he broke things off with her a few days later.

After their breakup, Jazmin buried herself in the internship. For her, romance and work became two mutually exclusive concepts. That summer she'd learned how to design and code cell phone software. Interns held exclusive rights to any application they successfully pitched, launched, and sold. The app she created provided up-to-the-minute stats on women's collegiate basketball games. "She Shoots, She Scores" took root locally.

Temple and Saint Joseph universities were the first onboard. The University of Pennsylvania followed three months later. Then, the app went viral, expanding to include all women's collegiate sports. Colleges up and down the east coast sponsored it. When the app broke into the Big Ten, Jazmin sold the idea and its code to start Tech Philly. The sale provided her with the seed money she needed.

Eventually you'll have to deal with him, especially if you plan to adopt Destiny.

Seriously. Can we please talk about anything else?

Frustrated, Jazmin fiddled with the thin gold chain she always wore. A gift from her dad.

Fine. When are you coming home? Rose Mary typed.

Pfft

Jazmin mumbled several expletives. She used her foot to swivel from side to side in the office chair. Her phone binged again. Rose Mary could be like a dog with a bone sometimes, never letting up.

Agree to disagree and put the past in the past.

Whatever.

LOL You and mom are more alike than you know.

Bye. Love you.

Jazmin sent the text message quickly and then stuffed her phone in the back pocket of her jean leggings. She didn't feel like rehashing the same argument with her sister. Heading out of the office, she went in search of Ms. Vicki. Unfortunately, as soon as she stepped into the showroom, Vicki pointed toward the stack of papers on the countertop.

"Drop those off for me."

Jazmin walked to the display case. "I still think doing business with that firm is a bad idea." She tucked the oversized envelope under her arm and ignored Vicki's stern stare.

Since meeting Micah Clarion the other night, Jazmin had done a little research on the law firm of Stein, Martin, Randolph and Associates. Some of the clients they'd chosen to represent were reprehensible. Additionally, over the years several female employees had filed complaints against Nathaniel Stein. He'd been accused of making one woman uncomfortable by commenting on her wardrobe. Another said he'd asked her to do menial but labor-intensive tasks while she was pregnant. A third woman alleged she'd been black-balled for leaving right at six o'clock to pick up her son from the aftercare program at his school. After separating from the firm, the woman had a hard time finding comparable work in the city.

Vicki waved off Jazmin's concern as she maneuvered her wide hips around the counter. "It don't make me no never mind," she replied.

Jazmin fell in step behind Vicki who pushed aside the velvet divider and entered the walk-in storage closet. Vicki retrieved a measuring tape along with a notepad and a plastic baggie full of safety pins. Apparently, the storage room's organization system worked for her.

"I don't have to like the men in charge to do business with their law firm."

Without saying goodbye, Vicki walked away with her chin high in the air. Jazmin shook her head and rolled her eyes to the ceiling. She returned to the office where she stuffed the contract papers along with her certified letter into her purse. After reapplying her lipstick, she headed for the back door. Outside, a strong wind blew. Crunchy dead leaves and litter created hurricane swirls at her feet. She opted to take the bus rather than walk the seven blocks to the law firm against the wind. As soon as she boarded the bus she texted Brenda and Rose Mary her good news. Right away, Brenda brainstormed photoshoot looks. The two friends discussed colors and fabrics. It scarcely felt like twenty minutes had passed when an automated voice announced, "Next stop, Broad."

Out of habit, Jazmin gripped the worn fabric strap above her head. The city bus lurched forward. Jazmin made her way to the rear door which opened at the same time the bus's hydraulics depressed. She stepped onto the sidewalk.

Micah.

Jazmin tripped over an uneven, raised slab of concrete. "Shit!" She'd spent so much time thinking about which silhouettes would make her appear taller and skinnier that she'd forgotten to consider what she would do if she ran into Micah Clarion while dropping off Vicki's paperwork. Now, there he was. The man from her nightly sex fantasies paced back and forth in front of his office building.

Chapter Six

Micah shoved his cell phone in his coat pocket. One of the senior partners, Everett Randolph II, had called Micah's father to gloat. The two men were fraternity brothers, but their goodwill and allegiance ended there. The Randolph family had longstanding ties to Philadelphia's abolitionist history. While attending Temple Law Micah quickly learned how close-knit the city's influential Black families were. As an outsider, he rubbed Everett Randolph II the wrong way. It didn't matter how many cases he won. The fact that he was better at his job than the man's son only further incensed his boss. Now, because of the phone call, Micah's father believed that Micah had dropped the ball. That he'd failed to deliver Tech Philly and its developer in a timely manner. No one seemed to care that it hadn't even been seventy-two hours. His bosses had assigned the task to Mr. Randolph's son, Rhett. They'd offered him the same incentive they had offered Micah, junior partner. Rhett's dad convinced the other partners it was better to have two dogs in a fight and they'd agreed.

Micah stopped pacing. He was determined now more than ever to land the promotion. Maybe he'd work from home for the rest of the day. On the way back to his condo he could stop by 5th Street Hosiery and Lingerie Boutique under the pretense of picking up the contracts. Jazmin might be working and have information on how to get in contact with J.J. That is, if the store were open. He turned his wrist to check the time on his black and gold Invicta when a siren's wail compelled him to look up. He locked eyes with Jazmin at the same time a hand clamped down on his shoulder. He turned his head slightly and his expression hardened when he saw who the hand belonged to. Rhett had followed him downstairs and outside. Dismissing the interruption, Micah stepped forward to place himself out of reach.

He watched as Jazmin threaded through the crowd, tossing out apologies to strangers she jostled. She squinted against the fluorescent glare of sunlight breaking like waves off stores' display windows. Micah couldn't take his eyes off of her. Her dark skin glowed in the refracting light. Everyone else seem dull by comparison. Several men who stood nearby smoking cheap cigars and talking loudly also noticed her. One let out a low whistle. She ignored him and instead blessed

Micah with a smile that made his heartrate increase and the tension he'd felt moments earlier lesson.

Refusing to be ignored, Rhett asked, "Clarion, how're you handling things?"

The muscle in Micah's jaw tensed. "Go. Away."

"Don't be a poor sport," Rhett began. "Who's she? Not your usual vanilla latte." He'd followed Micah's gaze and spotted Jazmin walking in their direction.

Micah shoved his hands in his pockets lest he strike the boss' son.

"Good morning. I would've sent a courier," Micah told Jazmin once she was in earshot.

She pursed her red-painted lips and blew her breath into her bare palms. "It's no problem."

The chilled air had left her cheeks naturally blushed. Also, the form-fitting leather jacket, while fashionable, wasn't doing much to ward off the wind.

"Let's get you inside and out of the cold."

He placed a light hand on her back to usher her forward, making sure his body served as a protective barrier between her and Rhett.

Jazmin stiffened but after a beat, he felt her relax.

"Everett Randolph III." The jerk shoved his hand in her path. "Mike and I work together."

She accepted his handshake and responded politely. Micah noticed she didn't offer her name and there wasn't any warmth to her expression. She'd earned a point in his book. If she caught the emphasis Rhett placed on his last name, she didn't make it known. Together, the three of them re-entered the office building. Jazmin wiped her feet on the mat and removed her hat.

"Why don't we go upstairs to the offices? I'll get you a cup of coffee to warm you up."

He surmised that it wouldn't be long before Rhett found his way to the boutique and Micah didn't want the man sniffing behind Jazmin for any reason. She didn't respond right away to his invitation, and Micah's stomach twisted into knots. He looked up and found Rhett watching them. Micah jerked a thumb toward the door.

"Weren't you on your way out?"

"Yes. Yes. I have an early lunch meeting."

Rhett nodded brusquely in Jazmin's general direction. He tucked a pair of loose dreadlocks behind his ear. They'd escaped the tightly woven braid hanging down his back. Rhett headed through the double doors and back outside. Micah couldn't hide his smug grin. Rhett would probably walk around the block before returning. He'd been in such a hurry to rub Micah's nose in the promotion, one he thought already belonged to him by birthright, that he'd left the office without bothering to put on his coat. When Micah turned his attention back to Jazmin, she was scrolling on her phone.

"Well, is there an opening for me in your schedule?"

A tiny smile peeked through her otherwise stony façade. She possessed beautiful lips, full and lush and she'd painted them fire engine red. They were the type of lips he'd like to kiss and continue kissing until she was breathless.

"Yes. I'll stay. Just for a little while."

"Wonderful." He gestured toward an elevator that would take them to the law firm's suite of offices on the eighth floor.

He and Jazmin waited patiently while a large group disembarked. When it was their turn, he allowed her to enter first. The black and white wedge sneakers she wore lengthened her shapely legs and drew his eyes to her round, perky butt. Micah closed the heavy outer door, then pulled the metal gate across. He pushed the button for the eighth floor and the elevator groaned. It slowly lifted.

Alone together, the space felt intimate. Jazmin watched the numbers overhead while Micah watched her. Under his examination her left foot started to tap. The heat between them cracked and sizzled like wood on a fire. He knew she also felt sparks because her disloyal foot began beating faster and she'd started fiddling with her necklace.

Suddenly, and without warning, gears squealed and then the elevator dropped slightly. Jazmin positioned her arms out in front of her to brace for the worst. When nothing happened, she darted to the far side of the elevator and took hold of the guard rail. Her knuckles paled as they gripped the cold metal. The overhead numbers flickered then went out, but the doors remained closed. Although dimmer, the lights had stayed on.

"We're okay," he said, pushing the open-door button repeatedly. "This old thing gets stuck all the time."

Her face blanched. Worried, Micah hit the red emergency call button with his fist. *Brrrriiiinng*, an old-fashion, rotary telephone sounded.

"Hello," called out a crackled male voice through static.

"Hello. Sir, you have two people stuck in the South elevator between the seventh and eighth floors. One male and one female."

"Sit tight. Damn wind knocked out the power."

"How long?" Jazmin croaked.

"Not pregnant, are you, Miss?"

"No, sir."

"Good. No need to call the fire department. We're working on it. We'll get you out of there in no time."

She nodded as if the man could see her. The static-filled call muffled, and then there was only silence. The man on the other end of the call had turned off whatever outdated two-way CB radio he was using. Jazmin's chest began to rise and fall at an increased rhythm.

Micah wiped the tiny beads of perspiration dotting his forehead with his pocket square and took off his coat. He folded then draped it neatly over the guard rail. She needed to calm down otherwise she might have a full-on panic attack. His baby sister had been prone to them during adolescence. Micah approached Jazmin slowly like he would a wounded but still danger-ous animal. He lightly suggested she sit while moving her bag's strap from her shoulder.

"Take this off. It's heavy," he added.

Next, she handed up her jacket. He placed it over his. Afterward, she slowly lowered herself to the lami-nate floor.

"Thanks," she whispered, gazing up at him.

"No problem."

Micah looked away from her long lashes and dark brown doe eyes. After a few seconds, he turned back. He'd always been a glutton for punishment.

"We're in this together, literally." He smirked.

***

In response to his corny joke, Jazmin chuckled softly. She smiled up at him before looking away. Fear still gripped her. She tried breathing in through her nose and out through her mouth, Lamaze style. For someone who prided herself on being in control, this was a nerve-wracking experience; to have her body rebel against her brain. She knew she was safe. She knew the elevator would be up and running shortly, yet her body continued to react irrationally. To her amazement, Micah Clarion unbuttoned and rolled up his sleeves before sitting down beside her on the floor.

"If you want, you can stretch out and rest your head on
me. It might help."

She searched his eyes for something malicious but found only kindness.

"You're having a panic attack. My sister suffered from similar episodes when she was little. Don't worry. It'll pass."

Jazmin hesitated and then cautiously curled herself into the fetal position. She found the floor's coolness soothing. She rested her head on his thigh and felt the tight cords of muscle. Her breathing slowed as she started to relax. She released a soft hum of pleasure.

"It's little things like this that will get a guy laid. Like when you get home and see your man has vacuumed."

"Really? Good to know."

Her eyes nearly popped out their sockets. Had she said that aloud? "Um...." She struggled to find anything to say that would save face. "So, I hear."

Micah laughed, a deep, rich sound. Straight from the gut. His laughter relaxed Jazmin even more, making her feel less overwhelmed. He might not be so uptight after all.

"I didn't mean to say that out loud. I'm sorry."

He placed his hand on her arm and squeezed it reassuringly. "No apology needed."

Jazmin closed her eyes. He smelled manly. It had been a long time since she smelled that distinct aroma. The musk of cologne and aftershave mixed with the spiciness of a man's deodorant. She counted the months since her last semi-serious relationship. Had it really been close to a year? Her days were mostly solitary other than spending time with Destiny or dropping in on Vicki at the store. She worked from home. Usually, she spoke with clients over the phone or via video conference. It hadn't bothered her much until now. She paid herself a generous salary and she could
pick the clients with whom she wished to work, rather than taking on whoever happened to call or looked her up online.

Why did lying on the floor with a complete stranger shine a spotlight on a hole she didn't realize she had in her social life? She'd had plenty of male friends, although, she ghosted guys after the fifth date as a general rule. In Jazmin's experience most men developed feelings after that milestone, even those she hadn't slept with. They wanted to introduce her to their sisters, or invited her on weekend getaways, or talked about plans three months in the future. After date number five, she cut all ties and never looked back. That way she was able to protect herself from getting dumped first. Or worse, falling in love with someone who more than likely would break her heart like Reggie had.

Jazmin opened her eyes and tilted her head. Micah Clarion was not the type of man you ghosted. He'd shown her genuine kindness without the slightest hint that he wanted something sexual from her in return. She had no business having nightly sex fantasies about him. She didn't need to link herself with anyone associated with Stein, Martin, Randolph and Associates. She knew that as a young, black, female tech entrepreneur she would give the law firm tons of positive publicity if she stood by their side. Unlike Vicki, Jazmin refused to do business with anyone whom she wouldn't be caught with during the light of day.

As far as Micah was concerned, if she had any sense she'd sit up and scoot to the far corner of the tin can they were stuck in. But today... today, she felt like throwing common sense and caution out the window. He hadn't shown any despicable traits like his bosses. Hadn't her sister reminded her again and again that not every man was Reggie?

A shroud of loneliness covered Jazmin. The other night, while watching Brenda and her friends reconnect, she'd been reminded of how lonely being a single parent could be. She'd devoted the last two and a half years of her life to work and to taking care of Destiny's needs.

Turning on her back, Jazmin reached up and ran her fingers along Micah's jawline. His short intake of breath turned her on. Flutters of excitement swirled in her belly that she couldn't ignore. It tickled its way down to her toes. Maybe all she needed was one kiss to get him out of her system. Just one taste. Afterward, there would be nothing to fantasize or dream about.

I deserve a little fun.

She started to sit up, but Micah raised his knee, effectively bringing her closer. She rewarded him by tugging on his ear and guiding his head down. His eyes closed just as she pressed her mouth against his. Jazmin nibbled and sucked gingerly. She tested his level of willingness once more when she applied a bit of pressure before biting his full bottom lip. The act elicited a low moan. He pulled her up and sat her on his lap. Her body melted against his chest. The hard length of him pressed against her ass.

Jazmin had noticed his biceps when he'd first taken off his coat. She was a sucker for well-toned arms and Micah had all the right artillery to lift a curvy girl like her up and fuck her against a wall. As the kiss deepened, he held her close. His free hand gently kneaded her lower back. His touch sent shivers of anticipation over her body. Jazmin's chest swelled with renewed confidence.

No more nausea. No more lightheadedness. Her earlier fear had dissolved almost completely and in its place was the control to which she was accustomed. She placed her right palm against his hard pectoral muscle and, with the slightest bit more pressure than was polite, pinched his nipple. He pulled back. His eyes slowly ignited until they blazed with desire. She treated the other nipple. Micah inhaled deeply. Jazmin beamed, pleased she'd found an erogenous zone. Taking things farther, she pressed her mouth to the column of his neck and kissed a trail down to his starched collar while still teasing his chest's taut points beneath his undershirt. He grasped her wrist firmly to halt her assault at the same time he swept his mouth over hers. This time, a soft moan escaped her mouth.

Damn, he was a good kisser! Cradled against his chest she felt secure. Safe.

Brrrriiiinng. The emergency phone pierced through the intimate haze surrounding them and jolted Jazmin back to reality. They separated. Stumbling to stand, she watched Micah's chest rise and fall in rapid succession as he regained his professional composure. With deft fingers, he righted his shirt.

Heavens, when did she undo those buttons?

Jazmin followed Micah's lead and snagged her jacket from the railing.

Brrrriiiinng.

She pushed the red call button, hoping to stop the noise

"Hello?"

Jazmin forced her eyes to look ahead. Then, she turned her gaze to the floor. She stared everywhere but at Micah Clarion. Based on the heat pulsing between her legs, she knew one kiss wasn't going to be enough.

Chapter Seven

Micah grumbled. His good friend, Adam, shamelessly dragged his loot across the card table using both hands. Micah was an ace at cards but tonight he'd lost several hundred dollars and his inability to focus was becoming more apparent to his friends. He regretted driving to New York for this month's card game. It didn't help that Adam had taken the last two hands and sat across the table grinning like an idiot. Micah frowned. All he could concentrate on was Jazmin. He replayed last night's dream in his head.

She had beckoned and he'd come willingly. He'd crawled on all fours to reach her, only for her to place the ball of her foot against his chest. She was a mythical siren dressed in a silk negligee the color of black raspberries. While she'd gripped his pectoral with pale pink painted toes, he had begged for more. She raised her nightgown and her scent had filled Micah's nose. He caught a glimpse of the area between her thighs. Without panties, Jazmin's bare sex was on full display.

"I need a beer," Micah said, pushing away from the table.

"What's up with him?" an acquaintance from college asked. "Who's got his nose open?"

Adam coughed and sputtered. He sat down his drink and wiped his mouth, but the smirk remained. Micah shot his friend a warning glare. Five guys he'd known since undergrad turned to stare at him. To his credit, Adam recovered quickly and attempted to change the direction of the conversation.

"Anyone going to Leon's cruise ship wedding?"

Micah stormed into the kitchen while the guys discussed the poor timing of having a destination wedding in February. Once a month, they all gathered over cards. Tonight, they were in Harlem. The earlier comment about him being whipped had warranted nothing more than a cursory response.

Adam strolled into the kitchen a few minutes behind Micah. "I haven't seen you this worked up in a long time. Maybe you're losing your touch in your old age."

Micah rubbed the back of his neck. He regretted mentioning Jazmin to his best friend. They were both thirty-two, Adam just six months younger. Unfazed by Micah's gruffness, Adam examined the collection of hard liquor on the kitchen island before pouring tequila into two shot glasses. He pushed one across the countertop. They clinked glasses and then tossed back the clear liquid. Feeling the tequila warming his chest and flooding his senses, Micah gladly accepted the lime Adam offered.

Micah closed his eyes, but behind his lids Jazmin appeared. Her coppery bronzed shoulders made him want to trace kisses along her clavicle. Hips swaying in a seductive rhythm, she led him down a dimly lit hallway. His mouth grew as dry as cotton. Her nightgown was cut higher in the front. As a result, it dipped in the back as she walked, displaying twin dimples at the small of her back. A salty breeze from somewhere up ahead rammed into him and inflamed the scratches dream-Jazmin had left on his chest earlier. He passed through the open doorway of a bedroom bungalow that he didn't recognize. He found Jazmin sitting on the window's ledge. Micah never imagined he would be aroused by a woman removing her stockings. Nevertheless, when Jazmin unclipped her garters and slowly slid the nylon hose over her thighs and down her legs, he'd been on the verge of pulling himself out and relieving the strain she'd created. Even now, almost twenty-four hours later, Micah's heartbeat echoed in his ears as blood raced downward.

Dream-Jazmin had looked ethereal with the curtains flapping in the strong breeze around her like butterfly wings. After shedding her pantyhose, she'd crooked a finger and beckoned him forward. He'd practically run to her side. He lifted Jazmin so she sat on his lap. With her snuggled within the circle of his arms, his fingers had dallied inside her core, forcing her to lean against his chest for support. While he plucked and played, her nails dug into his biceps. In no time at all, Jazmin's head had fallen back and she cried out in blissful agony.

Micah opened his eyes and found Adam staring at him. The vision had felt real.

"I don't know what it is about this one," Micah admitted. "There's always been another lady waiting in the wings and that's the way I like it."

"I can't wait to meet her." Adam poured more tequila for himself while Micah waved off the offer of a second shot. Adam saluted him and gulped down the drink.

Loud laughter drew both of their attention to the foyer. Rhett closed the front door and hollered a greeting to the guys playing poker. He moved further inside the apartment. A slender curly-headed brunette clung to his arm. She looked young, probably a senior in college. Rhett often trolled undergraduate fraternity parties at Temple University. Micah wasn't surprised that the creep did the same wherever he went. Micah watched as Rhett whispered something to the co-ed who erupted in laughter. She nodded enthusiastically before heading into the adjacent bedroom where the other plus-ones were holed up. The glass wall gave the bedroom an artsy feel. Curtains hidden out of sight could be drawn to offer privacy.

Rhett strolled across the industrial-chic open layout and into the kitchen. His chest puffed out. His dreadlocks hung loose, over his shoulders. The neat braid he'd worn to work the day before was gone.

"*Boys*," he said, removing a cold beer from the refrigerator.

"Rhett, how've you been?" Adam answered. "Long time, no see."

"Just fine." He inclined his head in the direction his date had gone. "The night is looking up. Well, for some of us."

Micah didn't bother offering a greeting. Instead, he collected his and Adam's empty shot glasses and moved around the kitchen island. He rinsed and deposited both into the undermounted double bowl sink. From the corner of his eye, he saw Rhett drain three-quarters of his beer and roughly set the bottle on the counter. The hollow clink demanded attention.

"I heard you got stuck in the elevator with that jawn Friday morning." He twisted his lips to the side and shook his head.

Everett Randolph III pronounced jawn like it was a dirty slur rather than Philly slang for any and everything. Micah turned around fully. He was inclined to wipe the smirk off his rival's face for the way he drew out the word.

"What of it?" Micah demanded. If the boss' son was spoiling for a fight, he would oblige.

"She's a nice piece of ass, if you like the look."

This time Micah didn't have coat pockets to stuff his fists in. He rounded the island at the same time Rhett did, only Adam got between them first.

"Fellas," Adam put one hand on Micah's chest and leaned into him until he retreated a step. "We're all friends, here—"he pinned Micah with a stare — "remember."

"I'm surprised you didn't bring her tonight," Rhett continued, acting like Micah's show of anger didn't bother him. His flaring nostrils said otherwise, however.

Rhett ran his hands over his shirt, smoothing out invisible wrinkles. A half-wall hid them from the card game but anyone upstairs in the loft shooting pool had a clear view. A brawl would put them on display and that was the last thing either of them needed their fathers to hear about. Glaring, Micah bit back a retort. Rhett knew damn well he couldn't bring Jazmin around this crowd. He pitied Rhett's unsuspecting date. Hopefully, her age would suggest to the other women that she wasn't wife material, rather a toy Rhett would cast aside when he was done playing. The women at the party carried designer handbags, each worth over one thousand dollars. Many were friends who had known each other since childhood. Others had met at college. None of that mattered because they still slung passive aggressive barbs back and forth, especially those who'd already nabbed a husband. A few, like Eleanor, fired both barrels at unidentified female guests as soon as the targets were within earshot. Micah knew the women would have a field day with a single mother who managed a South Street sex shop and possibly stripped on the side. Thankfully, Jazmin hadn't told Rhett her name.

"How do you two know each other anyway?" Rhett asked.

"Why?" Micah's eyes narrowed to slits.

"Just a question. She looked familiar, that's all. I just can't place her face."

God help him if Jazmin actually were a stripper and Rhett had seen her dancing.

"You don't know her," Micah insisted.

Rhett smirked and waved him off. "It'll come to me." He rubbed the fresh stubble on his chin. "Will I see you next Sunday?"

"Yes," Micah replied. His jaw clenched.

Despite their fathers' dislike of each other, their mothers got along. The women discovered they'd been princesses for their respective states and were both former Miss Howard University. The families reunited to watch The Miss Universe Pageant every year. It was an excuse to force their offspring together for a pre-holiday party. This year the Randolphs were hosting at their sprawling Main Line mansion.

"Good luck," Rhett said, taking what was left of his beer into the adjacent room.

He called out a greeting to the ladies and immediately two flanked his side. Apparently, the brunette had found a friend.

"Lucky bastard," Adam mumbled.

Micah rubbed his hands over his hair. He knew what Rhett's comment meant. Their fathers expected a report on their progress in less than a week. It was time for Micah to rally. Hell, he shouldn't even be here. Jazmin was the key. She was his advantage over Everett Randolph III. Hurriedly, Micah headed for the hall closet to retrieve his coat. He should be working to convince her to set up a meeting for him with Tech Philly's creator, J.J., not fantasizing about her. He tossed out goodbyes to the card players who'd looked up from their hands.

"You good?" Adam called out to him from the kitchen.

"I'm fine."

Micah didn't look back to gauge his friend's reaction. He slipped on his wool coat. While Rhett spent the night philandering, he would set in motion a plan to gain Jazmin's trust. The front door slammed shut behind him.

"Whatever it takes," he mumbled to himself

Chapter Eight

Jazmin was restless. Strings of yarn from a hand-crafted dreamcatcher danced above her head, caught in the subtle gusts from the small fan clipped to her headboard. She sat up and threw off the woven knit Temple University blanket. Destiny's faint snores from next door blended in with the rumble of rain against Jazmin's window. Barefoot, she crossed the room and plopped down in front of a care package she'd received earlier that afternoon. Her sister, Rose Mary, had mailed the box weeks ago but because it was so close to the holidays, and because their small hometown post office was notoriously slow, it had taken over two weeks to reach Philadelphia.

Inside were finger puppets, oversized satin hair bows, and a mobile with tiny plastic stars. Jazmin also discovered a small tin filled with over a dozen pictures of her and her cousin Cicely. They posed with large swimming medals around their necks in one framed photo. Cicely had won gold for diving and Jazmin silver for fastest two-hundred-meter free style. Their toothless grins placed them around seven or eight years old. In another faded photo, Jazmin was blowing out eleven birthday candles. Cicely stood behind her with two fingers like rabbit ears positioned above her head. Jazmin smiled at the memory. At the bottom of the box she found a fiberboard mailing envelope along with couture red nail polish for her, kiddie lip glosses for Destiny, and a well-loved felt sunflower. The plush toy with its smiling face had been Cicely's favorite.

The fiberboard envelope contained a more recent photo of her cousin. Cicely had glowed while opening gifts at her baby shower. Her belly protruded proudly. Jazmin and Brenda had outdone themselves, decorating their apartment with bright yellow and pink balloons.

Jazmin's attention shifted from the photograph to her ringing cell. It lay on the nightstand. Laughing softly at the memories of friends playing ridiculous baby-themed party games, she pushed her hands against the carpeted floor to stand. It was a quarter past ten and only Brenda called at this time of night. She then remembered her best friend had left for New York yesterday and would not be back until ... Wednesday. Her sister's name flashed across the screen. As she pressed the green accept button, Jazmin silently prayed for things to be alright with her mother.

"Hello?" An ache just above her heart had her clutching the bedspread.

"Jaz, were you sleeping? Did I wake you?"

"No. I'm up. What's going on, Rosie?"

Jazmin sat down and scooted until her back pressed against the headboard. Her sister was up at five o'clock every morning and went to bed by seven. If she was calling this late, something was on her mind. Jazmin mentally tallied how much money she had in her emergency fund in case she needed to book a one-way plane ticket. She could be in Michigan before noon tomorrow.

"Is everything okay?" she asked.

"Yes. I just wanted to know if you got the box I sent."

Jazmin's heartrate slowed. "You scared me."

"Sorry. There's nothing to worry about. I'm fine. Mom's fine."

Jazmin pressed her palm against her forehead and breathed deeply. "The box came today. Thanks for the nail polish." She covered her bare feet with her Temple blanket.

"I also wanted to make sure—" Rose Mary exhaled— "you're over the whole Reggie and Cicely thing."

Jazmin had asked herself that same question recently. If she were being honest with herself, she hadn't been ready for a relationship with a man like Reggie, or any man for that matter. Everything she'd learned about sex growing up, she'd learned from watching HBO's late-night series Real Sex along with reruns of the first five seasons of MTV's *The Real World*. Their mother banned them from watching the reality series when she'd caught her youngest daughter practicing a risqué speech for an audition tape to join the cast. Jazmin was seventeen and a senior in high school.

"You know he told me that Cicely came on to him. That she'd called dibs. She told him that he deserved better." Jazmin ignored the tightness she always felt in her gut when she thought about her cousin's betrayal. "I was pissed when I found out they'd slept together, but not pissed enough to keep a father away from his kid."

"Okay," Rose Mary murmured.

"I just think he's a bad guy and selfish as hell," Jazmin added.

Her ex-boyfriend and cousin had bonded over music. Cicely slept with Reggie after a night of drinking. Afterward, she apologized repeatedly. At least, she'd cared about Jazmin's feelings. Reggie ended things with Cicely after four months. By the time her cousin discovered she was pregnant he'd replaced her with another soprano.

"Look, if he wants to get to know Destiny, fine. Go through the courts like I'm doing, or let's come up with a plan together."

"It's just that, well…" her sister's voice trailed off.

She could picture Rose Mary twirling her curly, auburn hair around her fingers like she always did whenever she was agitated about something.

"He seems to have turned his life around. He's gotten his Associates degree and he's pursuing a Bachelor's in music management. He even works in the prison library, shelving books," Rose Mary explained. "He attended anger management classes. What if—"

"You really need to stop reading his letters. He'll do whatever he thinks he needs to do to get paroled early. I'm sure it looks good that he's reaching out, trying to make amends."

Jazmin's ears warmed. She'd buried her anger and now her sister was dredging it up, forcing her to reexamine it. If Reggie wormed his way into Destiny's life, Jazmin feared he would stop the adoption from going through. She scooted to the edge of the bed and let her feet dangle. There was no way she was going to let that happen. He hadn't cared about Destiny when she was born and he sure as hell didn't care now. Reggie had only started sending letters this summer.

"What if he's changed for real? We had a great dad, and I don't want Destiny missing out because you think Reggie should suffer," Rose Mary finished.

"You think I've been holding a grudge all this time, pining away over some loser who screwed me over when I was nineteen?" The question spilled out in a whoosh of words. Jazmin's cheeks were hot, and she felt a fire leap to life inside her chest.

"Hold on, Jaz."

"Seriously? Is this you talking, or mom? Because it sure as hell sounds like mom."

"Calm down. Please."

Jazmin sprung off the bed. Her sister was right about one thing. They did have a great dad and a pretty stellar childhood too. Jazmin paced along the well-worn strip of carpeting beside her bed. Their mom had held things together with the help of Aunt Marie, their dad's little sister. It was only after Marie passed that their mom changed. She became incredibly strict, insisting her daughters and niece check in all the time. They could barely leave the house unless it was re-lated to school, work, or church. Her sister, always the people pleaser, had fallen in line. Cicely, on the other hand, had rebelled. She was angry after her mom died, and when she wasn't trying to get a rise out of Jazmin and Rose Mary's mother, her aunt, she walked around in a drug induced haze.

"Are you still there?" Rose Mary asked.

Jazmin unclenched her fists. Several beats passed before she answered. "I'm here." She'd left fingernail imprints on the palms of her hands.

Taking a few more breaths, she padded across the hall. She propped the photo of a very pregnant Cicely against a petite pink jewelry box on Destiny's dresser. She dimmed the lights and carefully closed the door before retreating across the hall to her own room.

Rose Mary exhaled, puffing air into the phone's receiver. "I don't want to fight."

"It's getting late, and I should go," Jazmin answered. Annoyed and frustrated, she'd turned on the robotic voice she usually reserved for nit-picking clients.

"Me too. Some of us have to work regular hours." Rose Mary laughed softly at her own joke.

"Night," Jazmin said.

"Goodnight. Text me tomorrow. I want to hear about everything, okay? More about this Millennial Award, who you're dating, how work has been...everything."

If her sister only knew about her wickedly sinful Micah fantasies. Still awake and more restless now than before, Jazmin knelt and reached under her bed. Her fingers roamed until they found a velvet box. She pushed aside the top and slipped her hands around her favorite sex toy, a powerfully petite wand massager. She needed a release. A way to deal with the pent-up energy and sexual frustration from her run-in with Micah. Her pussy clenched in anticipation as she discarded her pajama bottoms and panties. She climbed atop her mattress and kicked the covers out of the way.

Jazmin closed her eyes and delicately stroked. With small circles she rubbed her slick, sticky wetness over the tight bundle of nerves at the intersection of her thighs. She moaned lightly. Soon, however, the friction against her clit curled her toes. She increased the rhythm. Jazmin bit her lip so she wouldn't shout out curses. Heaven help her if Destiny woke and sought her out to see what was going on. Jazmin pushed the power button several times so the ice cream scoop top pulsed at intervals. She set the wand against her clit and imagined. Dream-Micah flicked his tongue against her delicate bud, and she shivered.

"Just like that. Just like that," Jazmin said in a hoarse whisper.

He gripped her hips to hold her in place while he sucked greedily. Her legs stiffened as she squeezed her thighs around the toy. She was determined to ride out the illicit pleasure storm. It took all her willpower not to shift her bottom or loosen her grip on the wand as she creamed and then splintered into pieces.

Jazmin lay very still while her breathing slowed, and the tremors dulled to a soft hum. No. She couldn't share her sex dreams with her prim and proper, perfect sister. Slowly, Jazmin's toes unfurled. She righted herself and lifted the sheets in search of her panties.

Chapter Nine

Micah kicked off his gym shoes and then crossed the apartment. He walked toward the eat-in kitchen, tossing his phone and keys on the dining table as he passed. The front door closed with a soft thud behind him. He'd managed to squeeze in a workout at the twenty-four-hour fitness center located in the basement of his building. The muscles in his arms burned from lifting free weights. Micah grabbed a bottle of water from the refrigerator. He gulped down most of its contents before he was forced to take a breath. Wiping his mouth with the back of his hand, he snagged a bag of pretzels from the pantry and then headed for the living room.

Ever since his bosses had offered him the opportunity to become a junior partner, they'd dumped more work on him. This morning, Micah planned to double check the fine print on several affidavits that'd been placed on his desk at the last minute. The claimants would arrive at the office before noon. Focusing on something physical usually cleared Micah's head.

Lately, however, legal jargon and deadlines clouded his mind.

Micah had just sat down on the sofa when his cell phone beeped. Dragging himself upright, he walked to the dining room to fetch the device. He tapped the phone screen and the image enlarged. Eleanor, his ex, had sent him a text.

Good news. I've selected a dress for the gala. It's emerald and fits perfectly with the art deco theme. I've attached links to different designer men's clothiers for your perusal. Yours, Ellie.

He ran his hands over his sweat-dampened hair and then rubbed his temples. Placating Eleanor was the last thing he felt like doing. He reread her message. Did she honestly think he needed help selecting an outfit? It wasn't difficult to choose men's formal wear. He would decide between a black tuxedo or a black suit.

No sweat.

Micah snapped a screenshot of the message and sent it to Adam. Of course, his friend replied within seconds with a chuckling smiley face. The question that followed, however, gave Micah pause.

Are you sure things are over between you two?

If Adam's question was any indication, Micah needed to be clearer with Eleanor about his intentions. She was doing him a favor, nothing more. She wasn't his and he definitely wasn't hers. He sent her a curt reply.

Eleanor, I am capable of shopping for clothing. I've done well on my own without assistance and have since I was fourteen. I'll be sure to complement your dark green dress.

Tapping his fingers against the phone's screen, Micah waited for her response. The three blinking dots staring back at him further added to his frustration. A full minute passed and still she hadn't responded. Annoyed, Micah snatched up his phone and stalked back to the sofa. He typed *J.J.* and *Tech Philly* into the internet browser's search engine. A grainy image of the tech guru popped up. Long box braids cascaded over her shoulder. They covered one eye and half her face. The Philadelphia Tribune along with The Temple News had run articles on J.J. after the nineteen-year-old beat out hundreds of male applicants for an internship at one of the city's largest tech companies. Micah had searched J.J. on the web countless times. Several news outlets covered her success. She looked different in each picture. Sometimes her hair was short, and her makeup overdone. Other times it was obvious she wore a wig. Each photo captured a plastic smile and impatient eyes. The woman clearly didn't like the spotlight.

Micah plucked the television remote from the coffee table and powered on the TV. Relaxing back against the cool leather, he closed his eyes. He didn't care that the television had last been tuned to The Weather Channel. He looked forward to the day when he no longer had to prove himself to the senior partners. He'd started to drift off to sleep when his phone chirped, alerting him of a new message. Grumbling, he read Eleanor's lengthy response.

Darling, I was only trying to help. You must remember this is the event of the season, not a kickback with friends on a boat cruising around Lake Michigan. Of course, I have full confidence that whatever you choose will be fine. We are always the best dressed couple in the room. I only ask that whichever clothier you pick, be sure to enlist the services of a female sales associate and send me pictures PLEASE before you make a purchase. Emerald is far from dark green.   XOXO

Micah set the phone face down, just out of reach. He decided he could say more by saying nothing at all.

*

Destiny sat quietly on the rug watching cartoons on her tablet. Jazmin had turned on a movie to distract the little girl while she tamed the tangled curls atop her tiny head. Jazmin parted Destiny's hair and oiled her scalp while lightly scratching and picking out threads of string and lint. To Jazmin's good fortune, Destiny seemed more concerned with the cartoon princess and singing frog on the tablet than with Jazmin who awkwardly twisted tufts of hair to form a lopsided braid. Her plaits looked nothing like the example braids Vicki had done on the left side of Destiny's head. This morning, she and Destiny had left home early so they could stop by the boutique. Vicki had graciously agreed to show Jazmin how to create long curvy snake braids for the umpteenth time. She was tired of the other preschool moms' judgmental side-eyed stares regarding her parenting skills.

"Hold still, please," she told her little cousin.

Jazmin knew she was taking too long. Unfortunately, being the youngest in her family meant she was inexperienced at doing hair. Whenever she, Rose Mary, and Cicely had dressed up and played "beauty salon" as children, Jazmin was always forced to play the role of client, never the stylist.

Vicki called out to her from across the room. "I've got a customer coming in early before we open—" she glanced at the clock hanging above the door— "bless her heart, thirty-seven and just had a mastectomy."

Vicki counted the money in the register, writing down figures in a weathered leather ledger. Twenty-five years ago, she opened the boutique to provide women with ample bosoms like herself better options than those available at the mall. Her shop carried bras starting at size 38 DDD. After a while, Vicki saw a need for custom designs and styles for asymmetrical breasts or women who'd triumphed over breast cancer. Rather than boring hospital-looking undergarments, she offered cutesy, delicate patterns and fabrics that made customers feel ultrafeminine and sexy.

"Did you think more about what I mentioned?" Jazmin asked. "You've been lucky so far because you cornered a niche market, but celebrity-endorsed lingerie brands, with their online-only stores and inclusive sizes, are driving brick and mortar boutiques like 5th Street out of business."

She'd encouraged Vicki to spice up her merchandise. Other South Street sex shops made a killing on BDSM toys and apparel, not to mention their sales on vibrators and dildos. Whether Vicki wanted to admit it or not, bondage, domination, sadism, and masochism sex practices and role-playing were trending, especially since the release of the *50 Shades Of Grey* movies.

Jazmin covered Destiny's ears with her hands. "We could start small with whips and paddles, nothing crazy."

Vicki pushed the register drawer shut. "It's bad enough I'm selling lubricant. If your man can't rev the engine, you've got bigger problems."

"How much longer?" Destiny whined.

Jazmin lowered her hands. To distract Destiny, she ooh◇ed and aah-ed. She pretended to be captivated by the cartoon love story. An alligator and firefly had joined the traveling duo. Just as the new friends were making their way home on a riverboat and the frog was positioned on bended knee, ready to offer the princess a wedding ring, Jazmin's cell phone alarm trilled. Both females jumped, caught off guard by the interruption.

Jazmin threw her hands in the air. "I give up!"

The alarm meant they needed to leave. Parents who dropped their children off at the daycare after nine o'clock had to bring in a doctor's note. The policy unnerved Jazmin, especially considering the monthly tuition rates. Destiny allowed her hair to be fashioned into twin puffs, Jazmin's signature style. In under fifteen minutes, they had their coats zipped, their shoes on, and they were out the door. They hurried down the sidewalk stopping only when they reached Jazmin's car.

"Let's roll," Destiny said pumping her tiny fist in the air.

Smiling, Jazmin unlocked the rear passenger door and then carefully helped Destiny into her car seat. She pushed the door closed and stood in front of Destiny's window for a moment before rounding the hood.

Chapter Ten

"Foul!" Micah blew into his coach's whistle. "Let's run it again."

His players took their positions. This year's group was good. Most knew how to dribble well enough to move down the court without looking at their feet. Micah had begun working with the youth sports league when he was a student at Temple. He, along with other college basketball players from around the city, had volunteered for two weeks in the summer. The student athletes ran sessions to develop the kids' fundamentals. They refereed scrimmages as well. When the summer program ended, Micah chose to stay on. He helped as much as he could between practices, road games, and classes. After injuring his knee, he visited the afterschool programs more and more.

Micah checked his watch. Fifteen minutes left. "Water break!"

The boys jogged to the bleachers. A few parents had arrived. Usually, the team practiced on Tuesday nights, but since they had a tournament game Saturday, he asked those who were free to come in and do a few drills. Running up and down the court with the boys had also allowed Micah to blow off some of the pent-up energy he had from earlier. In no time at all his frustration with his dad had lessoned. In addition, he thought about Jazmin every eight minutes instead of five.

Crazy enough, maintenance had the elevator up and running and the doors open less than ten minutes after the initial radio distress call. It had seemed as if time had stopped. That is, until the blasted phone rang, ending their make-out session. Without so much as a word to each other, they'd righted their clothing. Once they were freed, Jazmin shoved the contract papers into his hands and then she practically sprinted for the stairs. Over her shoulder, she had offered him a raincheck for the coffee. He didn't even have her number.

It was probably for the best. He was too old for cat and mouse games and, with Rhett also vying for the promotion, Micah needed to stay focused. He couldn't afford any distractions.

"Circle up!" he shouted.

The boys locked arms and formed a huddle around him. Swaying from side-to-side they began to chant.

"We work together!" Micah shouted.

"We work together!" the boys echoed.

"We grind together!"

"We grind together!"

Micah beamed. "We win together!"

Several of the parents along with younger siblings chanted from the bleachers. Some added a percussion beat by stomping their feet.

"We win together!" the boys answered.

"Bulldogs, on three!"

"One, two..." the boys rushed Micah. "Three!"

Chuckles erupted from deep within his chest. They spilled forth and erased thoughts of upcoming meetings and work rivalries. He'd needed this.

"Bulldogs!" The boys jumped up and down, pumping their small fists in the air.

Micah patted shoulders and praised players for their hard work. When most of the families had gone, he began picking up the practice equipment. He stuffed basketballs into an oversized nylon bag and then lugged the heavy sack into the storage room. When he re-entered the gymnasium, he noticed everyone had cleared out. Everyone, except Hector. The boy sat on the lowest rung of the bleachers. His head bobbed up and down to music that Micah couldn't hear. Hector was new to the team and Micah had only met the boy's grandfather once or twice. Even so, it wasn't like the older man to be late.

The double doors leading to the main entrance creaked open. Micah looked up at the same time the doors thudded against the wall. Jazmin strolled into his gym. His feet tangled together, and he stumbled.

Her eyes widened. As she neared, the faint smell of sweet berries filled Micah's nose. The scent set off a series of emotions. Anxiousness welled in his belly while warmth spread to his lower extremities. His arousal gained momentum.

Play it cool, man. Play it cool.

Jazmin stopped. She held hands with the little girl from the other day. Her daughter, he presumed. The little girl's hand slipped from Jazmin's grip, and she sprinted across the gym. She laced her arms around the boy's neck. Hector teetered to one side.

"C'mon. Let's go," Jazmin called out. Her eyes shone with amusement at the two youngsters play-wrestling.

Still, Micah noticed when her shoulders and chest shivered slightly. She wrapped the halves of her over-sized sweater tighter around her body. Although she had her gaze fixed on the children, Micah caught sight of the way she nervously played with the thin gold chain around her neck. His attention shifted to her mouth. He remembered the moans she had made when he kissed her neck. How she had fit perfectly in his lap. The feel of her body pressed against his. She remembered too. He was certain. If there weren't children present, he would be tempted to remind her just how much passion they'd shared. Instead, he followed her lead.

Micah motioned to the three-ring binder resting on the blenchers between them. "Are you an authorized pick-up person?".

"Whhaa...What?"

Finally, he had her full attention.

"I think so."

Jazmin cheeks flushed just as they had the other night when her daughter burst from behind the storeroom's divider. Micah sifted through the players' files until he landed on Hector Allen Lopez. Jazmin Johnson along with Victoria Fontenot were approved as emergency contacts and pickup people.

That's one way to get her number.

Bell-like giggles echoed throughout the empty gym. Both Micah and Jazmin's heads turned toward the sound. Hector galloped forward with the laughing toddler bouncing on his back.

"Ms. Jazmin's my neighbor," Hector said.

The peewee jockey patted the top of the young man's head. "Me too."

"Sorry. Destiny is too."

Her smile widened.

When the little girl walked into the gym, Micah didn't think she could get any cuter. He was wrong. With two missing front teeth, she was adorable.

"Are we good, *coach*?" Jazmin asked.

The knots in Micah's stomach tightened. He hadn't missed the hint of sarcasm in her tone. He preferred this feisty version of her over the embarrassed store clerk from the other day.

"I'll walk you all out."

"No. That's okay. We're good." Wrinkles like ladder rungs lined her forehead.

"It's no trouble." Micah grinned, ignoring her obvious discomfort. He zipped his gym bag before slinging the strap over his shoulder. "Come on guys," he called out to Hector and Destiny.

He and the children neared the reception area before he heard Jazmin's feet racing toward them. He pulled open the heavy outer doors and Hector scampered outside with Destiny still riding on his back. Jazmin exited with her chin high in the air. He laughed and then followed her out. The streets were fairly empty. Most of the boutiques and cafés had closed. A few people lingered near the bus stop. With plenty of room to run, Hector jogged ahead. He stopped at the corner and then spun in circles before heading back. Destiny giggled wildly.

"Where are you parked?" Micah asked.

Jazmin's teeth chattered. If she'd parked on the next block he would insist she put on his coat. Adrenaline from practice warmed him. Her plain white t-shirt and black sweatpants were cute but not appropriate for a stroll through Philadelphia in early December. Also, her floor-length grey cardigan with pockets covered in purple feathers was more fashionable than practical.

"I'm a few cars down. The black Nova." Jazmin inclined her head.

"I'm impressed."

She returned his smile. "You should be. It's a 1964 Chevy II Nova."

"How long have you had her?"

"Since I was fifteen. My dad gave her to me after I aced my driver's test. My grandpa worked on the assembly line at the Willow Run, Michigan plant where the first Chevy II's were produced in the 1960s."

Micah noted how her shoulders relaxed and how much chipper her tone had become.

"You're from Michigan. I knew I didn't hear a Philly accent. I have a brother who's a Michigan alum."

Her eyes flashed with humor. "I won't hold that against you."

She slowly ran her hand over the hood of the car. Micah studied the way she treasured the vehicle.

"My grandpa bought my dad a similar one when he was a teenager. I guess the tradition stuck. She was a hunk of junk when we started, but we restored her to her former glory on weekends and during school breaks and summer vacation. The August heat nearly killed us."

"You all did a really good job. Is your dad working on anything new?"

Jazmin's gaze lifted. For the first time he noticed her eyes brimmed with water. Micah's heart sank.

"He's dead."

"I'm sorry."

It felt like someone had Micah's windpipe in a vice grip, making it difficult to swallow.

"Don't be. Dad was a cop—Lieutenant Dillan Johnson Jr."

She offered him a forced smile that left Micah off balance. He shifted his weight from one foot to the other.

Jazmin continued, "He was killed in the line of duty." She looked over her shoulder to the children playing. "Ready, co-pilot?" she called out to the little girl.

Destiny grinned, showing off her two missing front teeth again. "Ready!"

Jazmin brightened.

"Listen," Micah began.

He contemplated the best words to apologize for what'd happened in the elevator without stating that he was actually sorry. He didn't regret their kiss one bit.

"About the other day in the elevator."

"Please, it's okay." Tightening her grip on the sweater, she tucked her chin down toward her chest.

"I don't normally do that sort of thing," he assured her.

"Too bad. You're good at it."

Yes, Micah most definitely liked her playful side.

"Hector! Destiny!" she shouted, grinning.

The preteen followed Destiny as she jumped through an invisible hopscotch grid. Jazmin unlocked the driver's door and Micah instinctively moved to hold it open for her. The ignition turned over with a gravely roar.

"How often do you get to open her up?"

"Not often enough."

Unable to resist, Micah reached in and cupped her cheek. He rubbed his thumb along her jawline. When she rested against the palm of his hand, letting him carry the weight of her head, he inwardly cheered.

"About that raincheck you mentioned?"

"I'll call you, okay?" she whispered.

Micah leaned forward and captured her mouth. He only meant to give her a sympathetic peck on the lips. Instead, his desire sprang to life like a lightning rod set aflame. He was ensnarled by the sweet taste of her strawberry lip balm. Jazmin clung to him, bunching the material of his jacket in her small fists. He felt intoxicated, overwhelmingly so.

Somewhere in the distance his foggy brain registered Hector's voice. "On your mark. Get set. Go!"

Jazmin pulled away first. She must've heard Hector too. Micah watched as she tried to catch her breath. Equally affected, he held onto the door frame for support while his heartrate slowed to normal. She looked over at him and her eyes twinkled flirtatiously.

Hector and Destiny reached the car. Jazmin drug her gaze away from Micah's in order to fasten the car seat's safety straps. The dome light above her head shined down like a theater spotlight. She'd clearly had a full day if the stiffness in her movements and dark circles under her eyes were any indication. Micah nudged the driver's door closed. Unexpected protectiveness made him step backward. His heel bumped against the stones outlining the grassplot behind him. Twisting the sports ring he always wore, Micah wasn't sure who was charming whom.

Chapter Eleven

Click

Sitting back on her heels, Jazmin adjusted the lens on her DSLR camera. She focused on a mixed media mosaic turtle climbing the Brownstone's stucco wall. She'd finished her latest project and since it was a beautiful, unseasonably warm Friday in December, she'd decided to add a few more images to her client's webpage. Philadelphia's Magic Gardens was the perfect attraction for anyone who enjoyed modern, unconventional art. The owner-artist had covered the outside buildings and land with mosaics.

Jazmin had hoped that spending time outdoors would take her mind off last night. She touched her cheek. She'd been surprised to run into Micah at Hector's basketball practice. However, not as surprised as she had been when he'd initiated that kiss. She hated to admit it, but she had appreciated his compassion. She was having a difficult time remembering why she'd vowed to keep things purely physical. In truth, she didn't fully understand or know how she felt. She had just liked being in his arms, and she had really enjoyed the kisses they'd shared.

Jazmin stood and checked the time on her smartwatch. She wanted to capture shots at the riverfront at dusk. The renovated Cherry Street Pier on Penn's Landing provided studio space for artists-in-residence whose work passersby could view in-process. The space also included food vendors and an artisan marketplace. If she hurried, she might be able to run inside and capture a few pictures before the vendors closed for the night.

Her phone rang as she reached the Nova. The Bluetooth stereo she'd installed a few years ago picked up the call at the same time Jazmin started the engine.

"Hello?"

"Jaz, you're a miracle worker. I'm looking at the site now. It's perfect," her client, Tiffany, gushed.

Jazmin pulled away from the curb. "Remember that when I ask for a free weekend stay."

Tiffany had tried for six months to promote her business on her own. She'd hired Jazmin to update her social media page in hopes of boosting traffic to the website. Jazmin had met Tiffany a few months back at Cherry Street Pier when Jazmin had stopped to admire her handcrafted dreamcatchers. For years, Tiffany had rented out her Old City studio loft to budget travelers in town on weekend getaways or to small groups.

Listed on several different travel blogs, her place had received rave reviews for its location, stunning décor, and cleanliness. The twenty-eight-year-old decided she was ready to venture out on her own. She'd grown tired of paying fees to host sites when she did all the work.

Jazmin had nixed the continued use of Tiffany's social media page in favor of a professional website. She'd also convinced Tiffany to sell locally made paintings, sculptures, and tapestries in her loft. Jazmin had spoken to several other regular Cherry Street Pier artisans. They'd agreed to have their pieces displayed. Tiffany received a small commission from each purchase. More importantly, the boutique handcrafted art made the rental property stand out.

"I'm calling because my offer on a new property was accepted. Me and two of my cousins are buying three apartments in Savannah, Georgia. They're fixer uppers. I'll need your help again once renovations are done. Do you work on out-of-town projects?"

Jazmin shifted into first gear as the Nova came to a stop at a red light. She hadn't taken assignments that involved travel in the past. Destiny was older now. Jazmin's lips twisted as she considered the offer.

"I've only been to the area once, maybe twice," she replied.

She calculated in her mind how much time it would take to learn Savannah's history along with Gullah Geechee culture and folklore. She would need to scout

out local artists and artisans. She didn't want to short-change Tiffany because she wasn't as familiar with the region as she was with Philadelphia.

"The property will damn near rent itself with three apartments surrounding a pool. It has private parking. It's close to downtown Savannah and within walking distance of a Kroger."

Tiffany's enthusiasm bubbled over, spilling through Jazmin's speakers. Ideas swarmed around in Jazmin's head.

"We would have to start small..." she began. "Guests would only be allowed to purchase some of the items they admire during their stay, like your handmade soaps and candles along with dreamcatchers and quilts. Once I get the lay of the land, we'll include works by local artists."

"Done!" Tiffany cheered.

"Slow down. I didn't agree yet."

"You'll think about it, right?"

"Yes. I have to go, but I'll call you in a few days," Jazmin told her.

Looking out the rearview window, her stomach grumbled as she backed into a parking spot along Delaware Avenue. This was her third attempt at fitting the Nova between a mini SUV and a motorcycle. To her relief, a jogger stopped to help guide her into the space. She waved and mouthed "thank you" to the good Samaritan at the same time her cell phone rang.

"Hey, Brenda," she said, recognizing her friend's phone number on the stereo display.

"Have I told you how much I love you?"

"What do you need?" Jazmin looked to the sky. She prayed for divine intervention to rescue her.

"How much I appreciate you?"

"Spit it out," Jazmin said. She clicked her tongue.

"Gregg needs help setting up a show in Northern Liberties. You know you want to come through. It'll be just like in college."

Exactly.

She and Brenda had spent too many Friday nights helping Gregg on one show or another. Back then, Brenda had harbored "more than just friends" feelings for him. She still did. Gregg, like Jazmin, had known Brenda before her transition. He'd studied technical production and management while Brenda had focused on dance and choreography. Lately, he'd been touring with a burlesque show that made stops in Washington D.C., Baltimore, and this weekend, Philadelphia.

Perhaps, meeting up for some girl talk wasn't a bad idea. Jazmin hadn't told Brenda about getting stuck in the elevator with Micah or about running into him yesterday evening at Hector's practice.

"What's wrong?" Brenda asked after several seconds passed.

"I ran into the lawyer from the other night."

"And?"

"Aaaannnddd," Jazmin drew out the word. "I might have made-out with him between floors seven and eight and again last night. The second time, he kissed me, though." She cut off the car engine.

"Come again?" Brenda's voice had risen several octaves.

Jazmin's next words tumbled out. "The elevator got stuck and of course I freaked out. He was nice, genuinely concerned. I got swept up in the moment and kissed him. You know how I get about tiny spaces and heights."

"Alright. Alright. Slow. Down," Brenda said. "Are you in the market for a man?"

"I'm busy. I already told you that."

In the new year, Jazmin planned to schedule an adoption home visit. She'd already submitted the application as well as had her fingerprints taken. Additionally, she'd sent off for a background check. The conversation with Rose Mary replayed in Jazmin's mind. She didn't know what she would do if Reggie showed up and demanded access to Destiny.

"Does your body know you're too busy to date?" Brenda asked, interrupting Jazmin's thoughts.

Jazmin opened her mouth to respond then, changing her mind, pressed her lips together firmly.

Brenda continued, "You like him."

"That's obvious."

"No, you *like* like him."

"Are we in high school? I haven't dated in a while." Jazmin shoved her camera inside its case. "By choice," she clarified. "He works for that shitty law firm. I'd sell my business before I'd help improve their digital reputation."

"Start there," Brenda advised, her voice serious. "Tell him who you are or, better yet, don't."

Jazmin's brows knitted together. Her best friend wasn't quite making sense.

"You never worried about hiding your job before and with good reason. Remember that one guy who wanted you to help pay his mortgage? What was his name?"

"David."

"Right, David. He cooked you that big meal for your birthday."

Jazmin nodded even though Brenda couldn't see her.

Brenda chatted away. "So, why not have fun without a commitment? No strings attached, like always."

"Like always," Jazmin muttered.

Funny, the idea of doing what she'd always done felt like someone was driving a knife through a cavity in her rib cage. A knife that came dangerously close to pricking her heart. Jazmin grabbed her phone off the passenger seat and switched the call from Bluetooth to speaker mode.

"Hold on a sec—" she looked down at her cell— "Brenda, Rose Mary is on the other line." She stepped outside.

"Wait, are you coming by—"

The call clicked over.

"Rosie?"

"He has kind eyes," her sister said in lieu of a proper greeting.

Jazmin had told Rose Mary the story of how Micah had caught her dancing like an extra in a music video. Rose Mary had requested a photo of him. Jazmin selected a screenshot from the employee page of his law firm's website. She'd expected a better reaction from her sister than "he has kind eyes."

"Rose Mary, let me call you back. Brenda is on the other line."

"Okay, tell her I said—"

Jazmin tapped the green button on her phone and the call clicked over.

"I'm back." She popped several quarters into the parking meter and then hurried toward the pier.

Brenda lowered her voice to a whisper. "What are you going to do? And don't say, Mister."

Jazmin laughed. Mister was her twelve-inch dildo.

"Here I am thinking you finally met a nice guy and turned over a new leaf," Rose Mary said. Her voice cut through Jazmin's chuckles.

Jazmin skidded to a halt. She had joined the two calls by accident.

Brenda crowed. Her loud laughter had Jazmin holding the phone at arm's length. "Hey, don't worry, he's a ho too," Brenda told her sister.

"Wait! He's not...I'm not," Jazmin stammered.

"Hold on. I'm going to need more wine," Rose Mary said.

Although her sister's connection became muffled, Jazmin could hear cupboards closing and a faucet turn on. Rose Mary was rinsing out her wine mug. Jazmin shook her head in amused defeat.

"Are we seriously about to do a deep dive into my sex life?" she asked.

"Yes!" both women replied in unison.

Jazmin huffed. Her otherwise stony mask cracked as her lip curved into a smile. Brenda and Rose Mary discussed Micah as if Jazmin weren't on the call at all.

Chapter Twelve

The pungent smell of bleach singed Micah's nose hairs. He looked up. The custodian had nudged open the outer office door with a plastic mop bucket. The dueling sounds of office chatter and tolling church bells must have drowned out the noise of the bucket's squeaky wheels.

"Evenin..." Micah cleared his throat.

He realized he hadn't used his voice in hours. He'd spent the day with his head buried in online law journals.

The custodian's head bobbed up and down while he plunged the cotton deck mop into the bucket. He sloshed murky soap water onto the floor. The fancy earbuds were a gift, he'd told Micah, from his grandson.

"Get on up! Stay on the scene. Like a sex machine," the custodian sang, unaware of Micah's presence.

Micah tried again, a little louder. "Evening."

Virgil looked up and smiled. A chipped front tooth gave the old man an impish charm. He tapped the phone that he wore clipped to his belt. The music stopped.

"'Eh, boss. You're too young to be holed up in an office. You need a lady. Someone who'll make you hurry home for dinner."

"I'm working on it." Micah crammed his digital note-pad into his already overstuffed work bag. "Have a good one."

"You too," the old man replied. Adjusting the volume, the first notes of "Darling Nikki" by Prince started to play.

Laughing at the song choice, Micah weaved his way around the Y-shaped cluster of desks. He waved good-bye to the lone paralegal across the hall in the firm's law library. Ahead, he spotted two out of the three senior partners, Nathanial Stein and Frank Martin. Their cologne preceded them, and their voices echoed off the walls of the otherwise empty corridor. All three men met at the elevator.

"Clarion, how youz doing boy," Frank Martin said, his Jersey accent coming through.

"Fine, sir."

"Just the associate we need," Stein interjected.

Micah turned to face the fifty-seven-year-old and youngest senior partner. Stein rolled an unclipped cigar over and under each finger on his right hand.

"Sir?"

Nathanial Stein's eyes took on a mischievous, almost devilish, glint.

"How're you making out? J.J. is a wily filly."

Seeming to appear out of thin air, J.J. had fattened a lot of purses in a short amount of time. Tech Philly's clientele was sparse, yet everyone she'd worked with said she was worth every penny. J.J. dabbled in app design and game development but her specialty was overhauling websites and rebranding.

"Micah and Rhett have the advantage over you or me." Stein nudged his partner with his elbow.

Micah noticed how Mr. Martin's neck warmed. Red splotches spread up and over his face. The elevator dinged and opened. Mr. Martin motioned for his business partner to enter.

"Going down?" he asked.

"I'll catch the next one."

Micah did his best to keep his expression neutral. He clenched his teeth to prevent himself from saying something he'd probably regret later. Mr. Martin reminded Micah of his high school's assistant basketball coach. How he acted whenever the head coach made an irreverent remark about a cheerleader's ass. The assistant coach never spoke out against the head coach. He never acknowledged Micah and the other boys' discomfort.

"My money's on you, son, not Rhett Junior," Stein added as the elevator doors closed.

Micah responded with a slight, almost imperceptible, nod. Rising in the ranks at a place like Stein, Martin, Randolph and Associates gnawed at him once again. He tightened his grip on his work bag. He decided to take the stairs rather than wait for the ancient elevator to return. Outside, his car share ride waited. He climbed in the back seat and then dialed the number to his parents' landline at their Chicago home. He wondered if his father's opinion of the law firm would change if he shared what had happened with Nathaniel Stein and Frank Martin.

Micah knew he should shrug off the irreverent, often racially insensitive, comments. He should chalk them up to Stein being from an older generation. Micah also knew that comments could go too far. The head coach of his high school's basketball team had crossed the line a few years after Micah graduated. Charges were filed by the girl's parents and the coach's career was over. His wife filed for divorce six months later.

If only someone had knocked some sense into him earlier.

Micah's mother picked up after several rings. "Hello?"

"Hi, Mom."

"Hey, baby! How are you? Is everything okay?"

"I'm fine."

In the background he heard his father's voice, "No one better be pregnant!"

Micah laughed loudly. His newlywed baby sister had just given birth to a little girl. Despite his warning, George Clarion was a proud grandpop, constantly posting photos on social media.

"Oh, hush. I can't hear," his mom lovingly complained. "Go on, Micah."

"I called to—"

"Did he make partner?" his father asked, his voice sounded lively and full of enthusiasm.

Micah pinched the skin at the bridge of his nose between his eyebrows. A headache threatened to take hold.

"I called to check in."

"Remind him pride comes before the fall!" his dad shouted in the background.

Micah shook his head. His mom hadn't heard him. She continued fussing at his dad. "Do you want to talk to him?

Here."

Micah pictured his mother offering his father the phone's receiver.

"I've got to go," he said loud enough to be heard over his parents' bickering.

"Alright. Bye, baby."

The title of junior partner would serve him well when he moved on from the firm. He'd just have to stomach Stein's behavior and the ethical neutrality of his other bosses for a little longer. Micah's chest tightened with discomfort. He needed to reel in J.J. as fast as possible. The next time he and Jazmin met, Micah planned to get her talking about herself, to open up more. He would share information too and hopefully after a while they'd feel more like acquaintances than strangers. He'd ask for her help when the time was right. Easy.

***

A gusty wind rammed into Jazmin. The trek to South Street was slow-going. Vicki had texted, insisting she come by the store. Jazmin passed stoops decorated with colorful twinkle lights. Apartment windows showcased children's artwork along with snowflake cut-outs. She enjoyed the way some of the residents and shop owners had decorated the quaint Queen Village section of South Philadelphia. The door's chime announced her arrival when she reached 5th Street Hosiery and Lingerie Boutique. She tugged off her scarf and hat at the same time the wind slammed the door shut behind her. Right away, she spotted the reason for the urgent message. A potted red amaryllis sat on the main display case. Vicki stood behind the counter, her Creole ancestry on full display. A loosely wrapped headscarf replaced her usual wig. Her natural light brown coils poked out from beneath the silk fabric. Her flushed face made the freckles on her forehead and around her nose more prominent.

Jazmin looked around. The smell of window cleaner and wood polish filled the air. A mop and bucket rested against the wall near the fitting rooms. Vicki was in one of her deep-cleaning moods. She got like that whenever she was frazzled or annoyed. Jazmin's "Micah situation" had pushed the older woman into a cleaning frenzy.

"This has to stop." Vicki rounded the corner. "I've *Googled* him. The man's not abusive or a criminal. He's an up-and-coming lawyer. You could do worse." She patted Jazmin's shoulder at the same time she handed her the store's cordless phone. "Lock up when you leave. I'm going upstairs to watch *World News Tonight*." Vicki collected her belongings before crossing the showroom and exiting through the back. She lived in the small apartment above the store.

On Monday, Micah had sent a beautiful arrangement. It had taken Jazmin's breath away. Fragrant jasmine blossoms cascaded over the sides of a beautiful vase decorated with gold weavings. Paper white narcissus and orchids dominated lush greens. Tuesday, a bouquet of pale pink roses and Casablanca lilies had been delivered. The attached note read, "For the Little Miss." Destiny had beamed when presented with the flowers that evening before bed.

Jazmin had assumed there would be no more deliveries after that, but she was wrong. It was Wednesday, a week since they'd gotten stuck in the elevator, and currently she was staring at a beautiful potted South African trumpet-shaped flower. It would bloom and re-bloom all winter. She leaned forward and inhaled the flower's sweet aroma. She knew far more than she'd like about flowers and gardening. Her grandparents had owned a flower shop. She and Cicely had practically grown up there. Her mother sold the business to help supplement her income after Jazmin's dad died. Then, a few years later, whatever was left went to pay the medical bills for her dad's baby sister, Cicely's mom.

Jazmin slung her purse onto the countertop. She found Micah's business card and dialed his cell number. She'd decided to tell him that while she didn't intend to do business with anyone at his law firm, she would be open to a physical relationship, if he were interested. Sex with no strings attached. It was all she had time for. Maybe after a few rolls between the sheets he would be out of her system.

Micah picked up after the third ring. "Hello."

"Hello, this is Jazmin Johnson." She fidgeted with the hem of her jacket.

"Jazmin, I'm glad you called." She could practically hear him smiling through the phone.

"Thank you for the flowers."

"Glad you like them. Have you eaten dinner? Let's grab a bite."

At that moment, Jazmin's traitorous stomach growled. She hadn't eaten since breakfast and, even then, she'd only managed to grab a bagel and some hash browns from Dunkin Donuts.

"Just something small," he continued. "I need to ask you something, and I'd rather do it in person than over the phone. If that's alright?"

She had hoped to say everything she needed to say now. She anticipated Micah having a question or two, but she would lay down the ground rules. They were nonnegotiable. When she wanted to fool around, she'd text him. He'd come over in the middle of the night and leave shortly after. Eating dinner wasn't—

Micah interrupted. "South Street Diner isn't too far from where you work."

"Sure, South Street Diner"— she nervously ran her gold necklace across her bottom lip. She needed to clear things up if he thought she worked full-time at Vicki's.

Chapter Thirteen

The diner was busy as usual. Conversations whirled around Jazmin. The enticing smell of mashed potatoes and meatloaf made her stomach rumble. She spotted Micah seated at a booth near the back. As soon as their gazes connected, he stood and remained standing as she approached. He looked good in his business attire, wearing slacks and a light blue collared shirt. The shirt stretched across his chest and outlined his tight abs, as well as showed off the well-toned arms Jazmin was so fond of. Sliding into the booth, she took the seat opposite him. She was so anxious; she scarcely felt the friction of the torn vinyl seats against her leggings. Beads of perspiration had formed on her upper lip. She hoped to get through the meal quickly, without hurting Micah's feelings.

Jazmin slipped one arm out of her jacket and then the other. After removing her scarf and hat, she spied Micah's wool pea coat neatly folded on the bench beside him. She felt like someone had tossed water on her face. The fog she'd been in when she'd first arrived lifted. She held back the urge to roll her eyes. The uninhibited man she'd met in the elevator was gone. Making out with her was probably a spur of the moment, random act of carelessness on Micah's part.

He raised his hand to get their waitress's attention. The older woman brought over ice water and took their orders. As soon as they were alone again, he directed his full attention to Jazmin.

"So, why are you single?"

Jazmin's forehead creased as she squinted at him. "Was that your big question?"

Laughing, he lowered his head but not before she caught sight of his flushed cheeks.

"No, just curious."

"Have you tried online dating?"

"Come on, it can't be that bad." Micah sipped his ice water.

"You've got your cheaters. Then, there are the guys who are single but still married. There are the single guys with fiancés or guys with girlfriends who are looking for a girlfriend for their girlfriend. Let's not forget the guys with live-in roommates."

"Maybe there's nothing going on. They could be friends just trying to save money."

Jazmin moved her fingers up and down, forming air quotes. "'Live-in female friends' is code for late night creeping."

Micah's smile widened. He leaned back and folded his arms over of his chest.

"I see your point."

Jazmin's mood lightened. It had been a long time since she had a normal conversation with a man.

"Do you have any horror online dating stories?" he asked.

"We don't have that much time."

"What's the worst one?"

Their waitress returned and set a large pepperoni pizza between them.

"Thank you," Micah said.

His manners earned him a smile from both Jazmin and their server. Jazmin waited until the older woman was out of earshot before answering his question.

"The worst... *Pussy Beard.*"

Micah choked on the bite he'd just taken. Wincing, he fanned his chin with his free hand. A string of hot cheese had landed there and scalded him. Jazmin covered her mouth to muffle her chuckles. Her eyes drifted to Micah's full lips. His tongue swiped at the corners of his mouth. Thoughts of kissing him flashed through her mind. Thankfully, Micah gave her the thumbs up, signaling for her to continue. She'd been seconds away from leaning over the table and stealing a kiss.

She began again, "Like Black Beard but I call him Pussy Beard. When he arrived for our date, I leaned in to give him a polite hug. His beard smelled like pussy, and it wasn't mine. He hadn't even bothered taking a shower or cleaning up before coming to meet me."

"Wow."

"Wow, indeed," Jazmin said between chews. "This is delicious, by the way."

"Glad you're enjoying it."

The waitress returned to check in and Micah ordered a beer, a Yuengling.

"I'll have the same," Jazmin told the waitress who nodded and then left to get their drinks.

"Beer, really? The women I know order top shelf liquor or high-end wine. They often choose their drinks to determine the amount of available funds in my checking account or to see if I have the right pedigree to be seen with them in public."

"You need to upgrade the company you keep." Jazmin held his gaze for a few seconds to let her point sink in.

A city bus's brakes squealed behind her and Micah's attention shifted. He continued to stare out the window over her shoulder long after the siren's wail had faded. Maybe he'd taken her words to heart. She quickly dismissed the idea. Who he dated really wasn't any of her business. Still, she felt a tinge of envy. She was grateful when their waitress brought their drinks. Sipping the cold beer calmed her rising jealousy.

Conversation between them flowed easily going forward. They discussed music album releases along with movies they'd seen recently. Jazmin sensed an invisible thread connecting them.

Micah took a final swig of his beer and then sat the empty bottle on the table with a clink. "I asked you to dinner tonight because there's a promotion at work that has my name on it. *If*, I play my cards right."

Damn.

Jazmin didn't want to be responsible for slowing his career but there was no way she could work for his law firm.

"What about you? Why are you single?" she asked, deliberately putting off revealing her true identity.

Micah held her gaze. "I'm very particular."

She wiped her mouth with a napkin and looked away. She'd felt heat rise up her neck, setting her cheeks aflame.

"How long have you worked at the boutique?" he asked.

"I started working there in college. I was eighteen, I think, maybe nineteen." She sipped her drink. "Vicki's more like a mother than a boss."

The truth was she and her mom had a falling out shortly after she started working at the store. She'd chosen a college on the east coast to get as far away from her rural, southwestern Michigan town as a scholarship would allow. It didn't hurt that her cousin Cicely had laid the groundwork by choosing Temple University two years earlier. Her mother had approved of her going. She believed her daughter wouldn't be homesick with family nearby. Her mom's opinion changed during parents weekend, sophomore year. Because she hadn't been able to afford to come the year before, Jazmin hadn't expected to see her mom that weekend. Mrs. Johnson went to the campus movie theater hoping to surprise her daughter at work. Of course, she didn't find her there. When she returned to the dorms looking for answers, Jazmin's roommate unknowingly snitched.

Geraldine "Gerry" Johnson visited almost every sex store on and around South Street looking for her child. By the time she found Jazmin at Miss Vicki's, she was furious. It didn't help that Cicely had gone rogue over Christmas break. After failing her classes and then losing her scholarship, she'd dropped out of school. Cicely decided to move in with Reggie, the DJ she'd just starting dating, instead of returning to Michigan. They produced a demo together and nine months later a baby.

Jazmin's mom insisted that Jazmin come home to finish her classes at the local community college. She could transfer to Western Michigan University in the fall. Jazmin refused and her mother left parents' weekend early. She would not speak to her wayward daughter until she came to her senses. The two hadn't spoken more than a few words to each other since. Jazmin was determined to always be there for Destiny and to make sure she never felt that level of abandonment.

Not wanting to think about the rift between her and her mother any longer and the consequences of the ultimatum still dangling between them, Jazmin changed the subject.

"Did you always know you wanted to be a lawyer?" she asked Micah.

On the other side of the restaurant cheering erupted and then the serving staff harmonized the "Happy Birthday Song."

"Yes and no," Micah said, raising his voice over the ruckus. "I played ball for Temple. I managed to make the starting lineup my junior year but then I dislocated my kneecap during a random practice scrimmage ."

Jazmin winced. "I'm sorry." She placed her hand over his and squeezed it lightly.

He glanced down but didn't pull his hand away.

"Worst pain of my life. Rehab took over a year. Not playing meant there was a slim chance of drawing attention from the NBA or any development team. I thought about dropping out but my father..." his voice trailed off as he shook his head. "It wasn't an option."

"Let me guess. Your dad's a lawyer so there was probably a big push for you to go pre-law?"

"Ding, ding."

He smiled but the mirth in his voice didn't quite reach his eyes. She understood about feeling pressured and not living up to a parent's expectations. Their waitress returned to clear away their plates and trash. Jazmin instantly missed the feel and weight of his touch when Micah released her
hand to take out his wallet.

"Table Eight, order up!" called a male voice from the kitchen. Their waitress raced off.

"Thank you," Jazmin said to Micah. "This was fun."

"We should do it again sometime."

She expelled the first part of her mentally rehearsed speech, "I've got a lot on my plate between work and looking after Destiny. I'm too busy for a relationship right now." Having only paused because it was necessary to breathe, her words felt rushed.

She remembered the intoxicating kisses they'd shared in the elevator. Micah Clarion was different from other guys she dated. Men usually ogled her large breasts or made offensive and aggressive overtures on first dates. She knew what to do in those situations. Her words would cut them to the quick and they'd still be apologizing while the door swung closed behind her.

"You're a stay at home mom? I guess that makes sense."

She finished the last of her Yuengling to cover up that she hadn't been listening. "What makes sense?"

"You're a dancer, right?"

"What?" Jazmin nearly dropped the bottle. She caught it before it fell onto the floor.

His light brown cheeks reddened, putting his olive undertones prominently on display.

"The night we first met, you and your friend were dancing." Micah's words stumbled over each other. "I apologize if I assumed incorrectly."

Crap!

He really did think she was a stripper, just like she'd told Brenda. There was no way she could fess up to being J.J.

"No. I am not a dancer, professional or otherwise. My friend is a choreographer for different dance companies up and down the east coast. We were just goofing off and I thought she'd locked the door."

"But you work at 5th Street Hosiery and Lingerie at least part-time?"

She shook her head. "I was doing Miss Vicki a favor."

His phone beeped and he looked relieved as he turned to remove it from his coat pocket. Though his shoulders relaxed, Jazmin's heartrate had picked up. She was flattered he thought she had the body and moves of a stripper, but she was also insulted that he'd jumped to conclusions.

Pressing the button on the side of the phone, Micah silenced his cell. "Well, you can't fault my logic." He released short chortles that sounded fake to Jazmin's ears when she compared them to his earlier laughter.

"Come again?" The temperature increased on her slow boiling anger.

"Those other ladies who came in as I was leaving, they were dancers?"

Sasha, June, and Phoebe were not Jazmin's favorite people in the world, but Micah shouldn't have assumed they were exotic dancers because they were wearing thigh-high boots and form-fitting dresses.

"How old are you?" Jazmin asked, frowning.

He tilted his head to the side and studied her for a moment. It was apparent the gears of his lawyer brain were turning, trying to figure out the angle in her line of questioning. She held his gaze.

"Thirty-two."

"You're making some grandpa-ish assertions. Are you always this judgmental or is it something you picked up in law school?" Jazmin didn't wait for a reply. "The three women who came in as you were leaving are dancers. Professionally. Trained. Theater dancers."

"I'm sorry. It's just—"

"It's just, what?" Her voice rattled with unchecked emotion. "First, I'm a stripper and then they're strippers. Anyone else you want to call a stripper?" She glared at him when he opened his mouth to respond. "For your information, there is nothing wrong with working in adult entertainment."

The conversation reminded her of the one she'd had years ago with her mother. Jazmin's mom also had rushed to conclusions about her daughter. Stripper was one of the gentler words her mom had used to describe her the day she found out she worked at Vicki's.

The waitress returned with Micah's card and a credit slip. "No rush. You all take your time," she said sweetly with a Jersey-Philadelphia drawl.

Jazmin stopped glowering at Micah long enough to look around the restaurant. There were several people seated at tables near theirs. She caught one woman openly staring. She was seated in a booth near the window with three small children. Jazmin lowered her voice and looked down at her hands.

"I should get going." She expelled a frustrated breath. She didn't feel bad about giving him a piece of her mind, but she hadn't meant to make a scene or embarrass him.

"I didn't mean to offend you, really. What you were wearing, what they had on..." His words drifted away with a heavy sigh. He wound his sports ring around and around.

Jazmin grabbed her hat and crochet infinity scarf. His scarf, cashmere, no doubt, lay folded neatly beside his coat. What would he think if she revealed the truth? Would he even believe her? Her mom hadn't listened no matter how many times Jazmin told her that Vicki's shop was different.

Jazmin had been dressed like a burlesque showgirl when she and Micah first met. No, he wouldn't believe her. Heavens... if he knew the truth, would he tell his bosses? Jazmin's ribcage strained against the pressure of her thumping heart. Nathanial Stein, Frank Martin, and Everett Randolph II could ruin her reputation and make sure she forfeited the Millennial Titan Award.

"Please, let's not end dinner this way...what does your family think of you living so far from Michigan?" he asked, his expression regretful. A stark contrast to the stubbornness lurking in his gaze.

She sucked her teeth. "Are you implying I need a protector, Mr. Clarion?" She knew he was trying to start fresh, but now she was spoiling for a fight.

Plucking a paper napkin from the table, he waved it in the air. "Call me Micah."

"I don't need a champion, Micah."

He stood and held her jacket while she slipped her arms inside the sleeves. Jazmin bit her bottom lip to keep her body and hormones in check. He smelled good and she was seconds away from melting into his broad chest. She stepped away to distance herself from him.

"Are you taking applications?" he asked.

Jazmin's anger began to dissipate despite her best efforts not to let him weasel his way back into her good graces. Fortunately, she still had her back to him so he couldn't see her expression. He didn't deserve to be let off the hook so easily. Micah must have taken her silence to mean she had softened, however, because he babbled on.

"You know, when I first moved out here from Chicago, I had a lot of arguments with people over the silliest things. Water ice, for example. Isn't that just a slushy?"

"It is," Jazmin said, nodding her head.

Her grip on her anger lessoned more. She'd had similar spats with friends who had been born and raised in Philadelphia. She thanked Micah again for the meal and then moved to leave.

"It's getting late."

His voice made her pause. "Don't forget you still owe me a raincheck for coffee."

Boy, he was cocky.

"Excuse me?" she asked, turning around.

Smirking, Micah casually shrugged on his coat. Brenda had been spot-on with her declaration that Jazmin had a thing for bad boys. Jazmin needed to remember that while his show of confidence turned her on, his earlier comments had turned her off.

"I thought this was the raincheck." Jazmin repositioned her purse from her left shoulder to her right.

"This was dinner," he told her.

Micah held her gaze and she felt her insides go mushy. Earlier, she'd convinced herself that there was no harm in a mutual, no-strings attached dalliance. They'd go their separate ways afterward. In that case, he didn't need to know who she really was. Jazmin was older now and could keep her emotions in check. Also, unlike with her mom and Reggie, this time she would be ready when Micah snatched away his affections and walked out of her life.

"Okay," she said softly.

Micah's smile widened, showcasing a dimple.

Mercy!

That little cheek indent might have her falling for him. It was just too cute. She didn't even like older guys. In Brenda's words, Jazmin liked her men young, dumb, and easy to dump.

"Let me give you my number. It'll make cashing in that raincheck easier," she told him.

He handed her his cell and she put in her contact information. When she handed it back, he tapped the screen and then her cell rang.

"Got it." She added "Micah Clarion" and saved his information in her contact list.

"See you soon, Jazmin."

The way he said her name made her shudder. When Micah looked at her the way he was looking now, she was able to see herself as he saw her. She felt beautiful through his eyes. Jazmin forced one foot in front of the other and headed toward the entrance. She reached the front door and, unable to resist one last look, turned.

Micah was watching her go

Chapter Fourteen

As soon as Micah stepped inside Cutz Barbershop, the familiar scent of bay leaves and leather greeted him. Two antique gumball machines sat beside a cream-colored leather couch and a worn coffee table. Newspapers along with men's fitness and sports magazines littered the tabletop. Micah had stumbled across the barbershop while in law school. There was nothing special about the weathered North Broad Street storefront. Not with its dirt-covered outer windows and cracked blue, red, and white pole. Nonetheless, the shop was the only place he'd found in Philadelphia that felt like Southside Chicago.

Micah got his hair trimmed every week and the same older men or old heads were usually in attendance. Sometimes, there would be a boy getting his first cut. His dad, an older brother, or an uncle would bring him in. Today, a little guy, probably no older than four or five, sat pressed against his Pop Pop's legs, his eyes wide. A pair of clippers buzzed, and the little guy jumped. He tightened his grip on the hem of his grandfather's coat. The other hand clutched a Hot Wheels race car.

Micah smiled at the two of them and nodded his head politely. "Good morning."

"Morning," the boy's grandfather replied.

The boy squeaked, "Good morning."

The shop's owner, Faheem, signaled Micah over with the wave of his hand. Faheem's signature Philly beard and goatee glistened under the fluorescent lights and were a sharp contrast to his bald head.

"What's up, Mike? How've you been?" Kassir asked, the only other barber willing to come in so early on a Saturday.

The young man's head bobbed in rhythm with the low hum of the latest chart banger. The music played from tiny overhead speakers. His hairdo, a Basquiat-inspired matted afro with loose dreads, was a popular high school trend and made Micah wonder about the kid's age as well as his barbering skills.

"I'm fine," he answered.

"You must be living right. You're dripping playa," Kassir complimented.

"Nah."

Micah didn't wear flashy jewels or gaudy accessories. He was too old to show off. He rotated his wrist to draw attention to his Invicta.

"This is a twelve-hour workday, and these kicks are student loans."

Micah raised one pant leg, revealing vintage Air Jordan sneakers.

Faheem laughed. His big belly bulged beneath his oversized white t-shirt. The barber swatted the chair in front of him with a clean towel. "He gets it, *counselor.* Take a seat."

Micah shook off his coat and laid it on the vacant seat at the next station. "Ain't nothing on me drip. It's all hard work," he said with finality before sitting down.

Kassir waved him off and then went back to talking with his client. Micah frowned. He'd been on edge since Wednesday night. He still couldn't believe how badly things had gone with Jazmin. Adam had laughed his head off when Micah told him what'd happened. Adam couldn't understand how Micah expected to win favors by accusing Jazmin and her friends of being strippers. Worse, Micah had doubled down by saying he wasn't at fault for having his head up his ass.

"If you're interested, I may have some side work for you," Faheem said, drawing Micah out of his musings.

Faheem always had a cousin, a friend, or a neighbor who needed legal advice. Ironically, talking about potential businesses was just another way to pass the time while getting a haircut. Nothing ever came of Micah's willingness to help.

Micah's phone vibrated beneath the cape that covered his clothes. Keeping his movements small, he patted his pockets. He didn't want to tilt his head out of fear Faheem would skip over his scalp with the clippers and cut out a patch of hair.

Finally, his fingers trailed over the smooth edges of his cell phone. He slowly raised his arms and read the text message. His brother Paul had arrived at Midway Airport. His flight would board soon. In a little over two hours he'd land in Philadelphia. Micah grinned. One down and three more to go.

While Faheem talked about a restaurant his cousin planned to open, Micah's thoughts drifted back to Jazmin. He was damn lucky she'd agreed to give him another chance. He intended to make sure the next time they were alone there'd be no talk of J.J. or work promotions.

His phone buzzed again and looking down he saw he'd received a message from Adam.

"Easy," Faheem warned.

Adam wanted Micah to meet him in West Philly to check out a rental property. Even if the spot was as perfect as Adam said in his message, Micah wasn't as confident as his friend. Hell, he didn't know if any of his clients would follow him from Stein, Martin, Randolph and Associates.

Faheem dusted off the back of Micah's neck. The barber spun the chair around so Micah could check out his reflection in the mirror.

"All done." He unfastened the cape's collar and lifted it away.

Micah fished a twenty-dollar bill from his wallet. He handed Faheem the money and stood. The two friends clasped hands and then embraced briefly.

"Same time, next week?" Micah asked.

Faheem nodded.

Micah made sure to smile and tip his head to the boy and grandfather on his way out The little guy moved toward Faheem's chair with the help of his Pop Pop's hand steadily pushing him forward. Outside, Micah wrapped his cashmere scarf tighter around his neck. He hurried toward the subway entrance located on the corner. He'd give Adam exactly thirty-five minutes.

After disembarking to transfer lines at City Hall, Micah was one stop away from his final destination, 30th Street Station. His cell reception and internet connection improved as the train slowly rose above ground. Accustomed to riding Chicago's L, it took Micah no time at all to learn the interconnected transit lines crisscrossing Philadelphia. He exited the train and entered the main concourse where he joined throngs of Saturday travelers. Around him commuters spoke in Spanish along with Mandarin and Pennsylvania Dutch. The smell of fresh baked soft pretzels from Philadelphia Pretzel Factory filled the air, and, as a result, Micah's stomach tightened. He considered making a detour toward the stand to get a chewy, hand-twisted, figure eight pretzel with mustard.

He spotted Adam up ahead. As Micah approached, his friend's eyes lit up.

"Glad you were able to make it," Adam said.

"Paul lands in ninety minutes so I can't stay long. Where is this perfect office space?"

"Next door." Mischief danced in Adam's eyes.

"What?"

"You heard me." Adam practically skipped toward the exit.

"You brokered a deal for an office space in Cira Centre?" Micah hurried to catch up.

Ten minutes later, a Cira Centre real estate agent let the two friends into a vacant rental suite. Micah slowly turned in a circle, taking in the expansiveness of the room. Adam had struck gold. The glass skyscraper adjacent to 30th Street Station was an iconic part of the city's skyline. Its location
in the University City district of Philadelphia was perfect for clients and commuters. Most subway lines, regional rail trains, as well as Amtrak had to travel through 30th Street Station. Their law firm would not only be easy to get to and from, but they'd be in an area populated with trendy stores, eateries, and bars. It was an ideal spot to entertain clients.

"How did you get this for half price?"

Adam placed his hand on his chest as if offended. "I am a lawyer, so I do know how to negotiate."

Micah groaned.

"Well, I definitely didn't accuse the real estate guy of being an exotic dancer, that's for sure."

"Very funny."

Micah ignored the light-hearted ribbing. "How much money is it going to cost us upfront?"

He knew Adam hated debt. The last time his friend had purchased a car, he put down a third of what the SUV was worth just to make sure the full price would be paid off in under a year.

"That's not important right now," Adam insisted.

Micah eyed his friend suspiciously.

"It's half the price, man. You can't beat that rate for this location."

"How? Much?" Micah over-articulated his words as if interrogating a difficult witness.

"Two years," Adam mumbled.

Micah snorted. After glancing at his watch, he briskly headed for the door.

"Hear me out, Mike."

Adam stuck his arms out to slow Micah's forward advance. He stood between Micah and the exit, and the closer Micah got to the door, the more Adam stumbled backward. His feet tangled together.

"You're clearly interested. Otherwise, why would you be here?"

Micah stopped walking. Adam had a point. Why was he here? He should be cleaning his apartment. Instead, he stood in the entryway of what could be his own law firm, staring out of a floor-to-ceiling window with breathtaking views of Boat House Row and the Art Museum.

"You've already handed in your resignation letter," Micah explained.

For Adam, there was no going back. Either Micah joined his friend on this ledge, or he would watch Adam live out their shared dream.

"Mike, remember law school? How we talked about opening a firm together? We even drafted a ten-year plan."

They'd completed the first step by both acquiring experience in corporate law. Now, after five years, Adam had moved on to step two.

"Before you decide there is one other location I want you to see. It's much cheaper, but you'd have to commute or relocate to Delaware."

"Come again?" Micah must have heard wrong because Adam knew how much he loved Philadelphia.

"The Hercules Building is in downtown Wilmington, and just a short drive from the train station. The cost of living and working in Delaware is cheaper, it's a tax-free state, and they're building up the riverfront area."

"We'd be on the front-end of the city's renaissance," Micah concluded.

"Exactly!"

Micah found Adam's energy and enthusiasm contagious. Despite his attempt to remain skeptical, he smiled. Yes. He could imagine it.

"Set a date for a tour. The Cira Centre is nice, but two years' rent is a steep price to pay for vanity." Micah reasoned that he might need to get accustomed to a cheaper lifestyle.

"Done," Adam shouted, approvingly.

Micah glanced down at his watch again and slipped past his friend. "I have to run."

He hurried down the hall toward the elevator. He planned to stop by his condo before meeting his brother at the airport.

"I'll call you later and we'll go over everything in detail." Adam's voice echoed off the walls.

A chime sounded and the elevator doors slid open. Micah entered and was suddenly hit with the weight of what it might cost him if he started a firm with his best friend. Was he ready to turn his back on everything he and his dad had worked for? Micah clenched and unclenched his fists His emotions tittered between exhilaration and debilitating anxiety and were leaning toward the latter. He stared at the overhead numbers. Small palpitations hammered against his chest. They increased in intensity and frequency. Micah counted aloud as the elevator descended. He cracked his knuckles, filling the silence with loud pops. He needed to get his shit together, namely his game face, before tomorrow night's pageant and pre-holiday party hosted by his and Rhett's parents. His father and Mr. Randolph were sharks. They would be able to smell deceit and double-dealing and Micah was starting to reek of both.

Chapter Fifteen

The clack of pool balls ricocheting off one another intensified Micah's headache. Allen and Aaron, his younger brothers, had started up another game. Micah leaned against the bar. He pressed a chilled beer bottle to his forehead.

Like teenagers, the Randolph and Clarion children had retreated to the basement game room. They'd chosen the ESPN network over watching *The Miss Universe Pageant* with their mothers upstairs. Micah's older brothers, Paul and Derrick, were sports enthusiasts like him, and were tuned into the talking heads on the flat screen above the bar. Yesterday, they'd dropped off their bags at Micah's place and the three of them had headed to South Philly to the Sixers game.

His brothers' eyes were also red. The five of them stayed up late. Allen and Aaron were the only ones not showing signs of aging out of all-nighters. The twenty-five-year-olds had even suggested they all go out this evening after the pageant ended. They were on winter break and eager to check out Philly's nightlife. The two would finish their MBAs in May.

The twins had taken a later flight, and, using the spare key Micah had left for them at the reception desk, had gained access to his condo. When he and their two older brothers returned from the Sixers game, they'd discovered the twins had hijacked his home. Not only had Allen and Aaron left a trail of empty chip bags and pizza crusts in their wake, but they had also hooked up their videogame console to the living room television.

The whole thing was reminiscent of how Micah and his brothers had grown up. When the youngest two were in the third grade their parents had thrown up their hands. They gifted their five sons the master bedroom, complete with its own bathroom. His dad had removed the king size bed and replaced it with two sets of bunk beds along with an extra-long twin bed and a futon. The space was big enough to accommodate the boys' energy but still small enough to forge strong bonds between them, his father later explained.

Micah looked over his shoulder and smiled at his brother Aaron who awkwardly tried to position the pool stick behind his back. Several twenty-dollar bills rested on the table's ledge.

Their baby sister was the only one who hadn't made the trek east for this year's pageant-viewing party. She and her husband had been excused from the get-together. It was still too early to travel with their two-month-old daughter, Daniella. Usually, Micah and Becca spent the evening playing spades with Rhett and his older sister, Valerie. This year, Micah would have to choose a different partner.

He looked up when he heard what sounded like elephants jumping. Rhett bounded down the steps. Micah's temples throbbed. Rhett had volunteered to fetch a fresh deck of playing cards. That was over thirty minutes ago. Undoubtedly, he'd been sucked into running an errand for his mother or Micah's. There was always a last-minute demand for more cooking oil, paper towels, and aluminum foil. Or the ladies would need someone to find matches, the Citronella candles, or anything else that came to mind. The women's husbands knew to stay clear. They were holed up in Mr. Randolph's office, probably smoking cigars and discussing their sons' futures.

After the run-in with Nathaniel Stein and Frank Martin, Micah had an even harder time reconciling his employment with the firm. When he'd first taken the job, his father had insisted that the experience would outweigh whatever moral dilemma Micah felt about the clients the law firm chose to represent.

"Someone has to defend the good guys and some-one has to defend the bad guys," his dad explained.

To make matters worse, George Clarion had out-right laughed when Micah had expressed interest in working to help fight educational injustice within the

School District of Philadelphia. Micah had just passed the bar exam.

"That's the problem with you Millennials, you always want to protest. Want to make a change? You make it by getting ahead. It's called generational wealth, son. When you control the money, you control the shots."

His father's voice soon took on an inflection reminiscent of Micah's late grandmother's Alabama drawl. "Ya'll don't know what it's like to have water hoses turned on you, or to be attacked by dogs."

Abruptly, loud static broke through Micah's reflections. The enthusiastic voice of Rhett's mother, Taryn, crowed. From hidden speakers, she beckoned them upstairs.

Allen cursed. The cue ball clunked off the pool table and hit the laminate floor. Aaron snickered as he pocketed the money despite his brother's vehement protests.

The Randolphs had installed cameras and speakers throughout the house two years ago. They no longer had children living at home and Mrs. Randolph felt more at ease now that she could pick up her cell phone and check any part of the estate's interior or exterior.

Micah stood. His brother Paul slid from the stool beside him and draped one arm loosely around Micah's neck.

"You good, bro?" Paul asked.

"If you mean have I recovered from taking moon-shine shots, no."

Paul chuckled and then belched. The stale bitter beer smell set off waves of nausea for Micah. He pushed his brother's heavy arm off his shoulder.

"Well, rest assured. *This* old man is turning it in early tonight," Paul told him.

"More women for us," Allen said. He and Aaron high-fived.

"You, and Derrick, and Micah, with your day jobs, health insurance, and fancy credit cards, make us look bad," Aaron added.

Paul corrected him, "You all don't win with the ladies because you two are dumbasses."

Micah enjoyed his brothers' banter. Smiling, he looked to the bar. Derrick drained the rest of his bour-bon and then pushed away from the counter. He'd chosen academia over law. Although, now a tenured professor, he still caught flack for not living up to his *full* potential.

Micah's shoulders slumped forward at the idea of disappointing their father. His smile faded. He followed Rhett upstairs. Bright-colored, framed, abstract line art hung on the walls. Rhett stopped outside his father's open office door.

Rhett cleared his throat and then knocked on the doorframe. "Mr. Clarion how are you, sir?"

"Fine. Just fine."

Rhett entered first. He and Micah's dad shared an intricate handshake significant to their fraternity. Micah repeated the ritual with Rhett's father. George Clarion's voice softened with concern when he looked Micah over. "Are you alright, son?"

"Yes. I had one too many drinks last night with Paul and Derrick. You know how they like their Wisconsin Dells' moonshine."

The smoke wafting from the humidor wasn't helping Micah's headache. In fact, it increased his queasiness. He'd never live it down if he vomited into the over-embellished stainless-steel wastebasket beside the door.

George Clarion nodded and smiled knowingly. "That'll do it."

"Attaboy," Mr. Randolph interjected. "Next time invite Rhett. He could use some hair on his chest." He paused to sip his brandy. "And other places."

To his credit, Rhett kept his face emotionless. Micah looked between father and son. Associate and senior partner. He actually felt sorry for Rhett. Mr. Randolph coughed to cover his amusement at his son's expense, but it took a full minute before his horselaughs subsided. Thankfully, Micah's brothers and Rhett's sister, Valerie passed by the open door. They were the perfect interruption.

Micah elbowed Rhett. "We'd better go too."

Just as they moved to leave, Taryn Randolph's voice screeched. "Come quick!"

"As if this is life or death," her husband muttered, his cigar flopping up and down from the corner of his mouth. "You'd think they were crowning the democratic nominee for president."

"She looks ridiculous," Micah's mother said as the small group entered the kitchen and adjacent living room.

Valerie sat next to her mother. "Who?" she asked.

Allen and Aaron along with Derrick ignored the women. They piled plates high with cornbread, barbecue brisket, potato salad, and Mrs. Randolph's famous collard greens. The women had outdone themselves with this year's spread. They'd included everyone's favorites, from macaroni and cheese to crab tempura sushi.

Stuffed from overeating earlier, Micah leaned against the half wall dividing the kitchen and the living room. His father and Mr. Randolph rested on matching wood-framed leather recliners. Rhett stood not too far off. His cheeks poked out like a chipmunk as he popped another spinach and bacon stuffed mushroom into his mouth.

Micah's gaze shifted to the television. He noticed that three of the five pageant contestants were carbon copies of each other: pale skin, hands on hips, long flowing hair, and dark red lipstick. The fourth contestant, Miss Thailand, had a soft bronzy glow to match her dress. South Africa stood out, however. Her deep brown skin glowed under the stage lights.

"She really should have put some heat on her hair. She might've been able to pull off a pixie Halle Berry cut. She would have had to grow her hair out beforehand though," Mrs. Randolph said.

"That Wakanda dress. She shouldn't even be in the top five with that getup," Micah's mom added.

He thought Ms. South Africa looked regal. She'd chosen a flashy number with a high collar rather than a sequined bodycon dress or beaded trumpet mermaid gown like the others. Fringe drapery jutted out from the ornate shoulder pads and fell like armor across her front.

"I think it's beautiful," Valerie said, voicing Micah's thoughts.

Both older women cut their eyes at her. Clearly this was a two-person, one-sided conversation.

"Her answer to the final question was good," Val continued, unphased. "Everyone needs to do their part to affect climate change."

"It was on trend," Rhett corrected.

"Shush, they're announcing the top t'ree."

Micah instantly recognized his mom's native Chicago accent. The refined Diane Clarion had left the premises. Micah lowered his head to muffle the chuckle that refused to stay put.

Valerie cheered when the host called Miss South Africa's name. Micah's mother stood as soon as the program cut to a commercial break.

"She's not beautiful."

She marched into the kitchen. Micah's now-wide eyes followed her. Her back to him, she poured a glass of lemonade. His mother couldn't be serious. The woman was stunning. In fact, she could be Jazmin's twin, if the beauty queen were a bit curvier. They shared the same low cut, natural hairdo and deep complexion. He looked to his brothers and realized no one seemed bothered by the comment but him, or at least they weren't showing it. He'd heard his mother express colorist views before, but, for the first time, her opinions genuinely disturbed him. Jazmin had been right to call him judgmental. At the time, Micah hadn't known it'd been hereditary. His phone buzzed, diverting his thoughts. Thoughts that were becoming increasingly difficult to digest. When Micah saw a message from Jazmin, he nearly dropped his cell.

She wanted to meet up for drinks. Amazingly, she hadn't held a grudge against him despite his dinosaur way of thinking. It probably hadn't hurt that he'd texted an apology when he arrived home after their dinner date on Wednesday and then again the following morning. He'd messaged her "good morning" every day thereafter. Until now she hadn't responded. It was just his luck that she wanted to get together the one weekend he had plans and wasn't pouring over legalese until his eyes clouded from fatigue. Micah hoped he didn't spoil his chances as he thumbed a reply.

Stuck at a family thing, sorry.

After hitting send, he prayed silently for a positive response. Several seconds passed before Jazmin's reply came through in the form of a Bitmoji, a digital caricature. Micah laughed aloud. She'd chosen a miniature cartoon replica of herself with a saber poking her character in the chest. The word "touché" written in red across the top.

Paul squinted at him before leaning forward to read over his shoulder. Micah stepped away from his brother's prying eyes. He wanted his brothers to stay out of his personal and professional business for as long as possible. Lucky for him, Jazmin wasn't put out. She also hadn't tried to guilt him into finessing his schedule to accommodate her like Eleanor would've. He knew he really should stop comparing the two women. Matter of fact, he needed to get his head in the game. She'd lit into him so fast Wednesday evening that he'd never gotten around to ask if Jazmin had J.J.'s personal number filed away somewhere since she helped out at the boutique on occasion.

He lifted his gaze when the pageant resumed. Miss South Africa crossed the stage to give her final word. The seductively high slit on the front of her gown showed off long legs.

The pageant host, Steve Harvey, asked, "What is the most important thing we should be teaching young girls today?"

Micah was left dumbstruck by the sexy musical intonation of Miss South Africa's accent.

Mrs. Randolph smiled at her daughter. "Women do need to occupy space, especially in business."

"Politics also," Valerie chimed in.

"They want a female president," Rhett explained. He rolled his eyes.

"Nonsense." Mr. Randolph sipped his beer and reclined farther back in his chair.

Micah noticed the tension in his jaw as well as the creases under his eyes. He stared at his wife and daughter, his gaze stern and unwavering.

Valerie tapped her phone's screen. She hadn't bothered looking up or acknowledging her dad's response. Rhett looked between his father and sister. "Please, let's not argue over who's the best candidate to represent the Democratic party."

"Did you know Miss Teen USA, Miss America, and Miss USA are all Black women? If South Africa wins Miss Universe, four women of color will have won beauty pageants this year." Valerie looked at her mother. "Look." She passed the phone and asked, "Can you imagine?"

Taryn Randolph patted her daughter's knee. "You were great at pageants, baby."

Micah quickly wiped the look of disbelief off his face. He hadn't known Valerie had participated in beauty pageants. He looked her over. Her height fit the mold as did the long, permed hair that fell to her shoulders. Valerie had her mother's pear-shaped figure though, complete with what the kids called turkey thighs.

"Serena has dominated tennis. There's also Misty Copeland and ballet. They are proof that standards change. Nowadays, it's not antifeminine to be muscular," Mrs. Randolph told her daughter.

"South Africa may be a twig, but Serena...baby got back!" Aaron chimed in.

Paul frowned. "Act like you have some sense. Like we let you out in public occasionally."

Allen heckled his twin and then munched on a stalk of celery. Aaron tossed a carrot at his brother's head.

"No roughhousing," their mother yelled from the living room.

"Yes, Mama," the twins said in unison.

The room calmed after Steve Harvey revealed Miss Mexico as the second runner-up. It was down to Puerto Rico and South Africa.

"South Africa!" Harvey's voice boomed a few beats later. Congratulatory theme music blared through the television speakers. Leaping to her feet, Valerie pumped her fist in the air. Mrs. Randolph clapped her hands. The camera switched to the audience. One couple dressed in what looked like traditional African clothing were on their feet cheering. Now that the show had ended, Micah knew it was only a matter of time before he and Rhett were summoned into their boss' home office like two schoolboys. Micah's stomach tightened with anxious anticipation. He needed to do something to stop the impending confrontation from taking place.

"Pops? Mr. Randolph?" Micah said over the celebratory ruckus. Valerie was now whooping and prancing. "I just received a message from someone who I believe can lead me to J.J."

Mr. Randolph sat up, turning his attention from his daughter to Micah.

"That's taking initiative, son." George Clarion's eyes beamed. "Go on. Go on. No need to stay."

"I've also made a list of comparable companies in the area who are willing to do the same job as Tech Philly. They have solid reputations."

The law firm had received a fax from J.J. She had politely, but firmly, declined their request to be taken on as a new client.

"I'll have that in your inbox first thing in the morning."

Mr. Randolph nodded. Rhett, on the other hand, glared at Micah. Things clearly weren't going the way he'd hoped. If Micah could avoid being raked over the coals tonight, he would.

"J.J. will be out of town for a week," Rhett blurted out.

Micah's head whipped around. "What?"

The declaration meant Rhett had stopped by the boutique and spoken to Victoria Fontenot or to Jazmin. Micah felt like a weight had been placed on his chest. As his anger climbed, he had a hard time catching his breath. The promotion was at stake. Also, he desperately wanted his dad off his back while he decided the right course for his future. Bit it was the idea of Rhett Randolph interacting with his woman that bothered him beyond measure.

His?

Micah couldn't explain why he felt territorial toward someone who had practically told him to go to hell the other night, but he did. The collar of his dress shirt suddenly felt tighter when he thought about benefitting professionally from his and Jazmin's relationship...er, *possible* relationship. He swallowed the wedge of guilt lodged in his throat.

"Maybe you just need to know the right person," he said.

Rhett's frown deepened.

Ignoring him, Micah typed a message to Jazmin telling her that his plans had changed. Now, the only thing he knew for certain was that the kisses they'd shared had left him rigid and nightly cold showers had done little to quell his desires.

Paul inched toward him and elbowed him in the side. "Shame the devil. You're ditching us to see some woman?" he whispered.

The corner of Micah's lip curled up into a smirk.

Chapter Sixteen

Jazmin jogged up the stairs. As the doorbell rang for the second time, nervous excitement washed over her. It tickled her arms and neck. Shivering, she slipped off a pair of plastic pixie wings. When she reached the top landing, she flicked her wrist, throwing them like a frisbee through her open bedroom door. They glided several feet before landing. A puff of magic dust or glitter accented the air. She frowned. She would have to add cleaning her room to her ever-growing to-do list. She closed the bedroom door. Although her days of playing intramural sports had ended years ago and she couldn't remember the last time she'd picked up a disc, her ultimate frisbee teammates would be upset if they saw how rusty her throw had become.

She slid her feet into a pair of furry flip-flops and then stepped outside into the entryway of the renovated Brownstone. The unheated foyer had her body trembling. She opened the door and an artic breeze whirled by Micah. It pushed Jazmin's top against her body, showcasing all of her lumps and belly rolls.

Apparently, she was destined to be embarrassed whenever their paths crossed. First, he'd caught her dancing at Vicki's shop and now this. Jazmin held down the billowing oversized Red Wings jersey until the wind settled. She could feel Micah's eyes on her. Looking up, she met his gaze. He'd cut his hair since she'd last seen him, and his goatee was neatly trimmed.

"Come in." Her voice cracked. Opening the door wider, she stepped aside.

The small hallway felt even more cramped when Micah closed the security door behind him. It also wasn't as chilly. Jazmin supposed the six-foot five-inch tall, muscular man wedged between her and a wall of mailboxes had something to do with the rising temperature. The Brownstone was made up of two bi-level apartments as well as a landlord suite. Jazmin and Destiny occupied the ground level and basement while their neighbor's unit had been split between the first and second floors.

"Destiny's still up and I canceled the sitter because you said you couldn't make it. I thought she'd be knocked out by now."

Jazmin paused to catch her breath. She knew she sounded like a bumbling idiot, but she couldn't slow down. She imagined being encircled in Micah's arms. She turned her gaze to the floor; she believed if she made eye contact longer than a few seconds, Micah would know all the dirty and scandalous fantasies she'd had of the two of them.

"I can take your coat." She inched around his large frame and pushed open her apartment door.

Jazmin was careful not to touch Micah when he handed over the charcoal grey peacoat; she remembered how things had been when they first met. The physical contact had sent an electric shock to her nether regions. She knew she would be a goner if that happened again, especially after the things dream-Micah had done to her last night.

Micah's unreadable features made Jazmin wonder if he was at all aware of the effect he had on her. She opened the closet door and draped his wool coat over a plastic hanger. She was careful not to disturb the multitude of scarves and mittens that littered the top shelf and were always on the verge of falling. To make sure the closet stayed shut, she pushed against it with her hip. When she turned around Micah's keen eyes looked her up and down. They eventually settled on her feet. Her skin flushed.

"Shoes on or off?"

"Whatever you're comfortable with," she responded, kicking off her flipflops.

She was grateful she'd gotten a pedicure yesterday afternoon. Painted red, they matched her vibrant red lip gloss.

"Follow me. Up here are just bedrooms and an office."

She waved him along as she led him downstairs. When they reached the bottom step, Jazmin caught a glimpse of herself in the mirror that hung on the back of the bathroom door. Red cookie frosting was smeared from her earlobe to her chin and a kaleidoscope of sprinkles decorated her hair. She and Destiny had an impromptu baking fight. The holiday cookies they'd made looked horrific but tasted delicious. She'd cleaned up most of the mess before Micah rang her doorbell, but she hadn't had time to freshen up. Destiny had agreed to pick up her toys and then head to bed if they could bake cookies for Brenda. Jazmin had hoped to have the little girl tucked in before Micah arrived.

"Dez," she called out. Jazmin glanced back over her shoulder at Micah. "I need a minute."

Destiny skipped over. "You remember Hector's basketball coach. Say hello to Mr. Clarion."

Destiny latched onto Jazmin's leg.

"Nice to meet you. You can call me Mike. How old are you?" he asked, stooping to the girl's height.

Destiny held up three petite fingers.

"Wow! I thought you were at least six."

She grinned then loosened her grip on Jazmin's leg.

"What's your name?" he asked.

"Destiny."

"Are those your toys, Destiny?" He gestured to the mess on the floor in front of the TV.

She nodded.

He walked into their living area and picked up a plush Donatello. "You like ninja turtles? I love ninja turtles. My brothers and I watched the cartoons all the time when we were six like you."

Giggling, Destiny shook her head. "I'm phree." A large gap where her missing front teeth had been slurred her speech.

Jazmin placed a loving hand on her shoulder. "Three and a half."

"Are you sure?" Micah crossed his arms over his chest, his tone serious.

She stepped forward. "Uh huh."

"My favorite turtle is Mikey because he likes pizza, and everyone calls me Mike. Who's your favorite?" Micah flopped down on the floor and folded his legs, one over the other like a pretzel.

"They all like pizza," Destiny informed him. She walked forward. "I like Donatello and I like April." She kneeled beside Micah.

Jazmin watched the pair. Destiny didn't take to strangers easily. The fact that she felt comfortable with Micah spoke volumes. Jazmin knew he was good with older kids. Hector had talked non-stop about Coach Mike during their car ride home. Jazmin was impressed he had won over three-year-old Destiny.

"Who's this next to April? I don't remember her." He pointed to a female action figure dressed in a ladybug printed catsuit and wearing a mask.

"Ladybug," Jazmin clarified. "She's from a different show. Ladybug helps April and Donatello save their friends."

Destiny pointed under the coffee table. "Shredder has 'em locked up."

Jazmin mouthed "thank you" to Micah.

He winked and then returned his attention to Destiny. Jazmin flipped on the bathroom light and stepped inside, careful to leave the door ajar so she could keep an eye on Micah and Destiny. She washed her face and then swiped clear gloss over her full lips. Next, she straightened her clothes, making certain to wipe away leftover dough and traces of flour. She would have to wait until morning to sweep. Looking her reflection up and down, Jazmin sighed. Tonight, she planned to tell Micah that Jazmin Johnson and J.J. were the same person. The conversation would be difficult without her protective J.J. armor which included a wig, false eyelashes, and a flawless complexion courtesy of Fenty Beauty foundation and contour. Jazmin took a deep bolstering breath. She turned off the light and re-entered the dual combo living room and kitchen space. Destiny and Micah played checkers. The little girl's tongue pressed against the inside of her cheek. She looked as if she were sucking on an invisible lollipop.

Jazmin had taught Destiny the game over the Thanksgiving holiday. It had quickly become the toddler's new favorite pastime.

When Destiny pushed a red chip forward, Jazmin cleared her throat loudly.

"No. Go back."

"No side-seat driving," Micah scolded. A mile-wide grin plastered across his face. "You can move there if you want to, sweetheart," he said softly.

Destiny looked at her and then moved the chip back.

"Good girl." Jazmin pointed to another piece and motioned for Destiny to jump over three of Micah's black chips. Destiny finished her turn on a square in his back row.

"King me!" she shouted.

Micah's mouth hung open. "Whhh…What just happened?"

He looked over at Jazmin who casually shrugged her shoulders.

"I can't move my other two pieces. She has me blocked." Micah pointed at the gameboard.

Destiny's face reddened as she tried to hold in her giggles.

"Mr. Mike, meet Destiny, the Checkers House Champion."

He squinted at the little girl. No longer able to maintain a straight face, Destiny unleashed a hiccupy burp followed by a loud belch, and then laughter. Micah's eyes smiled down at her.

"I think I've been hustled."

Jazmin moved forward to pick up the hysterical little girl. She stood Destiny on her feet and then placed an arm around her tiny shoulder. The pair grinned.

"We don't know what you're talking about," Jazmin told him.

"I demand a rematch." Straightening to his full height, Micah put his hands on his hips. "I'll even let you pick what we play, but no checkers."

Destiny tapped her pointer finger against her lips.

"Tooty Ta!"

Jazmin turned her eyes to the floor, fearing she'd give too much away. Unbeknownst to Micah, Destiny had just challenged him to a dance off.

"You're on." He offered Destiny his hand in order to seal the deal.

The little girl shook it enthusiastically. Jazmin pointed to the remote that rested on the coffee table. Destiny eagerly snatched it up and changed the television channel to a music program for kids. She scrolled through the catalog of songs until she saw the "Tooty Ta" avatar. She bounced up and down as soon as the song's theme music began.

"Just follow the avatar's directions," Jazmin advised.

Micah made a show of stretching. He raised his arms and then twisted his torso left and right. When he bent at the waist, his jeans stretched across his muscular thighs and his tight ass was on full display for a brief moment before he righted himself. When Jazmin looked away, she noticed Destiny watching her. Blushing, she refocused the little girl's attention to the television screen.

"You got this, Dez." She clapped her hands.

Micah stumbled at first, but then began to pick up the steps. In no time, he wiggled like the cartoon boy on the T.V. He placed his hands on his hips and stuck both thumbs up. Next, he thrust back his elbows, spread apart his feet and pressed his knees together. With his torso slightly bent and butt pushed up high in the air, Micah resembled the front half of a two-person horse costume. It didn't help that he'd just been instructed to stick out his tongue and then to close his eyes. Destiny did the "Tooty Ta" dance right alongside him. In unison, they spun in a circle. Jazmin couldn't suppress her laughter any longer and a piercing screech slipped out.

Micah's eyes popped open. When he made eye contact with Jazmin's reflection in the television screen, he released a low rumble. His laughter overshadowed the music and soon Destiny's bubbly giggles joined in. Jazmin wiped tears from her eyes and even had to take steadying breaths in order to stifle the guffaws that refused to stop.

Bouncing up and down, Destiny urged Micah to "Tooty Ta" again. Micah's eyes pleaded with Jazmin for help.

"Come princess, it's time for bed. That's enough dancing for one night."

"Ahhhh... I didn't get to clean up yet." Shuffling forward, Destiny drug her feet.

Jazmin usually couldn't bribe the little minx to pick up her toys. Rose Mary was right in her assessment that Destiny needed a man in her life. She'd glowed under Micah's attentions. If Reggie had really changed, Jazmin would agree to let him see Destiny. She would sit down with him, and, like adults, they could decide the best way to introduce him into his daughter's life.

"Give me five minutes," Jazmin told Micah. "Feel free to change the channel. The clicker is right there." She pointed to the remote resting on the floor beside the coffee table.

Destiny took hold of Jazmin's outstretched hand and the duo headed upstairs. The three-year-old yawned and then she raised her arms for a pick-up. Happy to oblige, Jazmin lifted up her little cousin and balanced the girl against her hip. The effects of the sugar had finally worn off. Destiny nuzzled Jazmin's neck. Upstairs, Jazmin helped Destiny change into her pajamas and then she tucked the sleepy-eyed child into bed.

"Good night," she whispered, kissing each of the girl's pudgy cheeks. Destiny was snoring before Jazmin reached the door.

Jazmin descended the stairs carefully to avoid the portions of the steps that would make a loud creak. She didn't want to wake her sleeping angel. At the bottom landing, Jazmin peeked around the corner. Her chest tightened at how natural Micah looked lounging on her sofa. She seldom brought men to her apartment and had never allowed a man downstairs. Micah and Destiny's earlier performance poked holes in her initial appraisal of him. The fact that he'd willingly done something as ridiculous as the "Tooty Ta" proved he was better suited for her than the young boys she'd dated in the past. Not only hadn't Micah seen Destiny as an obstacle to them going out, he hadn't shied away from spending time with her, either

Micah cleared his throat, jolting Jazmin back to the present.

"Are you going to ogle me all night?" His eyes held a playful glint.

Jazmin stutter-stepped into view. She quickly regained her footing and then wiped her clammy hands over her pants.

"Can I get you something to drink? Water? Beer?"

"I'll take water. Thank you."

Briskly, Jazmin moved to the fridge. Feeling like a teenager who'd snuck a boy in through her bedroom window, the cold air calmed her nerves and lowered the temperature of her overheated body. After removing two waters, she returned to the living room with a little more confidence. She handed Micah a chilled water bottle.

"She's going to be a heartbreaker, that one. She had me wrapped around her baby finger." He snapped his fingers. "Like that."

Jazmin sat on a stool a few feet away. "She gets it from me." She dusted invisible lint from her shoulder.

He gave her a knowing look. "You're modest. I like that." He sipped his water. His free hand tapped against his knee. "In all seriousness, your daughter is amazing."

"Thank you." Jazmin's voice hitched at the end.

She was certain her eyes glistened. She hoped Micah hadn't noticed how much the compliment had affected her. She and Destiny interacted like mother and child so there was no need to correct him. Jazmin hoped her dream of adopting her cousin's daughter would come true soon.

"So," they said in unison.

"You go first." Micah gestured to her.

Jazmin shook her head. "No, please. What were you going to say?"

Micah took a deep breath. "I wanted to apologize for my attitude at the diner. Tonight I saw someone who I deeply care about and respect in a different light."

Jazmin blew out a breath, making a "phew" sound. "That must've been hard."

He nodded. Silenced settled between them. Jazmin was glad they'd cleared the air.

"Do you want to watch a movie? I have a ton of DVDs and some are actually PG-13."

She followed his gaze as he looked past her to the VHS tapes and Blu-ray movies piled beside the television set. She and Destiny owned a ton of princess movies.

Micah laughed good-naturedly. "I can't stay long. I have to be at court early."

Jazmin tried to control the intonation of her words so as not to let her disappointment show. "Of course."

He drained the rest of his water. Slightly crumpled, the plastic bottle wobbled when he set it down on the coffee table.

"I stopped by to apologize, but also because I wanted to ask you something."

Jazmin sat forward. Nerves like bouncy balls ricocheted around in her belly.

"I'd hoped you had some clue as to how I could get in touch with J.J. or someone who works with her. The promotion I told you about depends on me negotiating a contract between my law firm and Tech Philly."

Jazmin opened her mouth to confess.

"I know it's a long shot. You don't even work at the boutique. Maybe not finding J.J. is for the best," he concluded.

Jazmin clamped her lips together.

"A good friend of mine thinks he and I should start our own firm. He's even scouted out properties here and in Delaware."

"Is that what you want to do?" She propped her elbows on her knees and placed her head in her hands.

Micah shrugged. "We've had this planned since law school. I rarely get to try cases that actually make a difference. I'd love to work for the School District of Philadelphia, making sure students' rights are protected."

Jazmin noted how Micah's eyes had brightened. How his hands moved in sweeping gestures while he talked. Knowing he wasn't a spineless scumbag whose only interest was helping the rich made sleeping with dream-Micah not so bad.

"That sounds awesome! I think you know what you want. What's stopping..."

Before she could finish her question, his shoulders slumped. His chest deflated like someone had poked a tiny hole in a balloon. Micah's glum expression felt like a punch to Jazmin's gut.

She didn't wait for an answer. "Look, the way I see it, you only get one life. There's no sense in living for someone else. If your heart isn't in it, and you can afford to do what you're passionate about, go for it. Not everybody has that luxury."

"You're right." Micah stood.

It was as if he had been waiting for someone to affirm his passion. Jazmin felt reassured now more than ever that keeping her professional identity a secret was the right thing to do. He'd be leaving his firm anyway. Setting her half full bottle on the coffee table beside his mangled one, Jazmin stood also.

"Hell, maybe there's a reason you're not able to get in touch with J.J. Maybe you're not supposed to land this promotion and stay at Stein, Martin, Randolph and Associates."

Micah nodded along as she spoke.

"Even if you did get someone from Tech Philly on the phone there's no guarantee J.J. would do business with your firm."

She prayed he didn't think her statement odd. She'd been anxious about his bosses' reactions to her fax. She mentally crossed her fingers. She hoped the letter would put an end to Micah searching for her. Then, she could move forward and explore her feelings for him without having to avoid the truth or outright lie.

"A fax came in the other day indicating just that. Of course, the senior partners won't take no for an answer. It only fueled their desire and made them push us harder."

"*Us?*"

"It's nothing."

"Nothing like…"

"One of my co-workers is also up for the promotion. He came by the shop the other day. You two didn't talk?"

Avoiding eye contact, Jazmin shook her head. Why couldn't she tell him the truth? She'd eavesdropped on Vicki's conversation with Micah's colleague. Even with his back facing Jazmin, the man had appeared too smooth, like William Holden in *Sabrina*. He wasn't exactly disrespectful to Vicki but when he'd asked about J.J. his words were laced with the kind of annoyance some people displayed when they hadn't expected to engage with a child while waiting in the checkout line at a grocery store.

Victoria Fontenot was nobody's fool and far from the warm sit and sip sweet tea on the front porch and tell me all your problems "big mommas" often portrayed in black cinema. Rather than "out" Jazmin, she'd told the man that J.J. would be out of town for a week. After he left, Vicki had grilled Jazmin, and, like always, she'd told her mentor everything. About Micah and his quest for a promotion; and, about the inappropriate way they'd met.

Micah interrupted Jazmin's thoughts. "I'm sure he'll be promoted anyway."

"Stein, Martin, and Randolph," Jazmin murmured to herself.

She should have made the connection sooner. The guy standing next to Micah the other day was Randolph III. No wonder the jerk was so arrogant. His dad was a partner. Fortunately, she'd kept out of sight when he'd come by the store. Jazmin had listened and watched from behind the theater curtain that served as the divider between the saleroom and storage area.

"I should get going. I need to find another route to J.J." Micah moved toward the stairs.

"Wait, what? You're still going to track her down? Why?"

He turned. "If I don't at least connect the law firm with Tech Philly, I will never hear the end of it and I definitely won't have my father's backing if I start a firm of my own. I can hear him now." Micah's voice deepened as he mimicked his father. "How do you think you'll do when you can't manage to find one person? Have you heard of a phone book or the internet?"

"I get it," Jazmin replied softly.

She knew all about the consequences of venturing out without familial support. No matter how many awards she won, she still wanted to hear her mom say, "good job, sweetie." Caught up in her own thoughts, she stared at the black and white laminate kitchen floor tiles. During her last semester at Temple University her mother and sister had been in a car accident. A fire truck, with only its lights on had barreled through an intersection and broadsided their car. Rose Mary had walked away relatively unharmed. She had minor scrapes and sprains. Their mother, however, had taken a heavy blow to the head. Doctors had induced a coma because of the swelling against her brain.

Jazmin fussed and cursed when Rose Mary had finally told her months after the accident had taken place. Her sister had remained steadfast in her decision to leave Jazmin in the dark. The doctors had assured Rose Mary that their mom would make a full recovery. To her way of thinking, there had been nothing for Jazmin to fret over. Rose Mary insisted it was more important for her little sister to focus on her final exams and graduation. All Jazmin could think about was Rose Mary seated in a hospital waiting room scared and alone, and their mother hooked up to machines. Jazmin had been reminded of their Aunt Marie's diagnosis and how she, Rose Mary, and Cicely were kept away. They were only told the truth during the last few weeks of Aunt Marie's life, after she had decided to forgo future chemotherapy treatments. Jazmin had been a child then, but she was grown now and expected her family to treat her accordingly.

Jazmin felt her face droop at the memory. She couldn't stop it any more than she could keep her traitorous bottom lip from quivering. Had she known about the car accident, she would have skipped her finals and caught a flight home. One tear broke loose. It traveled the length of her cheek. It fell into the grove of a smile line and then curved around her mouth. It came to rest on her chin. She moved to swipe it away. Before she could do so, Micah's hand covered hers. A different kind of emotion replaced the sadness. Reassurance. It spread slowly through her belly as their fingers interlaced to join hands. Micah tugged her lightly until her feet dislodged from the grass-like plush carpeting. He led her upstairs.

"I'm glad you were free tonight," he said once they reached the front door.

Jazmin had planned on the two of them checking out a club that'd reopened after a fire. Renamed, The Ten Spot, the lounge featured live music and spoken-word poetry upstairs. Downstairs was a bass-pumping, hip hop club. She had planned on looking sexy and being seductive. Instead, she was an emotional mess.

"Sorry we couldn't go out. Another time?" she asked.

"Definitely."

He leaned in and Jazmin knew straightaway he was going to kiss her. Still, when he brushed his lips against hers. She was unprepared for the tenderness he showed her. She melted against his chest. His kisses were feather light. She had never felt so raw and vulnerable while at the same time feeling understood. The kiss in the elevator had been driven by hormones, but this one was driven by something else.

Knowing he deserved the truth, she forced herself to separate from his embrace. "Listen, I have to—"

"You don't have to explain anything," he cut her off. "We all have family baggage."

He gently brushed away more tears. Jazmin shuddered at his touch. Releasing her hand, he stepped away. His eyes never left hers.

"I'm going to head home."

Nodding, she stepped around him. She opened the hall closet and retrieved his coat. Her movements felt robotic as her brain tried to figure out a way to tell him who she truly was. Micah slipped his arms into the jacket sleeves. He pressed his lips lightly against hers once more before opening her apartment door. Then, he was gone. Jazmin felt woozy. When she finally came to her senses and stepped into the Brownstone's outer entryway, she barely registered the chill.

Chapter Seventeen

Micah tried to hold in a yawn. The staff meeting had gone on for close to ninety minutes. Usually, he didn't mind but today he'd made plans with Jazmin. He wanted to get to know her better, and not just physically either. Hell, he could call a number of women if he were only interested in sex. Jazmin Johnson stirred something within him that he hadn't felt in a long time. He enjoyed her humor and easy-going manner. Still, it wasn't until Sunday night that he felt a real connection. She not only encouraged him to go after what he wanted, but he felt relaxed around her, as if he wouldn't have to pretend to be the best son in the room, or the best lawyer in the office, or the most successful boyfriend at the party.

He smiled at the memory of how shocked she had looked when he reached for her hand. In that moment, he'd felt like a preteen.

The only thing nagging him was an inkling that something was wrong. Studying nonverbal communication made Micah a damn good trial attorney. Jazmin had stiffened and turned away when he'd asked if she'd seen Rhett at the shop. Micah just didn't know why. Also, how had Rhett not been able to recognize her? It had seemed as if every male over twenty had their eyes glued to her ass when she'd stopped by to drop off Victoria Fontenot's paperwork. Himself included. The short leather jacket she wore showed off her hourglass figure. The look, combined with soft makeup had accentuated her natural beauty, and had made him hornier than hell. He had to employ mindfulness breathing techniques in the elevator so as not to embarrass himself when she'd laid her head on his lap.

Micah glanced over at Rhett who was seated between his dad and the other partners. All were nodding along with whatever the financial advisors were droning on about. In his custom-tailored suit and wearing a smug expression, Rhett looked like he'd been bred for the role of senior partner. The company letterhead would practically stay the same when he eventually rose to the same rank as his father: Stein, Martin, *Randolphs* and Associates.

Micah's phone screen brightened as a text message appeared from Adam.

Have you considered something might have happened at the store between her and Rhett, and that's why she didn't mention him?

The idea that Rhett may have done something stupid or said something offensive ignited Micah's anger.

He cracked the knuckles on his left hand. The popping noise drew the attention of the paralegal who scribbled notes beside him. Micah whispered an apology before he turned his focus back to the financial team. He applauded like everyone else when their spokesperson finished the presentation. Rhett glanced over at Micah who stared back at him angrily. The younger Randolph had the good sense to focus his attention elsewhere.

Micah had more questions than answers. He also knew he had to let them remain unresolved. Jazmin had told him that she didn't know J.J. and hadn't worked at 5th Street Hosiery and Lingerie Boutique regularly since college. He would have to track down the reclusive tech guru another way. He would leave Jazmin out of his professional dealings from now on.

***

Jazmin rubbed her aching calves. She must have walked all two million, seven hundred ninety-three thousand, two hundred square feet of King of Prussia mall in search of outfits for the Deerfield Foundation promotional photoshoot. The closer it got to Saturday the more nervous she became. The photographer had asked that she bring outfits best representative of her personality. Brenda had suggested Jazmin play up her unique brand of "geek chic."

Shopping took most of the day and Jazmin had visited all the major luxury department stores including Neiman Marcus, Bloomingdales, Nordstrom's and Saks Off 5th. Her efforts had paid off. She'd found a fashionable, casual day outfit along with the perfect boardroom boudoir look and a show-stopping couture number.

Kicking off her Adidas, she slouched farther down in the booth. She'd chosen a table on risers in the back with a clear view of the door. Micah had asked her to meet him at a Jamaican restaurant around the corner from Vicki's shop.

Not only had he texted when he'd gotten home Sunday night, he had also messaged her the next morning. More posts came throughout the day and the messages continued on Tuesday and Wednesday. Each time her phone binged, and she saw a message from Micah, a surge of giddiness took hold of her senses. Her cheeks hurt from grinning like an idiot. Never in a million years had Jazmin dreamed she'd be *that girl*. In the past, being in constant contact with a guy drove her batshit crazy. She despised having to come up with clever responses to endless queries of "What are you doing?" She and Micah had even started talking on the phone in the evenings after Destiny went to sleep. Micah's claim that he just wanted to hear her voice had turned Jazmin's legs to putty. As a result, his nightly calls were easily the best part of her day. Before meeting him, she only talked on an actual telephone with family members because they lived far away. Even Vicki and Pops texted.

Ironically, she hadn't seen Micah in person since Sunday night. He'd been super busy with online video conference calls during the day and business dinners lasting well into the evening. Whenever he had a free minute, he combed the city for rental spaces with his friend, Adam. The two hoped to open their firm within six months of signing a lease.

Jazmin's phone binged. She giggled. The message featured a cartoon Micah running on a tiny hamster wheel.

Meeting finally ended. Still up for an early dinner at The Reef?

Yes. Here now.

See you soon.

She sipped from her glass of ice water. Thank goodness she'd stopped home to drop off her purchases and take a quick shower. She'd arrived shortly after five o'clock and within minutes the small restaurant became crowded and the happy-hour crowd livelier. She looked at the three laughing women seated catty-corner to her. All were impeccably dressed, but one stood out from the group. She wore a white cable knit crop sweater and a contrast piping skirt. Patent leather black booties made the ensemble look comfortable, yet sophisticated. Brenda would say it was "Chanel-inspired."

Jazmin turned back to her glass of water. She couldn't remember the last time she'd gotten dolled up for a night out with her girlfriends. Hell, she doubted her friends still remembered her phone number. She had canceled on them more times then she'd like to admit. She'd given them a million excuses until eventually the invites had stopped.

Jazmin glanced up when the restaurant door opened, letting in a gust of frigid air. She recognized Micah the second his foot touched the parquet flooring. She waved to get his attention but then decided to slip her feet back in her sneakers and stand. He scanned the room. No doubt, he had trouble seeing her over the giants in business suits standing around the bar. Just as Jazmin moved in his direction, the crowd shifted left and she and Micah locked eyes. She smiled. Butterflies fluttered in her belly.

Her excitement was short-lived, though. The *Vogue fashion model* from the other table materialized and rushed past.

"Micah!" the woman shouted.

Jostled and confused, Jazmin watched the woman practically launch herself into Micah's arms. If his face was any indication, he hadn't expected the assault. Regardless, a tinge of jealousy rolled up Jazmin's spine.

It was apparent he knew the woman intimately by the way she nuzzled his cheek.

"Mike, it's so good seeing you. How have you been? Where have you been?"

He peeled the woman's arms from around him. "Eleanor," he responded dryly.

It took a minute or so for him to wrestle himself loose. When his eyes found Jazmin's again, he stepped around the woman and then continued forward. Jazmin met him halfway. As soon as he reached her side, he pressed his mouth close to her ear. His breath tickled her neck.

He spoke in a low voice just above a whisper. "I got here as fast as I could."

At the feel of the heat on her neck, Jazmin's envy melted away. Yeah, Micah was smooth. He knew how to make her feel special. Also, she forgot about being fatigued from a long day of shopping.

The woman's eyes narrowed. Her angry stare focused on Jazmin.

"Who's this?"

It was plain she hadn't missed the intimacy of Micah's gesture. She trailed behind them, pushing aside tipsy men who stepped in her path. Micah turned when they neared the steps that led to their booth. Jazmin noticed he had positioned himself between her and the other woman. She also noticed that while his face remained neutral, the other woman's grew redder. Her perfectly airbrushed makeup had cracked.

"Eleanor, you're making a scene," he told her.

"I don't care." She shifted her weight to her other foot and crossed her arms over her chest. She snorted when Jazmin interrupted, tapping Micah on the shoulder.

"I'm going to go to the booth."

Micah nodded and then squeezed her hand. Jazmin passed by Eleanor's girlfriends on the way.

"She's always doing this," one woman mumbled.

The other awkwardly hobbled along. Her wedge boots were no match for her friend's fast pace. She slipped one arm in her jacket while holding two purses and what was more than likely Eleanor's coat, an expensive-looking, and no doubt real, full-length fur.

"I told you not to invite her," replied the first woman, who walked ahead.

Jazmin watched the scene from her seat. With Micah's back to her, she couldn't hear what he said or read his lips. She heard Eleanor loud and clear, however."I might not be around when you come to your senses. Who are you going to call when you get sick of this one?" She gestured to Jazmin before she snatched the fur from her friend's outstretched arm.

The couple seated at the table in front of Jazmin roared with laughter at the worst possible moment. They were oblivious to the drama going on several feet away. They made it impossible for Jazmin to hear Eleanor's parting words. By the satisfied looks on her friends' faces, whatever she'd said had been a doozy. The three women whirled around and pushed their way through the crowd. When Micah reached the booth, he flopped down in the seat across from her.

"An old friend?" Jazmin asked.

He nodded and then stared at the menu.

"I haven't been here in a long time. The food smells as good as I remember."

Jazmin wondered if Eleanor was the type of woman Micah was used to. If so, Jazmin knew she could never measure up. She would never fit into his Black bourgeoisie world. She didn't have a trust fund and hadn't pledged a historically Black sorority. Moreover, she hadn't grown up in Jack and Jill of America, a social and philanthropic organization. Social status withstanding, Micah would probably dump her after he found out she'd withheld her identity. Jazmin looked up to find his eyes watching her. He seemed to want to say something but before he could their server arrived to take their drink orders. After the young woman left, Jazmin leaned in as if to keep her comments from being heard by other diners. Micah followed suit.

"So, what was up with the Amazon chick who caused a scene?" she asked, unable to check her curiosity any longer.

He leaned back. Despite his calm exterior, Jazmin noticed him toying with the sports ring he always wore. She sipped her drink and put on her most innocent and chaste face.

She continued, "A word of advice: You're supposed to keep your women restricted to different area codes."

Micah's jaw dropped and his fingers stopped moving.

"That was an amateur move." She motioned between them. "You and me, we are never crossing the bridge to Jersey."

She could tell he didn't know whether to take her seriously. Deciding to toy with him a bit longer, she kept her expression neutral.

"The senior partners at my firm and Ellie's father do a lot of business together. I've known her a long time," he explained.

"Ellie is it?"

A different server returned with their drinks. Rum punch for her, and for him, Johnny Walker Black. Neat.

"So, how long did you two date?"

"Not long." He sipped his drink and met her stare head on.

***

The break in the interrogation allowed Micah a chance to gather his wits. Despite knowing damn well he was going to order the red snapper per usual, he pretended to look over the happy hour specials. He couldn't believe they'd run into his ex-girlfriend. He felt responsible even though he had no control over it. He had said a silent prayer of thanks that Jazmin had been out of earshot for Eleanor's parting words.

"Slumming it with a nappy-headed homegirl in public is a bad look for a future junior partner. You claim to be above the bullshit, but you're just like those bosses you hate," said Eleanor.

Steam had billowed from Micah's ears. He didn't care about the slanderous comparison she'd made about him. Eleanor's insults had stopped bothering him long ago. He was pissed that she'd brought Jazmin into their argument, a complete stranger. Before he was able to set Eleanor straight, however, she fired a second shot.

"Don't be late picking me up Saturday for the gala photoshoot. Ten o'clock sharp!"

His ex-girlfriend might as well have kneed him in the balls. Immediately, the pomp and circumstance of his bull-headed and self-righteous indignation vanished. Sunday night, Eleanor had called him. He'd just left Jazmin's place. Ellie had discovered that J.J. was doing publicity for the gala and she'd managed to convince the photographer to allow the two of them to stop by the shoot. It had been the good news Micah needed.

He sighed. He'd agreed to accompany Ellie to the photoshoot, and then to the New Year's Eve gala the following week. Hopefully, by early February he'd have is own firm or he'd have his promotion. Either way, he'd be able to wash his hands of Eleanor Deerfield for good. He just hoped the unexpected interruption hadn't blown his chances with Jazmin.

"Don't worry about Ellie." Micah laid down the menu. "How about we order appetizers and then get out of here. I was thinking it might be easier to talk in a less crowded place."

Jazmin sipped her drink. "Alright, but I want appetizers and *dessert*."

He placed his hand atop hers. "No problem."

When she squeezed his hand in return, his heart hammered against his chest. Jazmin covered her mouth and yawned with her free hand.

"How long did the "Tooty Ta" song stay stuck in your head?" she asked.

"Not long... if you want, we can take the food back to my place." She was clearly exhausted. "My condo's up the street, on the riverfront."

Jazmin studied him over the rim of her water glass.

He rotated his shoulders in response to her silent cross-examination. She would make an excellent attorney.

"Yes."

"*Yes*?" he parroted.

"Did you want me to say no?" Again, her lip curved up on one side, forming a playful smirk.

Their waitress approached.

"Thank you. Save me from myself," he said to the young woman who looked down at him curiously.

Jazmin snickered. Her laughter sounded just like her little girl, Destiny's bell-like giggles, but richer. The sound put his nerves at ease. He gestured in Jazmin's direction, indicating she should order first.

"I'll have the crab cakes, please." She handed over her menu.

"Red snapper with rice and beans along with a side of cornbread and macaroni and cheese." He glanced at Jazmin while the waitress jotted down their orders. "And rum cake."

"To go," Jazmin added cheerfully.

Chapter Eighteen

The moment Jazmin stepped inside Micah's condo it took her breath away. The windows on one wall offered views of the Delaware River and Benjamin Franklin Bridge.

"It's like standing in a constellation."

Smiling, she shrugged off her leather coat and placed it in Micah's outstretched hand before she slipped off her sneakers. When she bent over to position her Adidas against the wall alongside his Oxford leather boat shoes, she heard Micah's short intake of breath. Shivers of anticipation tickled the back of her neck and trailed down her spine.

Nervousness followed closely behind. Like a scout fanning kindling, it ignited slowly. She'd never wanted anyone the way she wanted Micah.

"This way," he directed.

Jazmin followed him around a table that could easily seat twelve people. It separated the living room from the galley kitchen. With stainless steel appliances, a double oven, and barbeque cooktop, it was a cook's dream.

"My sister would be in heaven." Jazmin ran her hand along the granite countertop.

"She's a chef?"

"Rose Mary is more than that." Jazmin shook her head when he moved to place a third crab cake on her plate. "I was always good at drawing. I even contemplated making art history my minor. Rose Mary, though, she's the artist in the family."

"Soooooo," Micah said, dragging out the word. "You're saying you can't cook?"

Jazmin playfully punched him in the arm. "I'll have you know, I bake very well."

He held onto her hand and interlaced their fingers. Thrilling vibrations traveled down her torso and beneath her waistband. Her breath hitched when their gazes locked. Not for the first time she noticed the flecks of gold shining in the deep mahogany pools of Micah's eyes. Pulling her hand back, she stepped away from him on wobbly legs.

"Good choice." Jazmin cleared her throat. "To ask for mac n' cheese."

The aromas that filled the kitchen reminded her of early dinners on Sunday afternoons growing up. Her mother was an expert at fixing comfort food. Jazmin watched as Micah scooped a decent-sized portion onto her plate before he expertly loaded the dishes onto his arm. His hands were large, and his palms calloused. Her heartrate quickened at the memory of him running those same rough hands over her back. Her nipples remembered as well. They tingled and then tightened, straining against the fabric of her bra.

Micah inclined his head for Jazmin to follow him into the living room where he sat their food on a vintage steamer trunk coffee table.

"Is this a Hartmann?" she asked. Horniness gave way to awe. "Did you know in *Live and Let Die* James Bond travels with Hartman luggage?"

"I didn't take you for a Bond fan." He headed back to the kitchen. "Can I get you a drink? I have water, beer, and soda."

She ran her hands over the glazed top. The faded traveling stickers had been preserved: Hong Kong, New York, Seattle, London. The owner of the suitcase had seen the world.

"Coke, if you have it, thanks," she said, not looking up. "My dad and I would watch *007* movies together whenever they came on television. Did you make this? I mean, did you do the restoration?"

"I wish. My sister's the D.I.Y. queen. She found that in the attic at my parents' house. I think it was my mother's stepfather's or maybe it was her dad's. I'm not exactly sure. Becca gave it to me as a housewarming gift."

"Well, she did a great job."

Micah returned and handed Jazmin a glass with ice along with an unopened can of Coke. "I'll let her know you said so."

He placed a cold Yuengling on the tabletop and then sat beside Jazmin on the mauve leather sofa.

"Do you like Bond movies?" she asked between bites. A soft purr of pleasure rumbled loose. "This is really good. Thank you for dinner."

When Micah didn't respond right away, she looked up. His pupils had darkened, and the tiny gold flecks had disappeared. His eyes were trained on her mouth.

"No problem. I'm glad you're enjoying yourself," he answered, at last. "I'm partial to the ones featuring Sean Connery."

His voice had sounded controlled but, if the way he was shifting around was any indication, he'd become aroused while watching her eat. No amount of Jamaican curry, jerk spice, or other seasonings could mask the musk of male sexual arousal. Jazmin smirked, happy that this time Micah didn't hide how their mutual attraction affected him. They weren't strangers in a store meeting for the first time. The intensity of his stare made Jazmin's sex clench while anticipation teased her newly awakened clit.

"It's not about the man playing Bond, it's about the story. It seems as if you're in need of *an education* in all things MI6," she told him.

Micah studied her for a moment. "Alright, which movie do you want to start with?"

Jazmin's phone rang, interrupting her response. She fished her cell out of her purse and frowned at the screen. "A scam. Probably."

"I hate those."

"I've been getting calls from Ohio, Indiana, Western Pennsylvania, you name it. If I answer, I only hear static." She shoved the cell phone inside her purse.

Micah pinched off a piece of cornbread and popped it in his mouth. His tongue swept crumbs from his bottom lip. Jazmin thought back to those same lips on hers and the feel of his tongue feasting on her neck. Heat radiated inside her belly. She placed her fork on her plate and then looked him up and down.

"Do you want to change? You can't be comfortable."

While she had dressed for a relaxed evening out, deciding to wear an oversized black, silk tunic blouse and leggings, Micah was still dressed for the boardroom. The tailored suit fit him well, but she preferred to jump his bones without fear of wrinkling his clothes.

He chuckled. "Sure. Give me a sec."

His touch sent sensual tremors straight to the points on her chest. Her tits were goners. The buds saluted him at full attention.

Micah handed Jazmin the remote before he departed. As soon as he was out of sight Jazmin's phone rang again. The familiar tune let her know the caller was her sister. After locating her cell again, she tapped the red end button, sending her sister's call to voicemail. The last thing Jazmin wanted was another lecture about Reggie and second chances.

Jazmin finished eating while Micah changed. Afterward, she gathered her dirty dishes and carried them to the kitchen. She'd just finished rinsing the silverware when she looked up and saw Micah. He'd changed into loose-fitting sweatpants. They sat low on his waist, showing off the V-muscles along his hips. He walked forward. Jazmin's heartbeat synced with the ticking secondhand of the analog clock above her head. Her panties dampened in anticipation.

Chapter Nineteen

"Snacks?" Micah asked, ten or so minutes after the movie had started.

Cuddling a beige sofa pillow, Jazmin shook her head. Of course, he'd chosen *Die Another Day*. Halle Berry had it all, sun-kissed skin, big boobs, toned abs, long legs and well.... Jazmin had one out of four. That wasn't too bad. Who was she kidding? She was an Oompa Loompa compared to Halle
Berry's Jinx.

Jazmin moved her right foot in a small circle. She repeated the motion with the left. Her ankles ached. She felt Micah looking at her but instead of turning to face him, she trained her eyes on the giant flat screen. The monstrosity had to be seventy inches. She squirmed under his appraisal and squeezed the pillow tighter. To her shock, he leaned over and then casually raised her legs. He placed them on his lap. Words of protest faded as he kneaded and rubbed her feet with strong and deliberate strokes. She sighed and sank into the sofa's buttery leather. Micah pushed his thumb deep into the arch of her left foot and dragged his finger from heel to sole.

She moaned. One by one he tugged on each toe, lengthening and squeezing the tip. Afterward, he massaged the area just beneath the pad. With a sweeping motion he rubbed from the center to the side. She sighed heavily. The aches from a day spent on her feet melted away.

"Are you a reflexology expert?"

Micah winked. "I know a few things. One of the guys who lived in the dorms moonlighted as a massage therapist on the weekends. He told anyone who would listen the way to wooing a woman was through her feet. Out of politeness, I took the reflexology pamphlet he passed out. I read the thing more times than I could count on one particularly boring twenty-hour train ride from Philly to Chicago. However, you, Jazmin Johnson, are the first woman I have ever used this knowledge on."

"Well, you can definitely quit your day job, Mr. Clarion."

His confession about her being the first and only recipient of his wonderful foot rubs danced around in her mind.

He couldn't be serious, could he?

Again, she moaned softly when he dug into her arch.

"Shush and watch the movie," he demanded, playfully.

She complied. Micah massaged the inner side of her foot. He took his time, alternating between soft and hard strokes. Jazmin bit her lip, enjoying the pleasurable pain he caused. Next, he pushed into a pressure point somewhere along the curve, by her heel. At the same time, he pressed into an area between her ankle and Achilles. Jazmin immediately felt a slight but stimulating sensation at her pelvis. She squinted at him. His expression hadn't changed, however. He focused on James Bond and Jinx exchanging witty quips laced with heavy inuendo. Micah continued kneading her muscles as if nothing had happened. When he pressed down hard on the side of her foot, near her pinky toe, her pelvic muscles pulsated without warning. The sensation moved lower as it intensified.

"Goodness!" she said in a loud whisper.

He looked over at her. On the screen the hero and heroine were getting it on. Embarrassment warmed Jazmin's cheeks. She still didn't know if he had done it on purpose. If not, she had just sounded like a prude.

Holding her gaze, Micah dug a knuckle sharply into a spot beneath her big toe. An unexpected orgasm crested over her. It crashed into and ignited what felt like every nerve ending below her waist. Jazmin struggled to keep her facial expression neutral. Failing miserably, she turned her head away, looking everywhere but at Micah. Though the orgasm ebbed as quickly as it had hit her, its intensity made her muscles quiver with aftershocks that she was certain she'd feel next week. When Micah loosened his hold, she snatched her feet away and pulled herself upright. Once confident her face wouldn't betray her, Jazmin met his gaze.

"You okay?"

Jazmin didn't even know a foot massage could induce arousal let alone an orgasm.

"I'm fine."

"Is everything... are you..." his voice trailed off.

"I'm fine, really."

Her voice sounded falsely confident even to her own ears.

Fuck it!

She scooted over until her body was flush against his. If he were that good with his hands, she couldn't wait until they came together between the sheets.

If being herself resulted in being pigeonholed, so be it. She would tackle that problem later. Jazmin caressed and then squeezed his thigh. His short intake of breath bolstered her confidence. She grinned shamelessly. He studied her a moment. Before he was able to find his voice, however, she leaned in and pressed her lips against his, snatching away whatever he was about to say. She pressed into him, chest to breast. Jazmin could kiss Micah forever. Tonight, however, she wanted more than a make-out session. She squeezed his pec at the same time she pushed on his chest. He fell back against the soft cushions of the sofa.

She positioned herself over his lower abdomen. A mix of shock and amusement chased each other across Micah's face. The weight of his arousal pressed against the juncture of Jazmin's legs. The points of her breasts tightened even more. They begged to be stroked. She moaned softly as they brushed against her shirt. The thrilling sensations had returned and tickled the area south of her waistband. She wrestled his t-shirt over his head while he tried unbuttoning her top. With one button remaining, Jazmin stilled his hands.

"What is it?" Micah asked, concern lacing his voice.

"Nothing."

He sat up on his elbows. "What's going on?"

Embarrassed, she looked to the ceiling. "I'm just weird about my stomach." Great. She'd messed things up.

"What?"

"And my thighs and my arms."

She could keep going. Her stomach was the meatiest part of her and the feature she hated most. The only parts of her body she liked were her boobs and her booty. She shifted to accommodate Micah as he sat up fully. He gently took hold of her chin and turned her face toward him.

"I happen to be a fan of your stomach, your thighs, your arms, your feet. Legs. Hair. Nose. Should I go on?"

Her posture relaxed. His dimpled smile dissolved her worries and set off the butterflies in her stomach.

Accustomed to their fluttering wings, she breathed easily. Micah was good for a girl's self-esteem. He brushed his lips over hers and when she nibbled and increased the intensity of the kiss, he squeezed her bottom.

"Do you want to finish the movie?" he asked.

She smooched him on the cheek playfully. "I want" —she nibbled his earlobe— "to watch"—she placed the palm of her hand over the tented bulge of his pants— "you cum."

***

Heat flared in Micah's eyes. He pushed aside the halves of her blouse, revealing her black lace-covered bra and bodysuit. He kissed the tops of her breasts. Desire flashed in her eyes. Again, she caught him off guard when she pushed him back. This time instead of straddling him, she stood. Micah licked his lips as she wiggled out of sheer knit, chiffon leggings. Black Spandex panels covered her from the knees down. The leggings reminded him of the movies *Flash Dance* and *Mad Max Beyond Thunderdome*.

"You're beautiful," he told her. Gratitude filled her eyes.

After a few seconds, her face grew serious. "Just so we're clear, I always use protection and I get tested regularly."

He nodded in agreement. "I never have sex without a condom, either; and I usually get tested every three months or so. Even if I've been dating the person exclusively, or if I'm single."

Jazmin smiled. Lowering slowly to all fours, she straddled him again. Her round ass pushed high in the air.

"Good." She placed her hand over his crotch and rubbed his erection. "Take off the sweats."

He quickly did as he was told. Jazmin only stopped her strokes so he could slide the sweatpants over his hips and off. Once free, she took his cock in her mouth. He mumbled an incoherent response. She held onto him with two hands as she licked and then sucked the tip. His breathing became ragged, and his brain fogged over. He gripped the edges of the sofa frame until his knuckles paled. The sight of her red-painted lips encased around his shaft was downright pornographic.

"Mercy," he moaned.

She swirled her tongue around the sensitive top, all the while watching him as he watched her. Her eyes blazed with confidence. When he tilted his head back and closed his eyes, her movements slowed. Jazmin admonished him with a tsk.

"One more thing. I say when you cum. Understand?"

The meaning of her statement slowly dawned on him while a desperate cry of release lodged in his throat.

"Mmmmhmm," he grunted.

"I can't hear you, love." She roughly inhaled just the tip of his erection.

"Yes!" he shouted when she drew him into her mouth.

Jazmin intended to kill him. His world spun on its axis and he grew lightheaded as all the blood rushed downward. Her hands increased their rhythm and his toes curled. Without warning, she closed her lips around his thickness and drew him into her mouth fully. Her head bobbed up and
down as she pulled him in and out.

"Ah, fuck yea!" he exclaimed.

After several minutes, she released him. Micah made sure to place his arms at his side. His erection was long, thick, and wet from her mouth. He didn't dare relieve the tension she'd created. Leaning forward, she kissed him on the mouth fully. He heard a tiny click while their tongues intertwined like snakes. She had unsnapped the crotch of her bodysuit.

"If we were at my place," she whispered in his ear, "I'd have tied you down."

Shivers traveled down Micah's spine. He thought he might embarrass himself and cum early when she dragged her acrylic nails down his chest and across his arms. The woman was a witch or some other mythical being. Not human. No human should be able to exert so much power over another. Heaven help him. He had enjoyed every minute of her domination.

His penis swelled as Jazmin crawled over him. He was positive precum had dampened her ass when it brushed against his hard-on. Rather than positioning herself on his stomach or pelvis, she rested above his shoulders. His tongue thickened with excitement that simmered to a boil. His throat was so dry he couldn't produce a single droplet of saliva to soothe and slake its rawness.

"Be a good listener," Jazmin instructed while reaching one hand over him.

She grabbed the armrest and lowered her dripping bare sex onto his face. Straightaway, Micah latched onto the sensitive bud at the apex of her folds. He lazily nibbled. Beads of sweat freckled his forehead. The resolve he'd been clinging onto splintered.

"Go on, touch yourself," she instructed.

Eager to comply, Micah gladly took hold of his engorged cock. He pumped his hand up and down his shaft while she greedily lowered her body so that her pussy covered not only his mouth but part of his nose as well.

"Get it, baby!" she cried.

He increased his efforts threefold, sucking like a man possessed. He'd give her the moon if she asked.

"That's it, baby, yes!" Not before long, her rhythm became erratic. "Cum, Micah!" She bucked against his mouth.

Jazmin unleashed a banshee-like wail. The dam within broke and Micah erupted. White hot fire shot out and covered his stomach. He flicked his tongue against her delicate bud, setting off a new wave of convulsions. She whimpered, quivered, and then shuddered. Only after the last trembling sensations had passed did she climb off him.

***

Jazmin awakened the next morning to sun streaming in through the window. She couldn't remember when she'd felt so well rested. Dream-Micah paled in comparison to real world-Micah. Although absent from the bed, his masculine scent filled her nostrils. She sighed. The clock on the opposite wall read eight forty-five. Swinging her legs over the side, she made her way to the master bathroom. It was Thursday. Knowing Jazmin would be exhausted from her marathon shopping trip, Vicki had agreed to pick Destiny up from preschool and keep her overnight.

After taking care of her needs in the bathroom, Jazmin noticed that Micah was still nowhere in sight. She decided to search for her host so she could say goodbye and head home. She sifted through the mess of clothes on the ottoman at the foot of the bed. She located her bra and tunic and put on both garments before she padded into the hallway. Usually, dread rushed over her after sleeping with someone new. Mornings were awkward. She'd clumsily attempt small talk while impatiently waiting for the appropriate length of time to pass before giving an excuse for why she had to leave. Today, however, she felt at ease. While she needed to pick up Destiny and then get home to finish working on a few projects, she contemplated how things would be the next time she and Micah slept together. They could spend a languid day in bed, watching Bond movies and stuffing their faces with popcorn and sweets. Jazmin smiled at the idea of a lazy Saturday with the hunky hot-shot attorney.

A familiar tune rang out. It broke Jazmin out of her reverie. She'd heard it before, but her brain took a minute to recall how she knew the melody.

Micah's cell phone.

She followed the sound until she spotted him. His laptop lay open on the large dining room table. He was shirtless. She admired his powerful and sculpted arms which were arguably one of her favorite parts of his body. It didn't hurt that he also had a really big penis. Grinning, Jazmin remembered the sensual feel of him entering her. After the first time, she and Micah fucked several more times before passing out in blissful exhaustion. She rarely met someone who could match her stamina. One night with the handsome lawyer wasn't nearly enough.

She heard her own phone somewhere in the distance. It was behind her. She turned around and headed back to Micah's bedroom. Instinctively, she knew she'd received a text message from her older sister, Rose Mary. Her purse lay on the tall dresser beside the bed. Micah must've brought it in sometime while she had slept. He had also plugged it in. Where had he been all her life? Great in bed and considerate!

Dammit.

Jazmin needed to leave right now. She was thinking like a schoolgirl with a crush. At this rate, she was on track to falling for Micah. It would hurt that much more when he wound up hating her guts. She snorted at the irony of her situation.

She removed her cell from the charger and plopped down on the bed. Three missed calls from Rose Mary and two missed calls from random spam numbers. Jazmin steadied herself for the lecture she assumed her sister had written.

7:05 pm Why aren't you answering?

7:25 pm Reggie is out of prison, and he's headed your way!!

He says he's been calling you for days.

9:00 pm He's traveling by Greyhound. He wants to see Destiny.

10:50 pm Call me.

Jazmin's stomach muscles twisted, and the taste of acid filled her mouth. Before she could panic, however, her and Micah's unique brand of electricity made the hairs on her arms stand at attention. She looked up. Micah stood in the doorway.

"Is everything alright?" he asked.

"Yes."

The worry lines on his forehead didn't smooth out.

"Family stuff," she confessed. "I received bad news from my sister. I can handle it."

Jazmin hoped she sounded convincing because she didn't feel convincing. Maybe it was time to fess up and tell him the truth. It would be helpful to have a lawyer in her corner if Reggie absconded with Destiny.

"God, please don't let that happen," she silently prayed.

Chapter Twenty

"I'll call you later," Jazmin promised.

She stood and placed a soft kiss on Micah's lips. The lapping waves of the Delaware River serenaded their farewell. As he threaded his fingers together over the small of her back, she recognized the intimacy of their posture and delighted in how natural it felt. Reluctantly, she lowered her heels and ended the kiss. She rubbed the pad of her thumb over his lips, wiping clean the smidgen of lipstick she'd left.

Micah had invited her to stay for breakfast, but she'd declined. Jazmin hated rushing off but knew she needed to make a beeline for Vicki's shop. She hoped the older woman would advise her on what to do about Reggie. She pushed down her rising anxiety and met Micah's gaze. She hoped her mask hadn't faltered, that he believed she was trying to control her breathing because of the heat of their kiss or because of last night's tryst. Not because she secretly worried about her ex-boyfriend showing up out of the blue.

Jazmin stepped out of Micah's embrace as a dark-colored sedan cruised to a stop beside them. Brent, Micah's on-call car share driver, had shown up quickly. Thank goodness. Micah kissed her again and then opened the car door. She lowered herself onto the cracked vinyl seat.

"I'll see you soon," he said as the door slammed shut. Micah lightly tapped the hood and then Brent pulled away from the curb. While he waited for an opportunity to merge into traffic, Jazmin scooted to the middle of the seat. Her sore and aching thighs stretched painfully. Micah had worked her out last night and again this morning. Leaning forward, she clung to the passenger headrest for support. The sun-bleached evergreen tree dangling from the rearview mirror emitted the faintest scent of pine.

"Change of plans," she told the young man.

Slowing the car to a stop at a red light, he looked over his shoulder. "Shoot."

"5th and South."

The traffic signal changed and Brent expertly maneuvered across two lanes. Was he Evel Knievel disguised as a hipster? The other drivers hadn't had a chance to lock in their speed before Brent positioned the car into the first spot in the left turn lane. A revving motorcycle engine muffled the other drivers' honking horns. Brent pulled a U-turn, drifting the vehicle like a kart racer in a videogame. The green traffic arrow had just switched to a yellow spotlight.

"Are you a stunt driver?" she mumbled under her breath.

Once the car cruised at a steady speed, stopping every quarter mile or so at red lights, Jazmin settled back against the seat and relaxed. She pulled her ringing phone from her purse. Though the number began with a local area code, she didn't recognize it. Her heart thumped and it felt as if it might succeed in breaking through the barrier of her ribs.

"Hello?" her voice came out as a choked whisper.

"J.J.?"

"How can I help you?" she asked, sitting up straighter.

Brent's eyes found hers in the rearview mirror. He was about to turn the car west onto Christian Street. Jazmin braced herself for another showy high-speed maneuver.

When it didn't come, she expelled a whoosh of relief.

"All good?" Brent asked.

She gave him a thumbs up and pointed to her phone. He nodded and then returned his eyes to the road. Ten or so more blocks and she'd be at Vicki's.

The voice on the other end of the line blathered on, "My name is Everett Randolph III. I'm interested in learning more about your company's services. I work for a law firm in Center City. My bosses are interested in overhauling the firm's website along with their presence online."

"Where did you say you were calling from?" Jazmin already knew the answer but had decided to play along. Putting on her professional voice, she over-articulated her words while still maintaining a sweet lyrical cadence. "I'm only taking referrals at this time."

She tapped her foot while Everett III droned on about how lucky J.J. was to be considered for the job. She wondered how he'd gotten her number. Interested clients usually emailed her. That's why she'd sent over the fax, telling Stein, Martin, and Randolph that she wasn't available.

"Let's chat over lunch. How's this afternoon sound? *Boy, he was presumptuous.*

Jazmin gestured for Brent to pull over on the opposite side of the street as there wasn't any parking in front of 5th Street Hosiery and Lingerie Boutique. While digging around in her purse for her wallet, she listened to Everett brag about his position with the top brass at his firm. Funny, he never mentioned nepotism.

At last, Jazmin found her wallet. Brent waved off her attempt to hand him money, however.

"Already taken care of," he told her.

Holding the phone away from her face, she smiled politely and mouthed "thank you." Everett continued to yak in her ear as she pushed open the door and stepped out. Jazmin straightened and looked over the roof of the cab. Across the street stood Everett Randolph III. He was leaving Vicki's.

"What the..." her voice trailed off.

She whirled around. She hoped he hadn't recognized her. "I'm not taking new customers at this time." She fumbled in and out of professional-speak.

"This deal will make your year," he urged.

Jazmin walked in the opposite direction as Everett. At the nearest intersection she made a mad dash for the other side of the street, not bothering to wait for the signal to change. She ran out in front of a large white delivery van hellbent on making it through the yellow traffic light. The driver pressed down and held his horn. To her dismay, Everett looked around. Left and then right. Jazmin wished that she could shrink inside her coat. She was positive he'd deduced that J.J. was somewhere out in the open, possibly nearby. She fell in step behind a family of tourists.

Speaking even faster than before, Jazmin told him, "I'm sorry, but at this time it's impossible. Best of luck in your search."

She pressed the red end call button before shoving her cell into her purse. When she reached the boutique, she opened the door and slipped inside. Brenda stood behind the counter filing her nails with an oversized bedazzled emery board. On the countertop lay her phone. A local radio icon, Queen Mum, offered advice to listeners. He read wildly outrageous "Dear Abby" emails.

"What?" Brenda asked, silencing her cell and setting the nail file down on the glass countertop.

Leaning against the door frame, Jazmin stared at her best friend. Her accusatory eyes were narrowed slits.

"Tall guy? Long dreads? Did you give him my number?"

"Yes. He just left. He wanted to know if J.J. was back in town. He said that he had some business to throw her way. What?" Brenda rolled her eyes at the glower Jazmin pinned her with. "I didn't give him your personal number, just the business one. The one you set up that appears as a random local number to callers. Block him if it's that big a deal." She shrugged and went back to buffing her nails.

Jazmin stormed forward, closing the distance between them. "He works for Stein, Martin, and Randolph. The same firm as Micah." She wanted to ring Brenda's neck. "Micah doesn't know that I'm—"

"J.J.," Brenda finished, recognition lighting her eyes. Less than a fraction of a second later her brows scrunched together. "Look, *Cloak and Dagger*, you can't expect me to keep up."

Jazmin fell against the counter. Her upper torso rested across the cool glass. She softly banged her forehead against it in defeat.

"Where's Miss Vicki and Destiny?"

"Upstairs. Miss V wants us to pick up some lunch."

Brenda plucked the store keys from the hook beside the register and rounded the counter.

Jazmin's eyes followed her best friend. With a sigh, she pulled herself upright. She had never wanted to pursue a career in espionage.

Outside, the churches around them dueled. Bells tolled loudly, signaling the top of the hour. Jazmin and Brenda headed south toward the Italian Market. Many of the stalls and stores along Ninth Street had just opened for business.

Jazmin frowned when she had to step out of the way to let a jogger pass. An unseasonably warm day had brought more people out-of-doors than usual. The sun might be shining brightly but it was still a chilly December morning. The temperature lingered in the low forties. Jazmin roughly pulled her knit cap down over her ears.

A nasally cackle exploded from across the street; the sound snaked its way down Jazmin's spine. While accustomed to cell phone conversations swirling around her whenever she walked through downtown Philadelphia, it seemed as if this morning people were talking louder than necessary. Everyone was trying to be heard over the stranger beside them. Jazmin vigorously rubbed the space between her eyebrows. She had hoped to smother the seed of a migraine that threatened to take root.

A car's horn blared, and she slowed her gait. She looked over her shoulder and watched as an annoyed driver shouted from his window at a sedan inching along while pedestrians and oncoming traffic flowed by steadily. Several feet back, Brenda had stopped in front of a kettle corn stand. Pivoting, Jazmin slid into the line of people trudging along in the direction she'd come. Her sour mood lessened a fraction as she inhaled the refreshingly sweet and salty smell of hot oil that permeated around them. Puttering pops of kernels expanded and blossomed. Brenda selected pumpkin pie flavored popcorn while Jazmin pointed at a bag of caramel corn. Brenda happily handed over cash in exchange for their treats.

"You know, all work and *no play* make Jazmin Johnson very grumpy," Brenda said in a singsong voice.

A slow smile curled the corner of Jazmin's lip. A musical montage of last night's salacious acts played in her mind.

Jazmin looped her arm through Brenda's. "Oh, come on." They strolled side-by-side.

Taqueria La Veracruzana, a Mexican BYOB, was located up ahead, at the end of Ninth Street and across Washington Avenue. The trip through South Philly's open-air market, every five feet to peer through display windows. Or to haggle with an elderly woman in Mandarin. Or to squeeze and test the weight of oranges and other fruits.

When Brenda approached a store's narrow entryway, Jazmin moved swiftly and positioned herself in front of her friend. Faded postcards, dusty toys, miscellaneous tools and doohickeys along with other junk blocked sunlight from illuminating more of the store.

"Not today," Jazmin insisted as she steered Brenda away.

Although she nodded, Jazmin followed her friend's gaze as it shifted ever-so-slightly to the mannequin adorned in bright checkered-print leggings in the display window of the storefront next door.

"Hello beautiful," a man called to Brenda from across the street.

"Hi." She waved.

She blew a kiss in his direction. Within the span of a half step, her attention switched to a vegetable stand.

"Look, purple asparagus." She pointed and read the sign aloud, "Two for a dollar. I'm buying it."

While Brenda paid for the vegetables, Jazmin inspected the peppers. "Do you think you could stay with Destiny and me for a while?"

"What's going on?"

Jazmin's stomach flip-flopped. "Reggie's on his way here. He wants to see Dez."

Brenda mumbled thank you to the vendor and then tugged Jazmin into the street between two parked cars. She pulled her in close for a hug.

"Of course, I'll stay for as long as you need me."

While they hadn't been friends when she had dated Reggie, Brenda had picked up the pieces of Jazmin's broken heart after Cicely's betrayal and then again after Destiny was born.

Relief washed over Jazmin. "You're my Claudia Kishi, you know that?"

Beaming, Brenda pressed the palm of her right hand against her heart. "That's the nicest thing anyone has ever said to me."

The two friends continued down Ninth Street. Brenda had loved to read *The Babysitters Club* books as a preteen. Unfortunately, she had to hide her obsession from her parents. Grown-up Brenda did not; she indulged her desires. The series had been rebooted and made into graphic novels. Brenda owned every one.

"When Vicki and Pops find out they're going to want his head on a platter," Jazmin said.

"At the very least Pops will be on high alert. What if you stayed at a hotel for a few days?"

Jazmin mulled over the idea before she responded. "There's no reason why Reggie and I can't sit down and talk things over like adults." She'd tried returning his calls but quickly learned he'd phoned her from pay phones at various rest areas. "I've done nothing wrong. I won't run and hide."

At least that's the advice her sister had offered. Rose Mary also thought Jazmin should seek legal counsel as soon as possible to discuss her options.

"I plan on installing security cameras on both the front and back entrance of the apartment this afternoon. I'll have a live feed connected to my phone. I'll get a notification if someone sets off the motion or sound detectors," Jazmin told Brenda.

"So," Brenda began, bumping her hip against Jazmin's. "When do you see *your* Micah again? You're glowing and shit!"

Jazmin grinned. She was happy her best friend was back in town, if only for a little while. "He's not *my* anything and I don't know. With Reggie on his way here, the less drama in my life, the better."

Brenda looked her up and down. "But..." she drew out the monosyllabic word dramatically.

"Being honest will only fuck things up," Jazmin interjected, clicking her tongue.

Hadn't she and Micah passed the point of no return? If he knew her true identity now, he'd never forgive her and, despite her best efforts, he had wiggled his way past her defenses. She shook off the sentimental feelings and guilt that welled in her belly. After five dates she planned to end their relationship. If they still had a relationship by then.

"If you tell him the truth, he might understand and stand beside you when you face Reggie."

"I'm sure he'd hate me. What if I tell him, and he goes and tells his bosses about how we met? They may spread rumors. I could lose out on the Millennial Titan and two-hundred-and-fifty-thousand dollars."

"Whoa, slow down." Brenda waved her hands in the air. "You're stressing out over what-ifs. What if he's as decent a guy as you think he is? It's not as if you did anything pornographic and there's no video or digital evidence. You were having fun."

Jazmin shook her head. She'd fare better if things stayed the way they were for as long as possible. At the moment, she still had a handle on the situation. Micah didn't need to know any more than she wanted to tell him. She and Brenda joined the small crowd waiting to cross Washington Avenue, a four-lane thoroughfare.

"He's a grown man yet you're making choices for him like he's a child," Brenda said as she stepped onto the curb.

Jazmin didn't respond. She knew Brenda meant well but sometimes her straightforward, no-chaser way of thinking got on Jazmin's nerves. Brenda's life was as put together as her current ensemble. She looked sophisticated in an oversized blazer and linen t-shirt paired with bronze-colored silk pants. Tapered at the end, they lengthened her already long legs. She carried a designer purse that matched her designer boots. She'd styled her hair perfectly with blonde highlights falling in soft curls. Her good looks and outgoing personality commanded attention wherever she went. Both men and women were drawn to her.

After a minute of tense silence, Jazmin addressed Brenda's comment. "He seems like one of the good ones but Destiny is my priority."

She knew she was being selfish by not wanting to ruin the good thing she had going with Micah, but not everyone could operate without a filter. For now, she would do what she thought was best.

"So, you sleep with him and then push him away without any explanation?" Brenda asked. They'd reached the restaurant. "You're such a *guy*."

Chapter Twenty-One

Micah smiled politely as he accepted his third plate of food. Baked chicken and macaroni and cheese piled high atop his plate along with what resembled potato salad.

"Thank you, Miss Thomas."

Nassir's mother winked at him and then strutted off. *Swish. Swish.*

Micah averted his eyes, ignoring the sway of the woman's hips. The sound of her jean-clad thighs rubbing together drew the attention of several fathers and uncles in attendance. They were all mesmerized by the young mother's booty, especially with the intricate tattoo peeking out from beneath her low-rise jeans. He'd overheard her explain to another parent that the design, a flowering butterfly, was an homage to her roots. Native to Suriname, Metamorpha Elissa was the only one of its kind.

Micah crooked his head in the direction of the red neon sign above the entrance.

Adam sat across from him. He cleared his throat to get Micah's attention. "Do you even know if she's coming to this thing?"

Not for the first time, Micah questioned why he'd invited his best friend to the end of the season sports banquet. Adam claimed he needed to see the woman who'd brought Micah to his knees. Micah suspected he wanted a free meal.

Adam drummed his fingertips against the plastic tabletop. "Do you have a picture?

Micah shook his head. He'd have to remedy that the next time they were together. If there was a next time. Although she had messaged him when she'd gotten home, he hadn't really talked to her since yesterday morning. She'd replied to his texts with emojis or one-word answers. He hoped she wasn't putting their relationship on ice.

Adam sat back in the padded fold-up chair. He opened his mouth to speak but was interrupted by Micah's ringing cell phone.

His brother, Derrick answered. "Hey, Mike, how's it going?"

"I'm good. Shouldn't you be in class boring your students?"

Derrick laughed through a mouthful of food. "I'm still on sabbatical, little brother. I had to drop in and visit Princess Daniella."

With his phone's camera, Micah's older brother scanned the familiar living room and kitchen of their sister's Brownstone. Their brother-in-law waved and called out a greeting and then Derrick turned the camera on their two-month-old niece who slept peacefully in her mother's arms.

"You know I'm her favorite uncle," Derrick boasted.

"Bull. I'll jump on a plane right now if that's the case," Micah said.

"Is that D? Tell him I said, what's up."

Derrick switched the camera, so his face filled the display box. "Adam! We missed you the last time we were in town."

Micah noted some interference with their connection.

"Hold on, the twins are beeping me," his brother explained.

Derrick's face disappeared briefly. Shortly after, three of his four brothers appeared, each occupying a quadrant on Micah's screen.
"Mike, Adam, what have you been doing?" Derrick asked, continuing the conversation where they'd left off.

"Or, who?" called out the twins in unison.

"I'm waiting to meet her," Adam muttered. He sipped iced tea from a Styrofoam cup.

Unable to hide his smirk, Micah shook his head. Before he could blink, however, his sister and her husband filled his brother's tiny square on Micah's five-inch screen. The three of them jockeyed for space. Micah chuckled. "She's—"

"We need her stats," Allen interrupted.

"Forget stats," Aaron argued. "Tell her to bring that ass here so we can see her."

Their sister elbowed her husband and their brother out of way. "What's her name?"

"Jazmin. Now, I really have to go."

"Wait," Derrick called out. He stood behind their sister and her husband. "T Boz, Left Eye, or Chili?"

A rumble of laughter burst loose. This was the litmus test he and his brothers had used to describe females since they'd begun dating as teenagers. Looking up, he saw Adam's brows furrow in confusion.

"I have to go," Micah repeated in what he thought was an assertive tone.

He ended the video call before his siblings' antics got out of control.

"You good?" Adam asked.

Micah glanced around to make sure no one was paying attention. "The sex with Jazmin was fucking amazing."

Adam scooted his chair closer. The screech of metal on the tile floor blended in with the noisy conversations around them.

"I'm listening."

"I couldn't focus at work," Micah said aloud.

He'd wrestled with what happened Wednesday night. The sex had also been incredibly erotic. His version of unconventional sex usually involved fifth base. While he'd enjoyed himself, Jazmin's control over him proved she didn't fit into the mold for a potential girlfriend or partner.

"What's the problem?" Adam asked, as if reading his mind.

"It's..." Micah's voice trailed off.

Crap! He'd drunk the punch until he'd become brainwashed! Eleanor's outburst replayed in his head like a record stuck on repeat. He disagreed with her choice of words, but he knew what she'd meant.

"She's different from other women you've seen me with. The complete opposite of Eleanor," he explained.

"Hallelujah!" Adam's eyes twinkled.

Micah raised his Styrofoam cup to toast Adam's choice of words. After taking a sip of lemonade, he added, "I really like her, but..."

He hated thinking that Jazmin only fulfilled the role of a side chick in his world because she was too free and uninhibited in the bedroom or because she didn't look the part. She had too curvy of a body. Her boobs were too big. Booty too juicy. Hair too short and coarse. Her friends and associates too eclectic. Micah thought back to where they'd first met.

"But, what?" Adam interjected.

"She doesn't quite fit." He ran a hand down his face. "Never mind."

The first pinpoints of perspiration cooled Micah's forehead. He scanned the room and watched a toddler attempt to dribble a basketball that probably weighed more than him.

"What's next?" Adam asked.

Confused, Micah looked to his friend. He hadn't been listening.

"What?"

Reaching across the table, Adam picked up a copy of a flyer. "You've given your coach's speech. Check. The trophies have been passed out. Check. What's next?" He held up the paper for Micah to see. "Whoever made this is fired: Introductions, food and mingle, awards and conclusion. I need a detailed church-bulletin."

Micah laughed. "Next is the presentation of the special awards for leadership, most valuable player, most improved, and 'sweetish' shot."

Micah forked a piece of mac and cheese and then speared some greens. He chewed slowly, appreciating the combination of flavors.

"The only thing after that is to recognize and celebrate the boys who are moving up to the next division, ages eleven to fourteen."

The players' mothers had decorated tri-fold boards, highlighting their sons' academic and athletic achievements. They'd also put together a highlight reel, a mixture of still images and short videos. After the slideshow, Micah planned to call the boys to the front, present them with an award and a small gift, and then conclude the evening with brief remarks.

"She volunteered her portable projector and Bluetooth speaker," Micah said to himself. He turned in his chair and glanced at the media cart across the room.

"Do you think she purposefully arrived early to avoid running into you?" Adam asked.

He had voiced the words Micah was too scared to say out loud. Micah knew he'd enjoyed Jazmin's company both in and out of the bedroom despite his uncertainty about the nature of their hypothetical future relationship. He'd assumed the feeling was mutual.

"No way," he told Adam.

"Maybe, for her, the sex wasn't fucking amazing. I'd need details in order to say for sure," Adam leaned forward.

Micah wiped his mouth with a napkin. He set down his fork and rolled his eyes. Adam merely shrugged his shoulders in response.

"I'm going to grab some fresh air." Micah stood.

He ignored the sultry stare Nassir's mother gave him as he passed by. The hum of single mamas buzzed as he headed for the exit. Outside, coldness enveloped him. He hadn't felt so unsure and out of sorts over a woman in a long time.

A police siren wailed. A unique location, Landreth Apartments for Seniors was on the fringes of a section of South Philadelphia known as Point Breeze. The team had hosted its sports banquets in the basement hall for the last three years. The area had seen revitalization over the last several years, largely due to Kenny Gamble. His companies had built low-income housing and established schools in the area, but impartial real estate developers followed shortly after.

Micah watched two coatless teenagers run across the street. They turned the corner. Profanity and laughter echoed off the parked cars they disappeared behind.

Gentrification and pretty murals couldn't wipe out pre-existing crime and drugs that had plagued the area for generations. Pop-up beer gardens along with gastropubs and other restaurants only brought about a stronger police presence, and, accordingly, scrutiny of long-time African American residents and Vietnamese immigrants who lived in the area. Micah turned his head when he heard a creaking door swing open behind him. Adam strode forward.

"The mamas are circling," his friend said by way of an explanation.

"You know, what's happening in this neighborhood is happening all over? Do you remember the case I lost to Rhett in law school? The one with the elderly man who was in danger of losing the home that his family had lived in for generations because of unforeseen liens on the property?"

Nodding, Adam turned up the collar on his navy blue peacoat.

"If we open a firm, those are the cases I want to give priority to. I'm tired of helping people who already have millions in the bank," Micah said.

He pulled out his cell. Curious wrinkles lined Adam's forehead.

"Who are you calling?"

"I'm not quitting my job if that's what you're asking," Micah explained.

Her phone rang three or four times. He thought the call would go to straight to voicemail but then she answered.

"Hello?"

"Hello, Jazmin. It's Micah."

Chapter Twenty-Two

Jazmin spotted Micah as soon as she and Brenda rounded the corner onto South Bank St. He looked hot. On anyone else loose-fitting jeans paired with a Temple Athletics tee may have been simple and underdressed. Not on Micah. The material of his shirt stretched across his chest and biceps, showing off impressive muscles. Several women standing in front of the club entrance batted their false lashes and giggled loudly. He ignored them and walked to Jazmin. A tingling sensation swirled around her midsection as familiar butterflies fluttered.

Micah introduced his friend who rivaled him in height. The similarities ended there, however. Adam was broad-shouldered and beefy. Not American football beefy, either. More like English rugby beefy. His thighs were the size of watermelons. Adam, also, was clean-shaven, and his skin looked remarkably smooth. A stark contrast to his short, gelled, spiked hair. The only thing making him mortal was his slightly off-centered Kaepernick nose. He'd clearly broken it once or twice.

"Adam Goldberg. Nice to meet you." He stepped forward.

"Jazmin Johnson." She shook his hand politely. "You too."

Wearing a goofy grin, Adam swiveled to look at Micah and then back to Jazmin. "It's good to finally put a name with a face."

She smiled. The humor twinkling in Adam's eyes put her at ease. "All good, I hope?"

"It was," he replied.

Jazmin extended her arm in Brenda's direction. She waved her friend forward. "Brenda, you remember, Micah Clarion?"

They shook hands and then Brenda repeated the exchange with Adam. As the four of them took their place in line, Jazmin crossed her fingers and then silently prayed that Brenda would be on her best behavior tonight.

With his hand on Jazmin's back, Micah ushered her inside and up the stairs into the club. Low jazz music played. Men and women swayed to a sultry voice that crooned about having found and lost love. A fog of mint, mango, and watermelon hookah smoke filled the lounge. Jazmin found the sweet aroma intoxicating.

There were dinette-size tables strategically placed throughout the room. In addition, several booths and plush sofas lined the walls. Micah led their group to a vacant table near the stage. Jazmin and Brenda sat next to each other while the guys flanked either side of the circular booth. In no time a waitress made her way through the crowd and stopped to take their drink orders.

While Micah tapped his fingers against the table in rhythm with the music surrounding them, Jazmin noticed how Adam's thigh pressed against Brenda's. For the first time in months Brenda wasn't lamenting about men who spread their legs wide in tight, public spaces.

"I thought you hated manspreading," Jazmin whispered.

Brenda fanned herself dramatically. She looked between Adam and Micah. "I could get used to this man-sandwich."

Looking him over, Jazmin easily made out tawny beige washboard abs beneath the crisp, white, button-down shirt Adam wore. While the guys inquired about the available microbrews on tap, Jazmin studied the tribal tattoo that covered one of Adam's pecs. It traveled over the shoulder and down his arm. Shading and straight lines created mountainous peaks and crescent waves in a monochromatic Polynesian design.

"Jazmin?" Adam asked.

Her eyes darted upward. Her cheeks warmed. She hoped
he hadn't caught her ogling him.

"Mike never said how you two met."

Brenda hid her coquettish expression behind her hand.

Adam's incredulous eyes narrowed.

"You had to be there," Micah said.

"I'm not an attorney." Jazmin felt her ears grow hot and was grateful when Micah loosely draped an arm over her shoulder.

"She owns her own business," Brenda said, the pride in her voice unmistakable.

Jazmin's throat felt dry. She struggled to swallow and then shrugged, hoping to appear aloof. With remorse, a half-truth wiggled its way out.

"I started it in college. I promoted women's sports: scores and stats. Now, I help small businesses."

"Once I convince this guy over here to join me, we may call on you. Goldberg, Clarion, and Associates."

Their server returned with their drinks at the same time Adam outlined the law firm's name in the air with his hands as if the words were displayed on a theater marquee.

Micah corrected him, "Clarion, Goldberg, and Associates. C comes before G."

Adam took a swig from his beer. His boyish, lopsided grin hidden for the moment.

"Let me know if there's anything else," the waitress said, pocketing the cash Micah handed her.

"Are you saying you're in, brother?" Adam asked.

"Do you guys need to talk business? If so, we can go." Jazmin jokingly gestured back and forth between her and Brenda.

"Hell no." Micah squeezed her shoulder.

"Is that how you two know each other? Do you work together?" Brenda asked Adam.

"Mike and I both attended Temple Law. Though I knew *of* him in undergrad."

"Don't." Micah's voice held a playful yet threatening tone.

With her hands steepled in a prayer position close to her chest, Brenda clapped cheerfully. "Storytime!"

Micah's cheeks flushed. "C'mon, man," he whined.

"What did they used to call you? Chi Mike? Or was it, Mike from the Chi?" Adam didn't stop, even though Micah lowered his head in embarrassment. "This guy wore Chicago Bulls stuff all day, every day, from head to toe...." Adam's voice faltered as he began laughing at the unfinished joke. After his chuckles subsided, he resumed the story. "One day Chi Mike comes running into English class wearing a vinyl plastic-looking tracksuit. The swish of his Fila pants was so loud, I thought he was going to start a fire."

Jazmin choked on her drink. Cranberry juice and vodka burned her nose hairs as the cocktail threatened to shoot out. Shaking his head and chuckling at the memory, Micah handed her napkins and patted her on the back. She dabbed the front of her blouse. Behind them, the lead singer announced she and the band would return after a short break.

"My Chicago-style was *flyy*," Micah shouted over the applause. "I don't care what anyone says."

Brenda held Micah's gaze. "You've turned out fine." She jerked a thumb in Jazmin's direction. "Unlike this one."

"Jazmin told me you're a choreographer," Micah interjected.

Expelling a relieved sigh, she squeezed his hand. He had saved her from having to endure Brenda's favorite embarrassing Jazmin Johnson story, a spin on *The Country Mouse and The City Mouse* with a little *Ugly Duckling* mixed in.

Brenda smiled brightly. "Yes."

Adam turned to her. "Would I have seen anything you've done?"

"Well, I'm trained in tap."

"Okay," he responded while nodding his head.

"Though, I prefer *Kinky Boots* over *Giselle*."

"Okay!" He raised his beer bottle and their glasses collided with a clink.

As the four of them settled in, Jazmin kept one ear trained on their friends' conversation. Adam wasn't exactly Brenda's type, but her friend seemed at ease.

Through all her bravado, Brenda sometimes got skittish mingling with folks outside her theater crowd.

"Do you have weekend plans?" Micah asked, capturing her attention.

Jazmin shouted over the neo-soul that played loudly. "Not really. I've a work commitment in the morning and I'm still figuring out that family thing. What about you?"

She took a long gulp of her vodka and cranberry drink. She'd hoped to drown further thoughts of Reggie. She was thankful for the overhead swirling fans. Between guilt about lying to Micah, her fear of Reggie wanting to take Destiny away, and the alcohol in her drink, Jazmin's face felt sunburnt.

"Same. Just some work stuff," Micah mumbled, picking up a paper menu.

Jazmin looked over Micah's shoulder and then pointed to a picture of buffalo wings.

"You read my mind," he replied.

With her earlier apprehension fading, Jazmin snuggled closer. She was glad Vicki had insisted she come out. Brenda had been partially right. Pops had become overprotective when Jazmin delivered the news about Reggie. Surprisingly, Vicki had turned into a mother hen as well, so much so, that she hated Jazmin and Brenda's hovering. The older woman had taken on that assignment, herself. So when Vicki overheard Jazmin and Brenda talking about a double date with Micah and his friend, she promptly shooed them out the door.

Jazmin slid Micah's discarded menu toward Brenda. "Hungry? We should put an order in before the kitchen closes."

"I'll just order for the table. Cool?" Adam waved over their server.

"Works for us, as long as you include wings," Micah answered.

Us!

Jazmin's butterflies flapped their wings spiritedly. She tried to play calm and composed even though she wanted to cheer. Micah considered them an us!

"Roger that," Adam replied.

Brenda amended the order. "Wings with salt, pepper, ketchup, and—"

"Hot sauce," Jazmin finished.

She and Brenda shared similar goofy grins.

"Fried hard," they said in unison.

"Fried hard," Micah echoed. "There's no going back."

Jazmin looked over at him. "What do you mean?"

"Your wing order. It was definitely something only a true Philadelphian would order. Philly's in your blood. You're stuck here like the rest of us." He tilted his head in Adam's direction. "Love it or hate it."

Raising his bottle, Adam saluted Micah's words.

Jazmin leaned in and pecked Micah on the cheek. His comment had sparked an idea. Tomorrow, she would tell her story, her way at the Titan photoshoot. She lightly elbowed Brenda. They wore the same shoe size and Jazmin needed to borrow a pair of red bottom booties to complement the new casual daytime look taking shape in her mind.

"Let's check out what's going on downstairs," Micah suggested, scooting out of the booth.

Jazmin drained the remainder of her cocktail and followed. The plush tufted bench assisted in buoying her upright. Snaking one arm behind him, Micah took hold of her hand.

"Brenda, text me when the food gets here," Jazmin said over her shoulder.

Downstairs the crowd bobbed up and down to hip hop music. Heat clung to Jazmin's skin from all of the perspiring bodies packed so closely together. Unlike the upstairs lounge, the downstairs club smelled of sweat, spilled alcohol, and soapy disinfectant. Micah lead her through the melee. They were poked by elbows and bumped by wiggling butts. Eventually, they slid into a spot at the bar. Micah finished his drink and set down the empty glass while Jazmin rocked and rolled her hips.

"Do you want another drink?" Micah asked, raising his voice over the cheering crowd. The house DJ had put on the latest track from a local rapper.

"No, thanks."

Jazmin nodded her head in time with the beat. She rapped the opening lyrics with precision, mirroring the artist's delivery.

"Impressive," Micah said before turning to the grinning bartender who'd also caught Jazmin's performance. Micah slid a bill across the counter and waved off the young man's offer to find change. The fingers on his free hand trailed across the half-inch of flesh peeking out between Jazmin's shirt and skinny jeans. Splayed, they landed on her hips. Jazmin's chest tightened as her heart swelled. One song blended in with the next and the crowd grew denser. Beads of sweat dotted her forehead. When a string of girlfriends maneuvered their way through the packed room, she turned and pressed her body against Micah's to avoid being bumped or bruised. At least, that's what she told herself. She was positive he felt her hardened nipples because his eyes smoldered her with desire.

Setting his now empty drink glass on the bar top, he took hold of her arms and draped them over his shoulders. He molded his lips to hers. He sucked and nibbled on the bottom one, coaxing her to open for him. When she complied, he captured her tongue and feasted. Lost in the kiss, the booming hip-hop music faded. Jazmin tasted remnants of Micah's drink. The whiskey's lingering full-bodied spice mixed with cola sweetness. He deepened the kiss and a rasping moan escaped from her mouth. Micah pulled back too soon for her liking. He stared down at her, a puckish smirk lit up his face, like a kid caught sneaking back inside the house after an impromptu night out with friends.

Jazmin rested her head over Micah's heart. She felt her phone buzz in her back pocket but decided to ignore it. An early nineties slow jam played in the background. L.L. Cool J was one of her favorite rap-pers. She supposed she ought to tell him that Brenda had texted and that their food had probably arrived. Instead, she inhaled the earthy scent of his cologne and then closed her eyes. She'd decided to savor the moment for a little longer

Chapter Twenty-Three

Micah patted Destiny's back. The little girl made no attempt to pump her legs. She was content with him pushing her on the swing. Jazmin swung back and forth beside Destiny. Micah had intercepted the duo on Christian Street. They were headed to a mommy-daughter playgroup that met a few blocks from their apartment in the basement skating rink of Saint Charles Borromeo Church.

He held Jazmin's gaze when she caught him staring.

"We should get going soon, otherwise we'll miss skating," she told Destiny, breaking eye contact with him.

The little girl whined. "A few more minutes."

Micah had no idea why he'd driven past their apartment this evening.

Liar.

He knew he was whipped and didn't care. Wednesday night he and Jazmin had sex and then last night, they'd gone out with Adam and her friend Brenda. Here it was Friday, and, like an addict, he was back again, sniffing behind Jazmin like a puppy. There were a million places that he could have ordered take-out from beside The Sidecar Bar and Grill on the corner of Christian and 22nd Streets.

Jazmin righted herself and then slowed her swing. Although she didn't say anything, she didn't rush to leave.

"You can roller skate?" Micah asked Destiny.

She nodded her head. "I'm real good too."

"I bet you are. Are boys allowed in your playgroup?"

Destiny's tiny lips twisted as she thought about his question.

"Billy and James Jr. are boys. So, I guess so."

"You want to go roller skating with us?" Jazmin asked. "It'll just be a bunch of moms talking about revamping their preschoolers' curriculum vitae with music lessons and early reading videos."

Micah slowed Destiny's swing. He had no idea why he was fishing for an invite. He just knew he didn't want to part ways yet.

Jazmin's phone buzzed. Without hesitation, she put the call on speakerphone.

"Rosie?"

"He claims my tacos have all the wrong flavors. I quote: 'They aren't even fodder for pigeon food.'"

A crinkly sound muffled the call's reception. Her sister had crumpled a piece of paper, the news article, no doubt.

"Who claims.... what?" Jazmin asked.

She waved for Destiny and Micah to follow her. The little girl placed her hand in his and Micah wasn't prepared for his body's reaction. His abdominal muscles constricted. Jazmin glanced back and grinned at the two of them. All the while, her sister lamented about an unfavorable review in the Taco Tuesday bulletin of their hometown paper.

"I don't need negative press. It's bad for business."

"They say any press is good press," Jazmin volunteered.

"Contact the paper and demand a retraction," Micah suggested.

Jazmin's eyes widened. He mouthed an apology but grinned sheepishly.

"Lil' sister, who are you with?" Rose Mary asked.

As if she were going to bop him in the nose, Jazmin shook a fist at him. "Dez, say hello to Rosie." She handed Destiny the phone.

"Hi, Rosie," she prattled away. Of course, she gave a play-by-play description of her day, including the brief respite at the park with Jazmin's *friend* Coach Mike.

Jazmin fell in step beside Micah. She looped her arm through his and allowed Destiny to walk ahead.

"You know I'm going to get an earful, right? Usually, I wait six months before I introduce anyone to the fam," she told him.

Micah plastered on an innocent expression, which included batting doe eyes. Jazmin chuckled lightly.

"I can't remember the last time I dated anyone for six months," she said.

Micah harumphed. He was the last one to pass judgment, especially since his last real relationship ended two years ago.

"Well, it seems like I have a goal to work toward."

He pulled Jazmin close to his side. She rested her head against his shoulder. Once again, his stomach tightened. He couldn't hold back a mile-wide smile.

***

"Hold. Just like that. Tilt your chin down, a little more. Perfect," the photographer instructed.

Jazmin's cheeks ached. She did her best to follow Jean's directions. But with each flash that exploded in the makeshift photo studio, fluorescent dots, like soap bubbles, speckled her vision. She rested one hand on the mid-century acorn wood desk to steady herself. She shifted her weight and then looked down to inspect her pedicure as instructed.

"Dip your shades low," Jean said in a faux French accent.

Although the shoot had been slated for nine o'clock, Jazmin had arrived an hour before to put on her makeup and ready her wigs. She usually hated doing publicity. Always had. This morning, she was optimistic about the end product. Unlike other photographers she'd encountered, Jean seemed receptive to her ideas for the photo story.

She looked over the bridge of her oversized, cheeky sunnies just as Jean shouted "freeze." Posed at an awkward angle, she held her breath. She hoped to hide her bloated stomach. Last night, she and Destiny had shared a pizza with Micah after playgroup.

When Jaz balked, telling him he shouldn't waste the food he'd purchased from the restaurant down the street, he put the To-Go boxes in her refrigerator. He suggested she keep them and consider the food her reward for working on a weekend. The red velvet whoopie pies had Destiny cheering. Two against one, Jazmin conceded.

"Got it!" Jean yelled, pulling her back to the present.

Collapsing onto the rolling desk chair behind her, a few pink paper butterflies floated to the ground and landed at Jazmin's feet. The photographer's assistant moved quickly. She changed out the office props for a reproduction streetlamp and bench. The petite young woman swept the delicate origami butterflies into a trash bin.

"That was a cute touch," Jazmin told her.

She smiled shyly before returning to her task. By including desk items with Temple's logo on them, Jazmin's alma mater, it was clear Jean's photography assistant had done her research. She'd expertly transformed a plain conference room into a professional photography studio.

Jazmin removed her synthetic wig and ran her nails over her scalp. She was still recovering from Thursday night. She'd stayed out far past her bedtime. They didn't leave The Ten Spot until the club closed. She took a deep breath and then pulled her stiff body upright. With rigid movements, she made her way to the dressing screen. For the finale, she'd picked up couture dress boning from a bridal boutique that was going out of business.

When she stepped out and walked to her mark in the center of the room, the assistant's eyes widened. Jazmin grinned. A soft pink glow warmed the younger woman's porcelain complexion.

"Miss Johnson?"

"Eloise, right?"

"Yes, Ma'am. I think I have something you might like to try on."

"Please, call me J.J."

Eloise nodded and then ducked behind a clothing rack. The garments easily obscured all four feet of her. She reappeared a second or two later in front of a table cluttered with watches, bracelets, and rings. She selected a large velvet pouch and then moved around the table to hand it to Jazmin.

Bouncing the bag lightly, Jazmin tested its weight.

"Miss J.J., I think this would go perfectly with your dress."

Jazmin opened the pouch, removing an haute-couture pearl and crystal face mask. Refracted rainbows connected the pearls and crystals under the bright photography lights.

"It's beautiful."

While staring at her shoes, Eloise replied, "Since you're going without makeup and you're barefoot, it only makes sense to replace the wig. I mean, they'd see the real you, but not really."

"I've never done a publicity shoot without a wig." The veil face covering would offer her the anonymity she treasured. Yes, Jean's intern had done her research. "Thank you."

"'Louise!" Jean called.

Eloise's lips pressed together tightly at the same time her posture straightened. She raced off to talk with Jean on the other side of the room while Jazmin dipped behind the dressing screen. She admired her reflection. She felt as if she belonged on the movie set for the sequel to *Daughters of the Dust*. She could almost taste the salt breeze blowing in from the Atlantic and feel the sand between her toes. She'd have to plan a getaway with Micah. Maybe they could head north to Martha's Vineyard or south to Savannah? Thursday night's date couldn't have gone better. For the first time in a long time, she was thinking about amending her five-date rule. She put on the veil and then re-applied her signature red lipstick.

"Magnifique!" Jean exclaimed when she walked out and strolled to her mark on the floor. "I hope you don't mind, darling, but a few benefactors are on their way up."

"Of course." She wasn't surprised, especially with the gala less than a week away. She waved off any concern Jean had that she might not approve.

"Let's begin, shall we, mon chère?"

To loosen her up, Jean had Eloise turn on 100.3 WRNB, Philly's local station for R&B and hip hop. Jazmin closed her eyes and swayed to the music. It turned out Micah's friend Adam was a shitty dancer. He was a good sport though. His lack of skills didn't stop him from joining them on the dance floor. Song after song, he and his awkward, jerky movements had kept her and Brenda laughing.

Flashes of light compelled Jazmin to open her eyes and soon Jean was back to cooing orders. He had her twirl. Then she posed with her hands on her hips. She smiled and she pouted. Jean asked her to keep her face neutral. He also instructed her to try her best to appear overjoyed. Thankfully, the elevator chimed, distracting Jean and allowing Jazmin a moment to stretch and re-group. She angled her chin upward and then down, left and right. She rejoiced at the knots that popped and creaked. Jean had just started shooting again when the elevator doors squealed a part.

To her shock, Micah strolled into the conference room with his ex-girlfriend on his arm. Her chest pressed into his side and her hand clung to Micah's bicep.

A green haze fogged Jazmin's vision as heated jealousy washed over her. Unabashed fear followed closely behind. She silently pleaded for her feet to move so she could run out of sight, but her feet had frozen in place. Recognition lit Micah's eyes before the elevator's doors had shut behind him. With a broad smile, he unhooked himself from Eleanor's embrace and walked forward with determined strides.

"Monsieur, monsieur. You are in my shot!"

"Jazmin. What the hell are you doing here?" He smothered her in a hug before pressing his lips chastely on hers.

Jazmin's nipples tightened under the heat of his stare. She was confident he would have greeted her more passionately if they didn't have an audience.

"Ellie, get your friend," Jean demanded, his accent sounding more Jersey than Parisian.

Jazmin wished she could look away, but Micah's gaze had locked onto her. She couldn't retreat. Her heart sank into her stomach.

"I'm. I'm," she stammered.

"Where's J.J.?" he asked looking around the room and then back over his shoulder.

The elevator's chime sounded once more. This time when the doors opened Everett Randolph III entered accompanied by Eloise. The intern rattled off instructions, asking him to be mindful and not to step on any cables or wires that crisscrossed the floor. She pointed him toward a vacant director's chair. Everett ignored Eloise. His and Micah's eyes mirrored their surprise at seeing each other.

Heaven help me!

Feeling woozy, she swayed. She was grateful that Micah still held onto her elbow. Maybe she was too warm under the lights or perhaps she should have eaten something before driving to this morning's photoshoot.

"Miss J.J., can I get you a water? You look unwell," Eloise said. She rushed to the miniature cooler resting against the wall at the opposite end of the room.

Micah stared. He looked her up and down and then his face slowly morphed. A scowl replaced his cheerful expression. His pupils darkened and his eyebrows pinched together. Although he didn't say anything, his twitching right eye demanded answers. Behind him, Eleanor frowned.

"She can't be J.J.!" Eleanor said. "Jean, there must be a mistake."

Out of the corner of her eye, Jazmin saw the photographer's lanky arms flail in the air. "Let's take a break," he moaned.

"Micah, I can explain."

This time it was Everett's long, wagging index finger that caught her attention. He interrupted whatever words she was about to say next. "The *jawn* from the elevator, she's J.J.?" Everett doubled over and then peals of laughter filled the silence. He slapped his hand against one knee. The crease of his tailored pant leg remained firm.

Micah snatched his hand from Jazmin's arm.

"When we first met, I was embarrassed, and then you were contemplating resigning so I thought it wouldn't matter," she explained softly.

"You're J.J.?"

"Yes. I never meant—"

"You knew how much pressure I was under." His voice was low and lethal. "I told you how much I needed this promotion because of my dad." Micah's fingers worked overtime, spinning the gold band around and around.

"I know."

Jazmin was too much of a coward to meet his gaze. She looked past him instead. In the corner of the room she spotted Eloise, still frozen in place beside the open refrigerator, a chilled bottle of water in her hand. Jazmin's gaze traveled to the elevator. Everett had stopped laughing. He and Eleanor's ears perked up like two nosey cats. Jazmin took a deep breath and trained her eyes to the floor.

She whispered, "I would never have worked for your bosses"— slowly, she peeled the veil from her face and raised her eyes— "and because we hit it off, I thought—"

"You thought it would be better to decide what's best for me." He turned his back to her. "Unbelievable," he grumbled. "Everyone knows what's best for me."

"Micah, I'm sorry."

He spun around. His voice rose and then cracked when he responded, "You're sorry!"

His expression tensed and the wrinkles at the corners of his eyes became more pronounced. Knots of guilt gripped Jazmin's stomach and she felt as if she might vomit.

"I tried to tell you that night at the diner and then when you came to visit after your family's get-together." She took a step in his direction.

Raising his hands defensively, he stepped back, out of Jazmin's reach.

"I think we should go," Eleanor said gently. Reassuringly.

Micah nodded. He turned and strolled away, not bothering to look back. Everett tilted his head at Micah in silent acknowledgment before pressing the button to call for the elevator. Everett's round eyes held a hint of compassion. The elevator doors closed and then Micah was gone.

Jazmin looked at the delicate stones in her trembling hand. She sniffled. "Jean, I'm done. I hope you got what you needed."

Retreating, she set the veil beside its velvet pouch on the long table and walked to the room divider. Eloise had created a makeshift changing room. Jazmin's knees buckled. Stumbling, she clutched the tufted wingback chair in front of her. She fell against it before sinking into the overstuffed cushioned seat. They'd used it when shooting her in a sexy, boardroom boudoir getup. Jazmin, overwhelmed with guilt and sadness, barely registered the approaching clatter of stilettos. When she looked up, Micah's ex-girlfriend towered over her. Eleanor's knee-high leather boots made her appear taller than Jazmin remembered.

"I don't care who you are. Stay away from Micah. I can't believe I had to compete with you, a gnat... an insignificant speck." She gestured to the clutter surrounding them. "None of this will help you fit in. Micah and I go way back. Hell, I had brunch with his mother last week." Eleanor blew out an exasperated breath and placed her hands on her hips, accentuating her narrow waist.

Tears pooled in Jazmin's eyes and a bitter taste filled her mouth again. This time, she'd bit down hard on her lip to push down her rising pitiful sobs. She and Micah hadn't been dating exclusively, but it hurt to know he may have been seeing Eleanor. Or any other woman. Jazmin had definitely felt more than a physical attraction toward him and had thought the feeling was mutual. Had he just used her to get closer to finding J.J.?

"Whatever was going on between you two is over," Eleanor continued. "Stay behind the red curtain. The Wizard never did Dorothy any good." With that, she spun around on her heel and strutted back across the room. Eleanor didn't bother to soften her voice as she talked on the phone while waiting for the elevator to arrive.

"Micah, I don't know how Everett found out about today's photoshoot. Baby, you're going to have to come up with a believable explanation for Stein and Martin by Monday."

Jazmin closed her eyes. She had no idea what she'd do if Micah sold her out to his bosses to save his own skin. If Deerfield Foundation rescinded the Millennial Titan Award along with the prize money, her livelihood could... no, it *would* be ruined. Only after she heard the elevator's door squeal open and then close did she grip the arms of the chair and give in to the heavy sobs that had choked her voice.

Chapter Twenty-Four

Of course.

Reggie was there when Jazmin pulled up to her apartment. He sat on her steps like no time had passed between them. He hadn't changed. He'd neatly parted and plaited his hair. He even had a toothpick wedged between his lips. His dark brown skin looked dulled under the porch light.

Probably not much of a moisturizing routine in jail.

Jazmin softly banged her head against the steering wheel. She was exhausted from too little sleep and emotionally drained from her encounter with Micah and his girlfriend. The last thing she wanted to do was argue with Reggie over Destiny's future. Hadn't he received the Excel spreadsheet she'd emailed him the other day, detailing potential visiting schedules?

She grabbed her purse from the passenger seat. She would come out later to retrieve the garment bags, along with her makeup and wigs.

"You look good," Reggie said. His eyes scalded her as they roamed over her curves. "It'll take some getting used to, but the short cut suits you."

Unlike Micah, Reggie didn't stand as she approached. Jazmin pulled the halves of her jacket closed. A lifetime ago she would have considered his comment a compliment. Today, his words further weighed down her spirit. She started up the steps and Reggie made no attempt to move out of her way. The smell of stale cigarillo smoke and body odor assaulted her senses. Jazmin brushed past him and unlocked the outer door.

"Come on," she said over her shoulder.

Inside, she neither offered Reggie water to drink nor did she ask to take his coat. In fact, she grimaced when he slumped onto her sofa. She'd have to Febreze the hell out of it before Destiny got home. Sighing heavily, she perched on a stool several feet away. All she wanted to do was take a bath and fall into bed. She hoped sleep would rid her mind of everything that'd happened, if only for a little while.

"I see you still have that old junker," Reggie said, capturing her attention. "I know a guy who'd offer you a real good deal for parts. He has an online business that caters to car nuts who rebuild—"

"Hard pass." He clearly didn't remember how much the Nova meant to her. It was like he was asking her to sell off memories of her father. "Let's talk about Destiny."

He scanned the room. "Yeah, where's my kid?"

"She's with a sitter." Jazmin felt a migraine coming on. She touched her fingers lightly to her temple. "How are we going to make this work? Do you want to come by in the evenings and then maybe—"

"Baby, slow down."

Jazmin flinched and then she pinned him with a glare. "You lost the privilege of calling me baby when you slept with my cousin."

Looking down at his shoes, Reggie appeared contrite. "You've created a good life for her here. A home. Now, she needs a family." He paused dramatically. "I want to be part of that family. You, me, and Destiny." He raised his eyes to meet hers.

"One step at a time," Jazmin said coolly. Destiny's family included her and Brenda, along with Ms. Vicki and Pops. Still, Reggie's words held merit. "We can co-parent."

"Yes." He puffed out his chest as if he'd come up with the idea.

Jazmin raised a hand. "Stop." She had no intentions of playing house with him. "You can't stay here."

He waved her off. "We'll take things slow. The important thing is to make sure Destiny knows we're both here for her."

She nodded. Maybe there was something to Rose Mary's theory that Reggie had grown up. He certainly wasn't talking like the boy she'd known.

Loud banging interrupted her thoughts. Jazmin strained her neck as she peered over Reggie's head. She tried to see what was going on out of the street-level window behind him but couldn't. It slowly dawned on her that the banging was coming from someone pounding on her outer door.

"Jazmin! J.J.! Open up!"

Crap!

Anxiousness rustled in Jazmin's belly like leaves on a blustery fall day. The stool clattered to the floor when she stood. Dashing across the room, she took the basement steps two at a time. Reggie was on her heels.

***

Micah pounded on the door again. The Nova sat across the street, so he knew she was home. The initial shock had worn off and now he wanted answers. His heart raced and the longer he stood on her steps the more enraged he became.

"Open up! We need to talk."

When Micah heard footsteps bounding in his direction, he stepped back. A door creaked, and Jazmin appeared. He hated that his chest tightened. Her tear-streaked face didn't help matters. He decided to put even more distance between the two of them by relocating to the sidewalk.

She opened the door wider. "Micah, what are you doing here?"

A man appeared behind her. Micah ground his teeth. He didn't like that the stranger hadn't moved out of the shadows. When the man made no attempt to go around Jazmin, Micah's heartrate increased as he realized the guy was her guest.

What the hell!

"Who's this?" he snapped, feeling as if she'd poured a bucket of ice water over his head.

"You're banging on her front door, and you've got questions?" Reggie asked.

"Give me a sec, okay," she said over her shoulder before she returned her gaze to Micah.

The pitiful puffy eyes and pouty lip weren't going to work. She'd made a fool of him and in front of Rhett of all people.

Micah's jaw clenched. "We need to talk."

She nodded and stepped forward but the dumb-ass behind her took hold of her arm. "What's going on, Jaz?"

Micah's eyes shifted to the stranger's grip. Heat warmed its way up his neck. Evidently, this guy didn't value the use of his hands because Micah was a heartbeat away from breaking every bone in his left, the one touching his woman. He shook off the thought. Jazmin wasn't his woman anymore. If she'd ever been.

"Reggie, please." She pulled away.

"You fucking him?" he asked with a crude sneer.

"That's none of your business!" Jazmin looked away from Reggie and then down at Micah. "I know I owe you a better explanation. Can I please meet you later?"

Micah half listened. Reggie had pulled the security door closed behind him and stepped into view. His body now pressed against Jazmin's. Gloating, the fool smirked. Micah's fingers closed into tight fists. Standing at least six or more inches over the chump, Micah had the height advantage.

"It's time for you to go," Reggie said.

With a confused expression, Jazmin turned slightly. Her footing faltered and she would have stumbled down the steps and twisted her ankle if Reggie hadn't caught her.

"I got this." She planted her feet firmly.

He wrapped his arms around her waist. When she attempted to move away, he held tight.

"Let. Go."

"If she has to ask you again, we're going to have a problem," Micah threatened.

Jazmin wiggled loose and soon she stood just one step above Micah. Too close. Her unique scent of sweet berries filled his nose. Their gazes locked. When he saw tears pooled in her eyes, he swallowed hard.

"Listen to this guy." Reggie laughed. "Baby, you sure can pick 'em."

Jazmin descended the final step and placed her palms on Micah's chest. His fists unclenched.

"Please, go," she said.

Micah couldn't believe his ears. Was she choosing this punk over him?

"What?"

"Go, please."

"You heard her"—Reggie rushed down the steps—"Are you hard of hearing or just that pussy whipped? Get." He took hold of Jazmin's wrist.

This time when she pulled away, he tugged hard.

"Ow!"

Reggie released his hand at the same time Jazmin yanked free. She staggered backward and then fell to the ground. Micah's hold on his patience broke. Lunging forward, his fist connected with Reggie's jaw sending the jackass staggering backward.

Reggie touched the corner of his scraggly bearded mouth, and, seeing blood on his fingers, quickly recovered. He rushed forward and slammed hard into Micah's midsection. They fell into a couple of trash cans that had been set out on the curb. Empty plastic soda bottles, paper towel rolls, fast food wrappers, and other debris littered the ground. Somewhere in the distance Micah heard alarmed voices. They'd drawn the attention of Jazmin's neighbors.

With Micah flat on his back, Reggie's fists slammed into his face. Reggie threw a right jab, a left, and then another right. Micah did his best to block the blows, but it was impossible to shift their positions or shove Reggie off him. He heard Jazmin's curses and saw distortions, shapes and shadows of her face, as she tugged on Reggie's jacket, trying to intervene. At last distracted, Reggie relented. He turned.

Without delay, Micah got to his feet. This time when Reggie turned back to pelt him, Micah leaned out of the way. The guy's right hook missed by inches. Before Reggie recovered from the forward momentum, Micah clocked him on the chin. Reggie hit the pavement.

"Stop. Stop it!" Jazmin yelled.

She shoved Micah. She pushed his chest again and again. Behind her, Reggie leaned against her bottom step. He shifted his chin left and then right. His heavy breathing mirrored Micah's.

"What the hell is wrong with you?" Jazmin shouted.

She shoved Micah once more before she turned around and walked to Reggie's side. Confused, Micah stared after her.

"Are you alright? Let's get you inside. I'm sure there's some parole rule about brawling in the middle of the street. I have some frozen peas you can put on your face." She helped him to his feet.

Micah's eyes widened. "Who is he?" he wheezed between pants of breath. His adrenaline still raced.

Jazmin scowled. "He's Destiny's father."

Chapter Twenty-Five

Ellie snuggled closer to Micah. She rubbed his arm. Her manicured nails, with their pink nail beds and white tips, had no accouterments, no fuss. The silence between them thundered. She threaded her arm through the crook of his. When he pulled away, she pouted. As he stood, she had no choice but to unwrap herself from around him. Her leg bumped the steamer trunk coffee table. The beer he'd just finished wobbled but didn't fall.

"Do you want to talk about it?"

"No," Micah said flatly.

He didn't want to explain how he'd gotten the bruises on his hands and face. Visions of him and Jazmin kissing swirled around in his head before he could push them away. The other night, she'd moaned when he'd nipped her earlobe. He trailed kisses down her neck. Her skin had tasted sticky and sweet. The weight of her breasts had pressed against his chest. His fingers itched to tease their strained buds. Jazmin had no idea that he'd been seconds away from hauling her out of the club and taking her in the backseat of his car.

"I need another brew." He stalked to the kitchen.

He heard Ellie puff out a loud breath behind him. Glancing back, he paused to watch as she toyed with the diamond and white gold bangle on her wrist and then stood. He'd given her the gift for their one-year anniversary. Her purse along with a rolling suitcase and duffel rested by the door.

"What happened after you dropped me off?" she pressed, sauntering forward.

In the kitchen, she opened an overhead cabinet and removed two wine flutes. Micah stepped around her and started to say something, but his voice caught in his throat when he saw his reflection in the refrigerator's stainless◇steel veneer. He couldn't ignore the bruises around his eye and jaw. He opened the door and pulled out a lager. With the ridge of his sports ring he snapped off the cap. He heard Ellie behind him. She rummaged through his silverware drawer. It closed with a muted thump. He turned around and found her looking up at him expectantly. Micah remained mute. While she pushed a corkscrew into the soft bark of the wine cork, he flexed his free hand. He winced slightly at the pain brought on by the movement. His knuckles ached and purplish bruising had started to show.

She poured herself a glass of wine and then closed the space between them. She put her hand on his chest, over his heart. Smiling at his short intake of breath, she misread his waning grip on his emotions. She grinned just before brushing her lips against his cheek. Normally, she would wait him out. She'd give him a while to stop brooding. This evening, she had decided to charm him. Ellie had no idea she'd poked a bear. The wine's additional floral notes brought back memories of Jazmin. The full aroma of sweet grapes flooded his senses.

"Have it your way. I won't ask about your face," Ellie said.

Micah drained his beer slowly. She stepped backward and he watched her light brown eyes darken. Anger turned her peachy cheeks rhubarb.

"Aren't you going to ask me to stay?"

"I'm not in the mood," he replied. "Please, go home. I'm tired."

Things had happened quickly after he learned Jazmin's true identity. Rhett had hailed a cab and Ellie tugged him inside. They'd dropped Rhett off first and then stopped by her place. As soon as the car door closed, Micah paid the cabbie to drive him to Jazmin's apartment. He hadn't expected Ellie to catch a cab on her own. And he sure as hell didn't think she'd be waiting in the lobby of his building when he finally made it back to his condo. The dull pounding at his temples had intensified when he spotted her. From the looks of the small arsenal of bags she had brought with her, she planned to move in.

"Micah, I assumed we would fall into each other's orbits again. Things were good between us for two years. Marriage can wait. There's no rush if you're not ready. I support you focusing on your career."

He contemplated her logic but when he didn't respond fast enough Eleanor's lips narrowed.

"There's no point in dredging up the past," he said as he watched her transformation. "At the end, neither of us were good for the other."

Micah kept his expression neutral. Eleanor Deerfield was losing it. Her breathing had increased. He visualized her patience like a matchstick drug across a course surface just before the dry tip sparked. The glass left Ellie's hand and she appeared caught off guard by her actions. They both followed the fragile vessel's flight path as it slammed against the wall and then splintered into pieces.

"Shit. I didn't mean to. I'm sorry." She stretched her hand toward him.

He jerked away. His movements were those of a seasoned athlete. He was suddenly across the room and standing in front of the intercom system on the wall beside the door. He instructed security to come upstairs. Afterward, he opened the door, grabbed the thin handle of her case, and threw it out.

A chortle snuck its way out of Ellie's nose and mouth. "Don't be immature."

The muscles along his jawline flexed. If she wanted to belittle and mock him, he would show her what immature looked like. Micah collected her purse, keys and any other items of hers within reach. He flung everything out the door despite her increasing shouts.

"Stop! You're crazy! Do you know how much that cost?" She'd reached a piercing octave. Spit pooled in the corners of her mouth.

He allowed her to get out all of her bitterness and to say what she'd been holding onto. When he heard the elevator in the distance, he exhaled and then his shoulders relaxed. A short minute later, he stepped aside to let a uniformed guard enter.

Ellie stood her ground. "You prefer her? A nobody! I don't care how many websites she's made or awards she's won. She's not like me and you!"

"Stop," Micah's voice thundered. "There's no you and me. Not anymore. When will you get it? It's over."

A pang of guilt squeezed his chest when her eyes widened. Tears streamed down her cheeks. She wasn't playacting. Out of the corner of his eye, Micah saw a second guard emerge from the door leading to the stairwell. Behind the guard, Adam. The second officer hastily collected Ellie's discarded belongings while allowing the first guard to escort her out of the suite. Adam tiptoed around them with his hands positioned high in the air, making it clear he wasn't a part of the scene. Ellie pulled away from the guard's hold.

"Fuck. You. Micah Clarion." her crisp articulation of his name sliced the air like a knife through butter. She stormed off with her chin raised high.

Adam flopped down on the sofa. Micah's gaze shifted to the red wine dripping down the wall and then to the glass shards on the floor. While cleaning up the mess, he relayed to Adam all that'd happened leading up to him calling security.

"Damn," Adam said after Micah had finished. "Do you think Jazmin was with her baby's daddy this whole time or—"

"I don't know anything, anymore."

Micah took a swig of beer. His third.

Or was it his fourth?

The coldness of the bottle pressed against his tender joints felt good, soothing.

Adam shook his head. "She seemed really into you." He muted the T.V. news broadcast.

Micah crossed the room. "The icing on the cake is that ol'boy is an ex-con."

Adam covered his mouth. Micah thought his friend might spew beer through the gaps between his fingers.

"Seriously?" Pinching his shirt, Adam fluttered the fabric to shake off any excess wetness.

"Yep," Micah said more calmly than he felt. He sat down.

"Now that I know how you two met—I get that she was initially embarrassed—but why do you think she let it go on for so long?"

Micah shrugged. He had wondered the same thing. From what he'd learned about J.J., Tech Philly had an established reputation in Philadelphia. Jazmin shouldn't be hurting for cash. That meant she wasn't dating him just for his money.

"I dated a klepto, once," Adam said, interrupting Micah's thoughts. "She took random stuff too, things with little or no value. The final straw was when we were out to eat, and she slipped the silverware into her purse and then asked our server for another place setting."

Micah stared at his friend in disbelief. After a minute, the corner of his lip curved upward, and then a burp rose from deep in the back of his throat. A rumbly chuckle followed. He cracked up with amusement.

"What the hell, man?" he asked between gasps of air. His side hurt from laughing.

"I deleted all the dating apps on my phone after that."

"I guess things could have been worse," Micah concluded.

Adam set down his empty beer bottle. "You dated the one person on the planet who could help you get a promotion, and she hid her identity from you while she played house with her ex-con, baby's daddy who you decked in front of all of her neighbors. That's pretty bad."

Micah pulled air in through his nose and blew it out through his mouth methodically to stifle his childlike chortles.

"What a shitstorm!"

Adam released a deep belly laugh. For several minutes, the hilarity of Micah's situation rang out. Laughing with Adam decreased the tightness Micah felt in his chest as their loud guffaws subsided and their breathing steadied, he and Adam stared at the television quietly. Both lost in thought.

"Do you know what you're going to do about the promotion? And Rhett?" Adam asked after a while.

"No clue." Micah slumped farther down. "The promotion is Rhett's for sure. I just have to figure out a way to save face." Micah turned. "I can't resign. Not yet anyway."

Adam nodded curtly. His cheeks flushed as he kept his attention trained on the T.V. "I get it."

"I've got to rebuild my reputation. You know how it is." Micah knew his friend was pissed off. He'd seen that look before "She duped me. It's going to take more than a few wins in court to convince everyone that I don't have my head up my ass." Micah raised the beer bottle to his lips and sipped. His father's condescending voice echoed in his head.

Adam continued staring ahead. He focused on the muted news recap.

Micah pressed on, hoping something he said would resonate with Adam. "I've ignored my dad's calls. I don't even want to deal with what he's going to say." He gulped down the rest of his beer."C'mon, don't be mad."

Adam turned his head and stared at Micah like he'd spoken a foreign language.

"Mad?" Adam shook his head. "How long are you going to do this dance?"

Micah set his empty bottle on the coffee table. "What are you talking about?"

"You let other people pull your strings like a marionette doll. If you want to stay at Stein, Martin, and Randolph, then stay."

Adam stood. He picked up their beers and headed to the kitchen. Micah heard the clink of metal hitting metal. Adam had tossed the empty bottles in the recycling bin.

"You want another brew?" he called out.

Micah leaned forward and cradled his head in his hands. "No."

Chapter Twenty-Six

Jazmin did her best to smile and appear happy. She felt haggard but hoped her painted face camouflaged a night of tossing and turning. She'd agreed to speak to a Girl Scout troop at a local elementary school. She was part of a series of guest speakers picked by the nine-year-olds. Because tonight's group was small, only seven girls and one little brother. Jazmin had borrowed tablets from the neighborhood library and purchased a coding kit for each girl. The little brother along with Destiny sat in the back of the classroom. They colored and watched kiddie videos on Jazmin's cell phone.

"My job is to design websites, games, and software like cell phone apps. I must focus on details so the game or app functions like it's supposed to. When I make websites, I have to make sure when you click on a link that you're taken to the right destination."

She pushed a button on the overhead projector so the girls could see her computer's desktop. "I'm going to double click on this. See how it highlights? Next, I'm going to move my finger across the mousepad and let go when it's between the two snowflakes." A chime sounded followed by several more chimes as the girls mirrored her actions. "You've just used computer language or code to tell your app to make a snow flurry when you wave your hand back and forth over the sensor."

Smiling, Jazmin demonstrated how to create a flurry over the ice castle on her screen. Pride swelled in her chest, hearing the girls' oohs and ahhs. She only wished she had more time to do events like this. Walking up and down each aisle, she checked in on her tiny prodigies.

"I have to return the tablets to the library, but the kits are yours to keep."

The girls cheered.

After Jazmin was convinced the girls could play on their own for a bit, she sat down near the moms who chit-chatted and munched on cookies. A tall, lanky girl with big brown eyes and a nervous smile sidled up to her.

"We code in class sometimes when we finish our work early," she told Jazmin. "My mom says I have to be a doctor or lawyer, but I really like computers. Maybe I'll do what you do. Do you make as much as a doctor?" the second grader asked.

This, Jazmin hated. It was partially why she'd started concealing her identity. Because of her early success, people often thought of her as Scrooge McDuck. They didn't realize she had bills to pay and a child to raise, or that it took money to run a small business. As big as Philly was, it often felt like the small, one stop-light town where Jazmin had grown up. Everyone knew someone, who knew someone, who knew you. The difference, Philadelphia could be very dangerous. She didn't need a sign on her back that read "Rob Me" whenever she left home.

Jazmin noticed that the moms had stopped gossiping. They were waiting for her to answer, also.

"I still buy a lottery ticket every Wednesday." Jazmin forced a grin.

The little girl nodded and then skipped back over to her friends. After taking Destiny to the bathroom for a last minute pitstop, Jazmin politely bid the Girl Scout group goodnight. Destiny fell asleep in the car before Jazmin had driven four blocks. The softly playing holiday music distracted her from thoughts of Micah. She hummed along to the radio.

I wonder what he's doing right now. Is he with her?

As she pulled into a vacant spot a few doors down from the apartment, her brief respite abruptly ended. Reggie sat on her steps. She'd forgotten he would be waiting for them. Whistle-sounding snores filled the air. Jazmin looked over her shoulder at the sleeping preschooler. Because of how messed up things had gone the day before, she had agreed to allow Reggie to come by this evening. He'd meet Destiny, maybe tuck her in, and then the two co-parents would come up with a game plan.

Sighing, Jazmin's breath created a delicate cloudy swirl. The heated interior of the car had cooled. It was time for her and Destiny to get out. Jazmin slung her purse over her shoulder. She exited the car and then made quick work of gathering her belongings. After opening Destiny's door, Jazmin expertly unbuckled the harness and removed the safety straps holding her little cousin in her car seat. She positioned Destiny on her hip and then bumped the car door closed.

Reggie stood as she approached. He didn't, however, make a move to take his child or to take the overburdened tote Jazmin carried. She'd filled it with library tablets and Destiny's toys. She glared at him while fumbling with her keys. At least he didn't smell like a funky locker room, but faint traces of smoke lingered on his clothes and person. Reggie bent over to retrieve her fallen keys. Afterward, he unlocked the security door for her. She mumbled a thank you that she didn't mean. After exchanging her tote bag for the keys, she unlocked her apartment door and stepped inside.

Not bothering to wait for him, she walked down the short hallway and into Destiny's bedroom. She flipped on the lights. Destiny squeezed her eyes tight. They fluttered, but the little girl didn't wake. Although Jazmin hadn't heard Reggie's approach, she felt him standing behind her. She carefully unzipped the pink fluffy snowsuit and worked Destiny's arms and legs free. She decided to forgo pajamas. She tucked in her little cousin and placed a soft kiss on the child's cheek.

"She looks just like you and Cicely," Reggie whispered.

"All she got was my coloring."

"And your eyes."

Jazmin stepped to the side. This was his first time seeing his daughter. Jazmin's heart felt heavy in her chest. She pitied him. After all, he'd missed Destiny's birth, first steps, first words, doctor's visits, and other milestones.

"Come on," she said, turning and heading out the door.

Reggie followed. He'd left her stuff on the floor in front of the apartment door. Jazmin rolled her eyes. She was too tired to fuss. She would unpack everything in the morning. When Jazmin moved in the direction of the stairs, Reggie reached for her hand. She looked down at it and then up at him.

"What?" she asked, tugging it away and then smoothing her palms over her jean leggings.

"Thank you."

A smile slowly spread over her face. "Do you want coffee or something? I was thinking you should come by in the morning since tonight is a bust. Maybe again on Christmas Day if you can get away. I'm sure your mom has plans."

She knew she was babbling, but she'd never seen this side of Reggie. His softer side. She'd known the kid who was loud and boisterous and the producer who took music too seriously. This Reggie's eyes were clear, not hazed from long nights of drinking and partying. They held tenderness and understanding.

In one smooth motion, Reggie pulled Jazmin close and covered her mouth with his lips.

She pushed him away. Hard. "What the hell?" she exclaimed.

"C'mon, Jaz."

"It's time for you to go."

She brushed past him, bumping hard into his shoulder. She'd forgotten how easily he could switch from doting boyfriend to jerk.

"For ol' time's sake?"

She frowned at him in disbelief.

"We're a family," he added.

"Not that kind of family."

He shifted his weight and, when that didn't do the trick, he adjusted the crotch of his pants with his hand. Sucking her teeth, she opened her front door.

"Hey, don't forget that's my kid sleeping in there." He pointed in the direction of Destiny's bedroom.

Jazmin's heart thumped against her rib cage and her earlier fatigue vanished. Hadn't she feared he would try something like this? Reggie was mistaken if he thought she would allow him to snatch her out of Destiny's life without a fight. She was determined Destiny would never experience the level of hurt she did when Reggie rejected her. Even worse, when Jazmin's mother walked out of her life.

Reggie must have felt the change in the air, like the charge of electricity before a storm, because he threw his hands up in surrender.

"My bad. I didn't mean that how it sounded."

Yes, you did.

"It's time for you to go," she replied coolly.

Lowering his arms, Reggie smoothly ambled into the entryway. "I'll see you two in the morning. We should get a light dusting tonight, maybe we can play outside."

She closed the door without saying a word and put on the deadbolt.

***

Micah looked at his wristwatch. 10 AM. He'd been up before the sun, trying to clear his head. But nothing had worked. Not an early morning workout, not watching sports highlights, not channel-surfing. Since before seven o'clock, he'd been fighting the urge to see Jazmin. He needed...no... he wanted answers.

Unlike last time, Brenda opened the door. She let him know Jazmin and Destiny were around the corner at Julian Abele, a park. It wasn't a park at all, rather, it was an open green space for concerts and events. It had snowed an inch or two overnight and Jazmin and Destiny had ventured out early to take advantage of the small deluge. Brenda had seemed excited to relay the information to him and gave no indication that Jazmin had informed her of the skirmish between him and Destiny's father.

It took Micah less than five minutes to navigate the one-way streets and arrive at the corner of Montrose and Catherine. Now, he felt like a stalker. It was killing him to watch Jazmin and Destiny and the girl's father race around in circles, playing tag.

"That should be me out there," he mumbled to himself.

With Christmas just three days away, he wondered how Jazmin would celebrate. Would Reggie sleep over? The thought made Micah's stomach sour.

His cell pinged, and his attention shifted. Micah plucked the phone from the change holder. He clicked on the envelope icon. He'd received a reminder bulletin about the upcoming gala from Deerfield Foundation. As if he could forget. The bulletin included a brief biography on J.J. A glutton for punishment, Micah double tapped the attachment. It downloaded onto his phone.

There was no need to read Jazmin's bio, so he scrolled past it. He was sure his own research had given him the same details provided in the article. When he glimpsed the first picture from the gala publicity photoshoot he forgot how to breathe. She wore a man's button down shirt dress that had the first letters of the word "love" embossed on the front and the remaining letters on the back. The look was short and sexy and a nod to Philly.

The waist length wig with its bangs and braided headband made Jazmin appear younger. While talking on an outdated corded phone, she leaned against what looked like a dorm room desk. The photographer had captured her mid-laugh and, unlike many print advertising campaigns, her smile wasn't faked. Micah was certain. The lines above her nose wrinkled.

He scrolled on and damn near blew his cover by falling against the steering wheel and pressing on the car's horn. He slumped down in the driver's seat and prayed he hadn't been seen.

She wore a short, ombre auburn wig in the second photo and had dressed in the corset he seen her in when they'd first met. A snug, black pencil skirt hugged her curves and the stiletto red bottoms she wore lengthened her legs. The outfit could only be described as boardroom vixen. Jazmin appeared to be giving a presentation. He envisioned laying her across that conference table and kneeling in front of her spread legs. Shifting in the driver's seat, he lowered the heat in his Impala. The chillier temperature helped.

The last thing he needed was for someone to walk by and spot him sitting in an idling car with a boner.

He continued to the last photo and made sure to commit the picture to memory. This was the outfit he'd seen her wearing when he'd interrupted the photoshoot. Barefoot, with her face free of makeup, and wearing scraps of material pinned together, she looked otherworldly. The bright lights transformed the pearls and crystals on the face covering, and the resulting swirls of rainbows obscured her identity. The only indication it was the same woman from the other two photographs were her red-painted lips. The photographer had caught her mid twirl. Her laughing smile thawed Micah's icy armor.

The photo spread had been accurately labeled, 'Journey to Millennial Titan. More dreams yet to fulfill.'" He turned off his phone and tossed it onto the passenger seat. Although he was happy for her, especially her winning The Millennial Titan Award, he wasn't ready to forgive. She should have told him. Looking out the window, Jazmin trudged through the slush; She headed in his direction. He rolled down the window, grateful for the cold blast of air that hit him. It sobered him from thoughts of twirling tulle, lace, and satin.

"Micah, you need to leave." She put her gloved hands on her hips.

"That's what you're going to lead with?" he asked, grumpily. "No remorse."

Her shoulders slumped and his chest tightened at her somber expression.

"I'm sorry. I shouldn't have lied and thinking back on my reasons, I have no excuse. I was selfish, and a chicken, and I am truly sorry I hurt you. But right now, I need you to go." She looked back at Destiny playing with her dad. "I can't mess this up."

He looked past her when Destiny's bell-like giggles filled the air. Reggie pulled Destiny along in a plastic sled. Jazmin wasn't going to get off that easy. She turned her attention back to him. He glared. His heartbeat raced as he fired a barrage of angry words.

"I told you about my father and his need to steer my career along with the pressures I faced from my bosses. I confided in you and at no point in time did you think, maybe, I deserved to know the truth? That I didn't need another person acting like they knew what was best for me?"

Jazmin lowered her head. "Your bosses are horrible people," she mumbled.

"That's not the point," he replied through clenched teeth.

She flinched and sucked in a short breath. When she glanced up, the hurt in her eyes jarred him so much that he pulled back the reins of his assault.

He took a deep breath. He did his best to keep his voice lowered and his tone neutral. "I came here for answers, not to fight. You were supposed to be different, not cut from the same manipulative cloth as my ex."

"Tell me this," she began, her posture stiff. "If you had known who I was and I told you I wasn't going to help you, knowing what you knew then, would you have given me a chance? Introduced me to Adam? Your family?"

Micah stared at her. Though he was frowning, his frustration was with himself. The answer to her question was simple. He would have seen her as undatable and unsuitable. How well they got along and how much he liked her wouldn't have mattered. Back then, he thought she was single mother who worked at a risqué lingerie store during the day and stripped at night. If he had learned that Destiny's father was an ex-con, he would have fled for the Main Line and never looked back. Micah ran a hand over his hair. Jazmin wasn't playing fair. He'd thought all of those things before getting to know her. Before he cared for her.

"Would you have used how we met against me? To get me to help your law firm in exchange for your silence?" she asked.

Her words were like a punch to the gut. He wanted to believe that he wouldn't have resorted to blackmail. But the truth had his cheeks hot with embarrassment. He didn't want to admit it out loud, but he'd been *that* desperate. Hell, hadn't he sent her flowers in order to weasel his way into her good graces? He had run out of options when Ellie'd phoned him Sunday evening, telling him about how she'd arranged for him to meet J.J. at the photoshoot.

"That's what I thought." Apparently, Jazmin took his silence as confirmation that she'd been right to keep her secrets. "Goodbye, Micah." She lumbered back through the slush the way she'd come.

After rolling up his window, he slammed his hand against the steering wheel. He was better off without her. Despite what he *might've thought* or how he *might've behaved*, the reality was he'd never lied to her. Jazmin, J.J., or whomever she planned to pretend to be tomorrow, couldn't be trusted. Especially, not with his heart.

Chapter Twenty-Seven

Jazmin smiled at Destiny in the rear-view mirror. With one day left until Christmas, the little girl's excitement bubbled over. The toddler chattered away, not caring that her older cousin only responded with the occasional "yes" or "okay."

Jazmin glanced over at her buzzing phone. Reggie, again. He wanted to meet today even though they'd already arranged for him to drop by tomorrow. What was wrong with him? She'd already told him she planned to spend Christmas Eve decorating her apartment and finishing up the last-minute items on her to-do list. Just as Jazmin was about to let him know, in no uncertain terms, that she didn't have time for his foolishness, a crackly car stereo sputtered outside her window. Her head jerked up at the sound of the booming bass. Her car windows rattled. The youngster had parked a little too close for Jazmin's liking. Jazmin watched as Brenda held the door open for the girl. By the look on Brenda's face, she entered the post office without saying "thank you."

Brenda tugged her hood tight around her head and jogged to the Nova. Her breath created a puffy white cloud. She pulled open the passenger-side door and tossed a stack of junk mail onto the center console. Her tan skin tinted red even though she'd been gone less than five minutes. Plopping down onto the seat, Brenda rubbed her hands together.

Jazmin took in her friend's despondent expression. "What's up?" she asked, turning the heat dial.

Brenda pulled an envelope from her sweatshirt pocket and handed it over. The return address, written in elegant cursive, revealed the letter had been mailed from California by a Miao Yin. Jazmin turned the envelope over in her hands. Larger than the standard size, it probably contained a holiday greeting card.

"I don't understand why you're upset."

Brenda puffed out an exasperated breath. "It's from my cousin."

Jazmin handed back the envelope. She adjusted the radio so music played louder in the rear than in the front. Destiny sang along to the Chipmunks' Christmas song.

"It's addressed to Brandon Liu Jr.," Brenda said frowning. She stuffed the envelope back into her pocket. "I guarantee if *Princess* Maio Yin decided to change her name to something more American-sounding, she'd insist everyone honor that."

Brenda rarely spoke about her family. Jazmin put the car in gear and pulled away from the curb. Her best friend vented about the frustration of being reminded of her past self with whom she no longer identified.

"Since parachuting in from Hong Kong when we were teenagers, Miao Yin has always thought she was better than us, her American-born cousins."

"Parachuting?"

"My dad's side of the family is crazy rich. It's nothing for my aunt and uncle to send Miao Yin to California for boarding school, lease her a condo, buy her a car, and whatever else she needs. If me or my younger siblings moved to L.A. to chase a dream, we'd be on our own. And there definitely wouldn't be a cushy diamond accented parachute to ensure a safe landing."

Jazmin clicked her tongue. She could relate.

"She's been fascinated with the career of Anna May Wong since we were kids, after seeing the 1924 black and white version of *Peter Pan* with an Asian-American Tiger Lily. It blew our minds. I bet Anna May is the name she'd pick..."

"Hey," Jazmin interjected. "You can't let someone else's issues become your problems. Isn't that what you always tell me?"

At a stop light, Jazmin turned to look at her friend. Brenda shivered even though the inside of the Nova was sweltering. Outside, it had started snowing again. The windshield wiper blades swatted away fat snowflakes but were unsuccessful at stopping them from collecting on the glass.

"You're right." Brenda sat up straighter. "Her tune will change when she lands a role where she has to dance on beat."

Laughing, Jazmin shifted gears and turned onto Christian Street.

"Speaking of dancing, when are you, I mean, we, hanging out with Micah and Adam again?"

An aching tightness spread across Jazmin's chest. She'd done a good job of not looking sad in front of Destiny. Or crying whenever she had a minute alone. She'd put off telling Brenda about her fallout with Micah because she hadn't wanted to hear, "I told you so."

Brenda mimicked Jazmin's shrug. "What does that mean?" Turning in her seat, she pointed a bedazzled nail in Jazmin's direction. "Your lying caught up to you and now things are fucked up, aren't they?"

"Language." Jazmin angled her head in Destiny's direction.

Brenda mouthed "sorry" and then glanced over her shoulder at Destiny. "Are you excited about tomorrow?" Pumping her fist in the air, Brenda soon had Destiny chanting. "Presents! Presents! Presents!" Their joy infectious, Jazmin grinned despite the jumble of emotions she felt. For now, she chose to ignore Brenda's accurate finger-pointing.

Since rooming together in college, it had become a tradition for her and Brenda to set up their tree on Christmas Eve. Neither traveled home for the holiday. After Destiny was born, they'd added baking German almond and buttery spritz cookies to the routine, a family recipe. A batch of Jazmin's German almond cookies never lasted more than a day or two.

***

Micah stared down at his phone again. He blinked several times to clear his vision. He reread the message. His sixty-eight-year-old mother, who struggled with emailing, had just texted.

It's the holidays, get your shit together and call your father.

Micah had already spoken with his little sister, offering his well wishes to her and her family. His niece had her first Christmas photoshoot, outfits courtesy of her five doting uncles. Wisely, Becca had taken a photo with the baby wearing a seasonal onesie from each of her brothers' respective alma maters. Micah's chest swelled with pride when he saw the precious infant wearing Temple cherry and white. Thoughts crept into his head of him and Jazmin, along with Destiny and a miniature version of himself holding hands. The four of them entered the Liacouras Center to watch the Owls play basketball. Taking a deep breath, he pushed the image out of his mind and then dialed his parents' number. After the third ring, his father answered.

"Son."

"Hey, Pop. Merry Christmas."

His father mumbled incoherently with what Micah assumed was a similar holiday greeting.

"Sorry I haven't returned your calls. I've—"

Micah's dad cleared his throat. A low rumbly chortle cackled through the phone's receiver.

"Save your closing argument for the courtroom. You've been sulking around trying to figure out how to get your head out of your ass."

Micah's shoulders slumped as he leaned against the kitchen countertop. He hadn't expected this. A lecture, yes. But this ribbing was humiliating, ten times worse than the tongue lashing he'd been avoiding.

"I have to go," Micah said.

"Whoa. Stop being so sensitive. There's a silver lining to this whole mess. I know you've been all over town looking at office spaces. It's a good idea to align yourself with Adam."

Micah nearly dropped the phone. Several awkward silent seconds passed.

"Are you still there?"

"Yes, sir. I'm here."

"You didn't think I knew Adam left his firm? I may not be practicing anymore, but don't count me out.

Hell, I bet you boys don't know that I lecture at the University of Chicago Law School on occasion."

Micah shook his head. He hadn't had a clue. Moving toward the fridge, he got himself a bottle of water. He gulped the chilled liquid while his father continued talking, explaining step-by-step how he and Adam should set up their firm. The iciness cooled Micah's fevered skin. Eventually, he got a legal pad and wrote down the contact information of several people he needed to call.

Micah felt a weight fall from his shoulders. Things were coming together, and he hadn't needed J.J. His father had found a solution. Sure, George Clarion would extract his pound of flesh over time. He'd gloat and remind Micah how his brothers hadn't needed help to succeed, but Micah could deal with that.

After ending the call, he crossed the room. The discolored patch on the wall caught his attention as he passed by the front door. The faded wine stain served as a visual reminder of the mess he'd made of his love life. He looked down at his cell phone when a familiar tone alerted him of a text. He took a steadying breath. Adam had messaged him a few times already. His brothers too. Everyone had seen the Millennial Titan photospread, and everyone thought it necessary to call and ask about Jazmin "J.J." Johnson.

Micah looped his gym bag's strap over his head and yanked open the door to his condo. He planned to sweat out his frustrations downstairs in the gym. He hoped to get rid of the nagging feeling in the pit of his stomach. Even if he wanted Jazmin back, which he didn't, she'd made it plain that she wasn't interested in reconciliation. Not for the first time, Jazmin's words played on repeat in his head. "I can't mess this up," she'd told him.

Chapter Twenty-Eight

The bubble bath was almost done. While Jazmin sprayed Destiny's back with water, the little girl wiggled her rump. The smell of pink bubblegum still hung in the air. Destiny had recently learned the chicken dance. As the water drained, Jazmin attempted to wash Destiny's face, but she squirmed away.

Gone was the mild-mannered, playful child. She wrenched herself from Jazmin's hold and moved out of reach. The little imp stared up unflinchingly. Jazmin was tempted to remind Destiny that Santa gave naughty boys and girls rocks instead of gifts but then decided against it when the three-year-old yawned. A tiny smile peeked out from behind Jazmin's frown. She hoisted the sleepy child from the water and wrapped her in a fluffy towel.

Destiny shifted in Jazmin's arms and, without warning, expelled a loud fart. Instinctively, Jazmin held the toddler as far away from her body as her arms would allow. The corners of Destiny's mouth turned up at the scowl on Jazmin's face. After a long pause, both females broke into laughter.

"Stinky butt," Jazmin cooed. Then, feigning ignorance, she belched loudly, echoing Destiny's earlier poot and setting off a new round of giggles between them.

"Excuse me," Jazmin said in a sing-song voice.

The little girl broke wind again. "'Scuse me."

Jazmin looked down affectionately at Destiny and then hugged her tightly.

"Aw," said Brenda. She stood in the doorway with one hand over her heart. The other clutched Jazmin's cell.

Jazmin smiled. She hadn't heard her friend come upstairs.

"Your cell's been beeping." Brenda placed the phone in her outstretched hand. "I'll take her." She lifted the towel-wrapped Destiny and cuddled her close.

The caller was Reggie. Jazmin's smile faded, and her lips pressed tightly together. He was outside waiting.

"I'll be right back."

Before heading out Jazmin made sure to grab a long wool cardigan off her bed. When she stepped into the cold, she stared at him in disbelief.

"You came empty-handed?"

Instead of replying, he removed a half-smoked cigarillo from behind his ear and sandwiched it between his lips. Jazmin fought the urge to smack the cigarillo out of his mouth when he lit the thing with a lighter from his jacket pocket. He had the good sense not to come up the steps or enter her apartment.

"Did you think I wouldn't find out?" he mumbled.

"What are you talking about?"

The first pungent notes of his cigar tickled her nose hairs, and the smell made her nauseous.

"You were always fiddling with computers."

He paused waiting for her to say something. Though she stiffened, she didn't reply to his arched eyebrow.

He continued. "I have a plan to get a new studio off the ground. One better than that hot box, hole in the wall I recorded in back in the day."

"I don't sing," Jazmin said.

Reggie snickered before taking a drag. "I know that." Angling his head, he blew smoke off to the side. "I thought you could front me the money."

"No." She stared at the plastic mouthpiece that held the tiny cigar together.

"No?" he asked, challengingly. His beady eyes were bloodshot.

"You heard me."

"It'd be pennies compared to the rest you're bringing in. I just need to get on my feet."

She'd heard this excuse before. "You're always counting on buying the winning scratch-off lottery ticket, or the next good beat, or a halfway decent producer."

He spat on the ground. "Watch it."

She tsked. *Or, what?*

He pointed the cigarette roach in her direction. "I'm not asking. The way I see it—" he tilted the stub toward the door— "you've been playing make-believe in there with my kid."

"You're welcome," Jazmin said. "I think that's the response you're going for."

"My name is on the birth certificate. Mine and Cicely's. Not yours. You've no legal claim. I could take off right now with her and you couldn't stop me."

"Bull—"

He cut her off. "Miss Millennial Titan. You must be feeling yourself. I would too if I were sitting on a quarter of a million dollars. All I'm asking for is a pinch. You won't even consider that."

"Wait one minute!" Jazmin shouted.

He flicked the last remnants of his cigarillo onto the sidewalk. The embers dissolved to ash seconds after touching the cold concrete. "I want it all."

She raced down the steps, stopping in front of him, getting right in his face. Her heartbeat echoed in her ears.

"Fuck you."

"No, sweetheart, pay me." Reggie seemed to find her anger humorous. His eyes shone with mirth. "Go to your big party and smile for the cameras." He leaned in close. The warmth of his stale breath grazed her cheek like a seedy caress. "You should wear that boujee lingerie number."

Jazmin gasped. Who on earth forwarded him the photospread? She took a step backward and crossed her arms over her chest.

"You terminated your rights when Destiny was still a baby."

"Says who? Cicely?" Reggie spun in a slow dramatic circle. "Where is she? Where's your proof?"

He waved off her glare. There was something he didn't know. After Cicely stopped calling months ago, Jazmin had filed papers petitioning for guardianship of Destiny. For now, Jazmin kept this piece of information to herself.

"You have until January second to hand over the cash or the kid."

She sucked in a breath. She hated that she'd flinched at his ultimatum. His predatorial smirk turned into a wide grin. She could see all thirty-two of his yellowed teeth. He seemed satisfied by her silence or maybe it was her refusal to argue further. He turned around and jogged across the street. He entered a narrow walkway between two brownstones. In no time at all, darkness swallowed him.

Jazmin's chin quivered. She stifled the urge to cry. A gust of wind swirled around her, and she tightened the belt on her sweater. A lump formed in her throat and saltwater stung her eyes. Her worst nightmare had come true. She bent at the waist and inhaled deeply. The milk and snickerdoodle cookies she and Destiny had made earlier for Santa threatened to reappear on the ground.

In through the nose. Out through the mouth. In through the nose. Lord, please help.

A throaty wail escaped as she reached back and gripped the cold railing. She sat down as the first convulsions began. Rocking back and forth, she wrapped her arms around her midsection. A passing car with its windows open and radio blaring informed everyone within earshot that the late-night on-air personality would take over after the commercial break. It was almost ten o'clock. After a few minutes, Jazmin stood. Carefully, she climbed the steps. Once inside her apartment, she headed down the hall to Destiny's room. Faint sounds of *It's A Wonderful Life* floated up from the basement. Jazmin stared at the sleeping little girl tucked in all the way up to her chin. Removing the phone from her back pocket, she thumbed a message to Reggie. She'd pay for his new studio space and equipment. Nothing more. He didn't deserve that much and she sure as hell wasn't going to give him cash. They would go to court in the New Year and he wouldn't protest her appeal for full custody.

Quietly, she closed her little cousin's bedroom door and then crossed the hall to her own room. With the back of her hand, she wiped away the tears that streamed down her cheeks. She walked to her closet and started pulling purses off the shelves. Over the years more than a dozen people had left notes or business cards on the Nova's windshield asking if the car was for sale. She'd always saved the inquires. She needed a safety net. Lawyer fees alone would drain her current checking account. Selling the car would provide a small cushion for her and Destiny to live off of if Reggie got slick. She sniffled and then straightened her spine. Wallowing was a luxury she didn't have and couldn't afford. She sat down in the middle of the pile of handbags and began methodically checking pockets.

She was a royal mess by the time Brenda found her forty-five minutes later. Jazmin sat cross-legged in a semi-circle of organized confusion. To her left lay scraps of paper and business cards, to her right were rolls of scotch tape and holiday wrapping paper. On her bed was a pile of shopping bags stuffed with toys and receipts. She looked up at her friend with tear-swollen eyes.

The color immediately drained from Brenda's face as she knelt beside Jazmin. "Stop," she commanded, softly.

Brenda smelled like cinnamon and vanilla extract. The scent was too close to home. Jazmin would give anything to be back in Michigan. She let go of her fancy ballpoint pen and sank against Brenda's chest.

"What's going on?"

Jazmin's shoulders shook. Brenda's fuzzy wool sweater muffled guttural moans.

"You're frightening me," Brenda said. "Please. Tell me what happened?"

Jazmin cried harder.

"Is it Micah?" Brenda patted her back. "I'll gas up the car. I think I saw some limes in the refrigerator and I'm sure you have extra-large trash bags. We can pick up a shovel on the way over to his place. He won't know what hit him."

Jazmin's sobs mixed with chuckles as she pulled away from her friend's embrace. "It's not Micah." She wiped her nose with the sleeve of her cardigan.

She then turned her gaze to a clump of carpeting. A blotch of pink nail polish had dried together. "It's over between us."

Brenda sat back on her haunches. "Okay."

"He popped up at the photoshoot."

Brenda blew out a breath.

Looking up, Jazmin added, "It gets worse."

By the time she'd finished the story, Brenda paced back and forth beside the bed. "What the hell is wrong with Reggie?" Brenda asked for the fifth time. "He thinks he can sell his daughter?" She flung a hand in Jazmin's direction. "You're okay with paying him off?"

"No. I'm not happy about any of this."

Jazmin had transitioned from the floor to the end of the bed. She felt a little lighter knowing she didn't have to shoulder this burden alone. "It's one way to get what I want, though. Paying him off and drawing up papers will only expedite the adoption process."

Brenda stopped pacing. Jazmin met her friend's gaze and shook her head, answering the unspoken question. Of course, Brenda pressed anyway.

"You need legal advice. Micah can help you."

Falling back onto a pillow, Jazmin closed her eyes. She envisioned being wrapped in Micah's strong arms.

"Once this Reggie business is done, everything will go back to normal. You'll see," she mumbled, struggling to fight back tears that refused to stop coming.

"What *normal* are you talking about? Working non-stop and flitting from one meaningless fling to the next? That's what you want to go back to?"

Without opening her eyes, Jazmin rose to the bait, "You're one to talk. You travel all the time. Who are you running from?"

The mattress dipped. Jazmin opened her eyes and sat up. She scooted over to make room.

"Maybe I'm running to someone," Brenda corrected. "Did you ever think of that? Maybe I continue to make this detour to Philly to check in on you and Dez."

Jazmin sighed heavily. "Please, don't let me hold you back. Go on. Live your best life."

"Don't worry, I'll be gone soon." Brenda sat with her back to her. "I took the job in New York. Rehearsals start on the seventh."

Jazmin felt as if she'd been slapped. "You're serious?"

"When you met Micah, you two seemed really happy. He put up with your craziness, which isn't easy." She looked over her shoulder. "I thought, 'finally, I can leave and know she'll be okay.' Destiny saved you from working nonstop. But Micah, he brought out the old you. The girl who stood upto her mom ten years ago. Whose light was blinding. I miss her."

Jazmin wiped away fresh tears. "I'm right here, y'know?

I'm not dead. Don't eulogize me yet."

Brenda clicked her tongue. "Then don't lay down and let this no-talent fool walk all over you."

Jazmin shook her head. "The stakes are too high. I can't risk losing Destiny."

Silence stretched between them. At last, Brenda responded. "I get it." She pulled Jazmin close. "I still think you should contact him."

"It's over." Jazmin rested her head on her friend's shoulder.

"Over-over? Or just sort-of over?"

"It's over-over," Jazmin said softly. A tear slid down her cheek.

Chapter Twenty-Nine

"What's up Frat?" Rhett asked, knocking on the outer office door.

Micah glanced up. Without answering, he dropped a carton of business cards into a trash bin. Micah could feel Rhett's eyes on him. He went back to emptying the contents of his desk drawer without saying a word. He'd come in early on a Saturday to avoid this very interaction. If the masking tape around Rhett's wrist and the stack of unfolded file boxes leaning against the glass door were any indication, Rhett had picked today to move out of the associates' office suite.

"Congratulations are in order, I hear," Rhett said.

Micah didn't feel like listening to him gloat. The jerk had gotten the promotion even though Stein, Martin, and Randolph had chosen one of the image consultants Micah had suggested as an alternative to J.J. The day after the announcement, Micah turned in his resignation.

He added a stapler to the box of office supplies he planned on keeping. Rhett stepped over the threshold but didn't come farther in.

Smart man.

"I'm sorry things didn't work out with you and your lady."

Micah flexed his sore knuckles. He had nothing to lose and wouldn't mind teaching Rhett an old-fashioned lesson with an ass whooping. Yet, instead of goading him, Rhett frowned.

"I talked to some of her clients, at least the ones who would take my calls. They were impressed."

"She's good at her job," Micah replied.

"Funny thing," Rhett looked around the room.

Micah ground his teeth. Jazmin was the best in the business. That was the whole reason the partners wanted her help. The last thing he needed right now was to listen to whatever salacious gossip Rhett had uncovered. The longer he stalled, however, the more Micah wanted to know what he'd found out. Finally, the pain-in-the-ass looked up. Micah hated that he'd held his breath in anticipation.

"I'm sure you know that J.J. worked with a lot of old heads."

Micah straightened his spine and leaned forward in his office chair. When looking into Jazmin's background he had pretty much discovered the same thing.

Her clientele consisted of green entrepreneurs along with men in their late sixties or older.

"They all talked about her with fierce loyalty. And not one person commented on her figure, or the smell of her perfume, or the way she walked. Not one." Rhett nodded as if preaching to twelve jurors. "That says a lot." He tossed Micah the roll of tape at the same time he pushed off from the wall. "Will I see you tonight at poker?"

Micah shook his head. He had no plans of driving to New York this evening. He'd also been impressed with J.J.'s resume and bootstrap determination. Still, he had judged Jazmin Johnson from the minute they met and even after he learned her identity. While she had worked her butt off and established a decent professional reputation for herself, both he and Rhett had benefited from their fathers' influence. Micah sobered. Although he didn't know all the details, he knew how difficult it had been for Jazmin when she'd lost her mother's approval. She'd worked hard and came out on top, tougher than ever.

As Rhett turned to leave, he threw another curve ball Micah's way. "Tell Adam I said congrats. You two make a good team. I'm hoping we don't meet on opposite sides of the bench."

Micah listened to his footsteps fade and when he couldn't hear them anymore, he sat back in his chair. Outside the office door, Rhett had left the unfolded cardboard boxes. Micah shuffled through the clutter on his desk until he located his phone. He dialed Adam.

"We need to talk," he said when the prerecorded voicemail directions ended.

Micah ran a hand over his face. This was the first of two hard conversations he would inevitably have. He dreaded the call he'd have to make to his father.

A little over an hour later, Micah and his regular car share driver, Brent, headed back to his condo. Traffic moved smoothly through Center City. He'd asked Brent to take the long way, past Jazmin's place. He hoped to catch a glimpse of her. During one of his midmorning runs he swore, he'd heard her voice in the distance. He'd almost gotten run over when he dashed across the street without looking.

"Slow down," he told Brent as they turned onto her block.

The Nova was parked out front, but the porch light was off. A For Sale sign in the driver's side window caught Micah's attention. Alarm bells rang in his ears. He couldn't think of a scenario in which she would willingly sell the car that she and her dad had started building together.

Destiny.

Micah said a silent prayer.

"Pull over!"

Brent expertly maneuvered to the shoulder of the road, but before he had a chance to put the car in park, Micah had yanked on the door handle. In a flash, he ran across the street. Horns blared when he darted between two moving cars. He could only imagine what Jazmin would think of him coming over uninvited. He mentally prepared himself for a barrage of angry words. Brenda opened the door instead of Jazmin. When she saw that it was him, her posture relaxed and the worry lines on her forehead and at the corners of her eyes smoothed out. The two of them had come a long way since their first meeting. Brenda stepped forward and the security door closed behind her with a thud.

Chapter Thirty

Jazmin's head fell back as she laughed. Pops had called "bullshit" on one of Vicki's stories. He insisted she'd made up the whole thing. While teaching Hector and Destiny how to play tonk, Vicki had casually revealed she'd been a high-stakes gambler. Vicki shared stories about her life every so often. Apparently, she'd made a fortune in Vegas before she'd been run out of town.

"You ain't never laid eyes on no Sammy Davis Jr.," Pops argued.

"Sam was on the run from the mob and needed to get hitched quick," Vicki said, laying down two cards. "I'd seen him cruising the Strip with King Cohn's girl, Kim. I slammed the door in his face. I'm no fool."

Pops set three cards face up on the table. "You'z a fool if you think I believe your jabbering."

Vicki shrugged her shoulders and then tossed out her remaining cards. She lovingly pinched Destiny's cheek. Pops grumbled and snatched a card from the deck.

"That's how you win, baby doll," she told Destiny.

Vicki had closed up the shop early and invited everyone over for a pre-New Year's Eve party. Brenda had stayed back at the apartment. She said she needed to pack for New York. Jazmin hoped the countdown-to-noon celebration followed by a six o'clock fireworks display at Penn's Landing would tucker Destiny out. Vicki and Pops had graciously agreed to babysit while she attended tonight's gala. Jazmin didn't need the little girl pestering the older couple as they tried to enjoy their evening.

Brenda had opted out of attending the gala as Jazmin's guest. She'd declared that she wouldn't be anyone's plus-one who she couldn't bed after midnight. She refused to reveal her plans beyond that. As a result, Jazmin was left to face Micah Clarion alone. She was positive he'd be in attendance. He would probably accompany Eleanor Deerfield, who was *the* black society socialite.

Jazmin had done a thorough internet search on Micah's ex-girlfriend after their first meeting at the Caribbean restaurant. Eleanor Deerfield had graduated with honors from the University of Pennsylvania. After graduation, she had modeled for a bit. Then, she attended Wharton School of Business. Rather than work for some Fortune 500 company, she started a home décor and organizing business. According to her website, she had a Rolodex of A-list clients. Included among them were models, wives of Major League Baseball players, and several professional singers. Eleanor Deerfield had branded herself and carved out a space in a niche industry, just like Jazmin had.

Jazmin blew out a sigh that made her lips vibrate. She patted her hair with the heel of her hand. She'd gotten her hair braided the night before and her scalp was still screaming. The braiders knew how to twist every strand of hair into a braid. She rose slowly and then crossed the showroom. If she planned to mingle with members of Philadelphia's Black elite, she needed to begin putting on her armor. She kissed Pops on the cheek and hugged Vicki and Hector. After swinging Destiny around in a circle until the little girl burst into a fit of giggles and promised to be a good listener, Jazmin was out the door.

The wind whipped against her face. She walked faster. She had stopped driving the Nova as much as possible once she'd begun talking to interested buyers. The person she'd settled on had offered her more than what she'd asked, and way more than the car's Blue Book price. Accordingly, she wanted to prevent additional wear on the interior and exterior. She'd paid for a professional deep cleaning in order to get out the barbeque sauce and chicken nugget stains left behind by Destiny. Yesterday, she transferred the title to the new owner. She delivered the keys by courier to his business. A truck would arrive in a few days to transport the Nova to a storage unit outside the city. The buyer had connections with Simeone Foundation Automotive Museum. He planned to store the car at one of the Museum's garages for the winter. She was happy about that. She'd hate to see a stranger cruising in her car while she tramped and bused around the city.

While waiting for the light to change at the intersection of Broad and South Streets, Jazmin watched a car-share driver zoom by. The driver reminded her of Micah's friend, Brent. For some reason, she had thought she'd feel better by now. She had never been the brooding type after a breakup. Then again, she was usually the heartbreaker. With Micah, it felt as if they'd both lost. She missed him. They'd gone their separate ways after the conversation at the park. That was nine days ago. Not like she was counting. The light changed and she plodded on. When she rounded the corner onto her block and neared her brownstone, she noticed a figure sitting on her steps.

Reggie?

If he kept this up, she was going to have to file for a protective order. She planned on renewing her membership at the shooting range. She and her sister had grown up around folks who hunted for sport. They had also been taught how to respect and handle firearms from an early age. As she drew nearer, she realized the person wasn't Reggie at all.

"Rose Mary?"

Her sister looked up and the happy recognition in her brown eyes mirrored Jazmin's.

"Took you long enough," Rose Mary said, standing. "Who else were you expecting?"

Jazmin rushed forward and almost sent her older sister tumbling backward. Burrowing her face into her sister's shoulder, Jazmin smiled as she inhaled. Rose Mary smelled woodsy with a little fresh baked bread mixed in.

"Didn't Brenda tell you I was coming?"

Jazmin shook her head. Happy tears rolled down her cheeks. "That bitch. Wait until I see her." She laughed.

Pulling back, Rose Mary examined Jazmin's face. She brushed away tears with her gloved fingers. "It looks like we've got a lot to talk about, brat."

Jazmin's smile widened at the pet name Rose Mary had bestowed on her when she was in kindergarten. It was short for bratwurst. It was the only food Jazmin wanted for lunch for a whole year after attending her first Octoberfest.

Rose Mary squeezed Jazmin's shoulder. "Brenda filled me in on the Reggie situation. I'm sorry. I should've listened to you."

"I don't even care about that anymore."

Jazmin realized she meant it. Reggie would always be Reggie. Once she'd had time to digest the situation, she'd made peace with the cards she'd been dealt. His ultimatum wasn't ideal, but it was a means to an end.

"What is it? No offense, but you look awful."

Jazmin hiccuped as a laugh escaped. "A boy."

"A *boy*?"

Tears continued to stream down Jazmin's face. "I'm in love with a boy who hates me." It was the first time she had allowed herself to say those words aloud or to even think them. She loved Micah.

Rose Mary squinted at her. "You didn't try to cook for him, did you?"

She grinned and shoved her sister playfully. "No."

The sun had moved from behind a cloud. Although it was chilly because of the wind, the sunlight warmed Jazmin's cheeks and her sister showing up had brightened her spirits.

"God, I missed you!"

"Let's go inside where it's warm. You can fill me in on why this boy hates you."

Rose Mary looped her arm through one of Jazmin's. With her free hand, she pulled a rolling suitcase.

Chapter Thirty-One

Micah patted his damp brow with a handkerchief. He saw Jazmin the minute she entered the hotel. She looked stunning in a beaded floor-length dress, as if she'd popped off the pages of *The Great Gatsby*. The gown clung to her curves and flared out at the bottom. He also liked her sexy new doo. The medium-size braids fell over her shoulders in waves before stopping just above the small of her back. She looked radiant under the ballroom's softened lighting and her diamond chandelier earrings sparkled. As she crossed the parquet floor, she drew the attention of several of the eligible bachelors in the room, and some married men too.

A large lump wedged itself in Micah's throat. He patted his forehead again. Across the room Rhett and his father eyed Jazmin. Glaring, the elder Randolph didn't hide his displeasure. The father and son duo had positioned themselves beside the coffee station alongside other lawyers and CEOs. Rhett acknowledged Micah with the tilt of his chin before he returned his attention to the conversations swirling around him. Micah didn't envy Rhett. No doubt his former co-worker was on the job. A few handshake deals would be made tonight. Micah's jitters returned as he watched Daniel Deerfield approach.

The older man clapped his hand on Micah's shoulder. "Good luck, son. You're up in five."

Micah nodded his head stiffly. Mr. Deerfield had allowed him to introduce this year's Millennial Titan recipient.

***

When the bathroom door slammed shut Jazmin had every intention of finishing her business and ignoring whoever had entered. That was until she heard a sniffle, followed by a hiccup, and then crying. Peeking through the gap in the door, she spotted a woman elegantly dressed in an emerald lace and tulle gown. The A-Line, one-shouldered number with its sweeping train, made her look like one of Destiny's storybook fairy princesses.

The woman talked on the phone via a Bluetooth earpiece. Her petite purse was too small to hold anything more than lipstick.

"I don't know what it is about him," she replied. "I always pick emotionally unavailable guys. I thought Micah was different."

Tossing her hair over her shoulder and out of the way, Jazmin leaned forward just as the woman turned to look into the spotlighted vanity mirror.

"When times were good, they were great." The woman tilted her head downward. "I know I push too hard—" she laughed softly at whatever comment the person on the other end of the line had made. "Okay, I can be batshit crazy."

The woman looked up, and Jazmin saw her face.

Eleanor.

Jazmin jerked back while mouthing silent expletives. On the other side of the stall, she heard the buzz of the automated hand towel dispenser. Leaning forward again, she stared through the gap between the door and the stall wall.

Eleanor blotted her rouged face as she sniffled and cleared her throat loudly. "You don't get it. My mother swears I'm defective because I'm not married with kids already. As if an M.R.S. is a degree."

Was it ridiculous to stand on the toilet seat like they did in rom-com movies so her feet wouldn't be visible?

Jazmin shook her head. It probably wasn't a good idea, especially not with her inclination toward clumsiness. She might fall in.

"I was so lonely when Micah and I met. My grandfather had just passed and less than a week or two later Daddy was diagnosed with cancer. Dating Micah was a welcome distraction and Daddy liked him so much."

Eleanor crumpled a couple of tissues and lobbed the ball into a nearby trash bin. "I miss being with someone, companionship, you know?"

Jazmin couldn't stay in the bathroom all night.

"I'm pathetic," Eleanor drawled.

Taking a deep breath, Jazmin pushed down on the toilet handle with her foot. She stepped out. Their eyes met in the mirror. Eleanor's shock promptly turned to an icy stare.

"You're not pathetic," Jazmin said, walking forward.

"Charlotte, I've got to go." Eleanor tapped a button on her earpiece.

Taking up a position at the sink beside her, Jazmin washed her hands.

"Go on, say it," Eleanor instructed.

Jazmin looked at her in the mirror. "What is it you think I want to say?"

Eleanor sucked her teeth. "You won, alright?"

Jazmin shook her head. Micah hadn't so much as said hello or stood within six feet of her. The dinner dishes had been taken away and dessert eaten. The program was almost over. The last thing was for Eleanor's father, Daniel Deerfield, to present Jazmin with her award. She would give a short speech. Afterward, the men would loosen their ties and the women would kick off their shoes. Everyone would dance and drink their way into the new year. It hurt too much to be near Micah and have him ignore her. Jazmin planned to stay for an appropriate amount of time and then say her goodbyes and head home. She'd never been good at brushing elbows with high society, and she couldn't pretend tonight.

"You're wrong," Jazmin told Eleanor. Her shoulders slumped forward. "It's over between us."

Puffing out a breath, Eleanor placed one hand on her hip. She turned to face Jazmin head-on.

"Look," Jazmin began again, not backing down. "I overheard your call. I just wanted to tell you that you're not pathetic. You put yourself out there. You just didn't get the return on your investment you expected, as my sister would say."

"I think I would get along with your sister."

Jazmin mumbled to herself, "Probably. You both are wound pretty tight."

Eleanor arched an eyebrow. A beat passed and then her lip curved up at the corner, creating a tiny smirk. "I'm sorry for my bad behavior."

Jazmin accepted the small peace offering with a nod. Ellie collected her clutch and walked to the door. She paused.

"In case you haven't noticed, Micah is in love with you."

Jazmin opened her mouth to refute the claim but then thought better. She kept her trap shut.

"He's been watching you all night. He was never that way with me. While he can be as stubborn as a mule sometimes, he never stays mad long. I hope you two work things out."

Speechless, Jazmin just stared.

As Ellie exited, Rose Mary entered. She held together the two halves of her slinky black dress. She had balked at wearing the strapless gown because of the thigh-high slit, but it was the only thing in Jazmin's closet that fit.

"Excuse me," she said to Ellie and then turned to Jazmin.

"Hurry up. They're waiting on you to take your seat."

Jazmin quickly dried her hands and followed Rose Mary out of the restroom. Applause erupted as the two sisters came into view. Jazmin flashed a plastic smile. The uproar of clapping drowned out the clicking of their heels on the wood floor as they rushed to their table. Once they were seated, Micah strolled to the podium. A shocked Jazmin barely registered the feel of Rose Mary's pointy elbow digging into her side.

"That's him?"

"Uh huh."

"Does he have any brothers?" Rose Mary asked, playfully.

She'd strung her words together with a familiar whimsical midwestern drawl.

"Four, I think. There's a sister too. Younger."

While Jazmin felt the breeze created by Rose Mary fanning herself, she couldn't unglue her gaze from Micah. He looked stunning in his black tuxedo.

"All that fineness ... and he's got brothers. I might have to stay out here a while longer."

Jazmin looked back at her sister. She couldn't hide her shocked expression. "Cross your legs and keep your panties on," she said, grinning.

Rose Mary leaned in close and covered her mouth with her hand as she spoke into Jazmin's ear. "Look who's talking." She handed her a napkin. "You've got a little drool on your chin." Jazmin elbowed her sister in the side, but Rose Mary's giggles didn't fade.

Chapter Thirty-Two

Micah gripped the sides of the podium with clammy hands. Removing a handkerchief from his pocket he patted his palms dry and then wiped the sweat from his brow. He scanned the ballroom until his eyes found Jazmin's. He noted how her breath hitched and the color drained from her face.

"Good evening." He cleared his throat. "Good evening," he repeated.

Murmurs of "good evening" echoed throughout the room.

"My name is Micah Clarion. I have the pleasure of introducing our Millennial Titan. This month I've gotten to know Ms. Johnson personally."

The woman seated next to Jazmin squeezed her hand. Surprisingly, Brenda wasn't Jazmin's plus-one. He wondered about this but was grateful she hadn't brought another man. Perhaps, there was a chance what he was about to do would work.

"I won't go into details, but I can tell you our first encounter was unusual to say the least." He watched

Jazmin's cheeks flush. "From that day forward, it seemed as if I put my foot in my mouth again and again, or simply made an ass of myself." Micah waited until the laughs quieted before he continued. He leaned forward and lowered his voice as if he were going to reveal a secret to the crowd. "I agreed to a dance-off against a three-year-old and embarrassed myself badly. I may be able to Chicago step, but the 'Tooty Ta'.... Let's just say, I failed."

The eyes of the mothers in attendance flashed with humor.

"Being around Ms. Johnson is like meeting your favorite celebrity or sports idol. Your brain shuts off. I think most of us in this room can attest to how talented Ms. Johnson is. We know she received accolades in her late teens and early twenties that many twice her age will never see in their lifetime."

He began listing the awards Jazmin had won while still an undergraduate at Temple University. The audience nodded their heads and clapped when he turned the page of his speech and continued reading off her achievements. Dramatically, he paused to catch his breath.

"We'll be here all night," Micah joked, reaching for the bottle of water that rested on the podium. He took a small sip.

"There is more to Jazmin Johnson than you can read in tech magazines and newspaper clippings. She's kindhearted. She volunteers in her community and actively seeks out changes to things others would pass by. Ms. Johnson doesn't wait for the city to clean up the vacant lot next to a park. Instead, she gathers rakes and trash bags and knocks on her neighbors' doors. She has helped to create multiple community flower gardens throughout South Philly."

Micah once again waited for the applause to die down. "Did I mention, she's funny as hell and a fierce feminist? Brothers, you don't want to be on the wrong side of an argument with her. Trust me. She will let you know where you and your wrong backside can go."

He noted that Jazmin's guest nodded her head in agreement. The two women shared the same smile and warm brown eyes.

"I, of course, didn't know any of this when I first met her. How could I? I had my ego blinding me. My pride and arrogance along with my own agenda held me back from being able to see beyond her beauty."

Micah paused. He made sure his voice held the conviction he felt. "I misjudged you, Jazmin. Crazy enough, you gave me another chance and then another after that."

Mr. Deerfield appeared at the side of the stage. He carried an oversized cardboard check. Two hundred fifty thousand dollars scrawled on it. He inclined his head encouragingly and mouthed the words "go on." Taking a steadying breath, Micah stepped forward and walked down the steps of the stage. All eyes tracked him as he headed in Jazmin's direction. He stopped just in front of her chair and handed her a plaque. The applause thundered for so long that Micah had to wave a hand in the air to settle the crowd.

"Some of you may already know that J.J. calls Philadelphia and the east coast home. What you might not know is that Jazmin Johnson is from Michigan. That means she's tough. Her spirit doesn't cower in the harshest of circumstances and she is passionate beyond belief. I came to know that person during these past few weeks and I fell in love with her."

There was an audible sigh throughout the room. "You deserve this award, baby. But you also stole my heart."

Lowering to one knee, he reached in his pocket and pulled out a large rectangular velvet box about the size of a candy bar. He tilted the microphone away and whispered. "I'm sorry." He motioned for her to take the gift.

Wide-eyed, she looked around the room. A cameraman streamed video of the two of them on the ballroom walls.

Her sister, Micah presumed, nudged her. "Take it," she whispered.

Jazmin took the box and removed the lid. Upon seeing its contents, her mouth formed the shape of the letter O. She pressed one hand against her chest. Her fingers trailed over a set of car keys.

Murmured whispers grew louder throughout the room as people asked about the contents of the box. Jazmin held the keys high in the air. Although tears pooled in her eyes, she grinned.

Micah raised his voice. "She's got gasoline in her blood, folks."

"I sold the Nova because I needed money," she said to the woman beside her. "He bought the car."

Her sister's fingers latched onto the tiny pink pearls around her neck. Her eyes flashed with disbelief and then they overflowed with joy. She swiped away tears.

Micah removed a smaller box from the inside pocket of his suit jacket. An eerie calm settled over the room.

"Jazmin Johnson, will you make me the happiest man alive and agree to be my wife?"

Jazmin's sister's hands flew to her mouth. Meanwhile, Jazmin leaned forward and, reaching up, cradled the sides of his head with her hands. Her lips covered his. Rowdy applause and cheers filled the room. Micah barely heard a thing. It felt as if he had cotton stuck in his ears. Or like he was swimming underwater. All he could hear was Jazmin's tiny voice.

"Yes."

Chapter Thirty-Three

Jazmin opened her eyes and then stretched. Her limbs entangled in Micah's wine-colored silk satin sheets. A sliver of sunlight streamed in between the curtains. It cast tiny rainbows on Micah's dresser and chest of drawers. Her thoughts drifted back to last night's gala. Never in a million years had she thought she would find her happily-ever-after prince. Sure, they had some things to work out. But Micah had assured her there was no rush. They could have as long an engagement as she wanted. She opened her eyes and instinctively rubbed her thumb against the halo ring with a two-carat oval cut diamond. She heard the shower turned off in the adjacent bathroom. Shortly after, Micah stepped out. A dark grey towel wrapped around his torso.

Her eyes widened as her gaze traveled down the length of him. The towel tented in response to her appraisal. Micah stalked toward her, stepping over his slacks which lay crumpled in a ball in the middle of the floor. Her dress rested nearby. As he approached, she inched backward into a seated position. Her back pressed against the headboard. She distinctively remembered clutching the frame at some point during the night as she ground herself against Micah's face. He discarded the towel and the mattress dipped under his weight as he settled on the bed. His eyes blazed with passion. The smell of mint shampoo filled the air around them. He took hold of her ankles and playfully yanked her forward. Jazmin emitted a tiny squeal of delight.

"I love you," he said, covering the length of her body with his torso.

He kissed her roughly and Jazmin moaned into his mouth. They both seemed insatiable since leaving the gala after-party. She reached up and placed one hand on Micah's chest. She groped his firm ass with the other. She squeezed it and then flicked her wrist, smacking one cheek possessively. He sucked in a sharp breath. Tilting her chin, Jazmin captured an erect nipple between her teeth. He had to peel her hand from his chest. He stretched her arms above her head. Pinned in place, she grinned. She enjoyed Micah taking the dominant role.

In and out. Micah thrusted. Each time, he went deeper. She thought things couldn't possibly feel any better and then he shifted his weight and rotated his hips. She cried out as he pounded against her G spot. Wanting even more, she wrapped her legs around his waist. Soon Micah's rhythm became rushed and sporadic. He unpinned her arms and placed her legs over his shoulders. Jazmin splintered a part. He followed closely behind.

Minutes later, a twangy ringtone pulled Jazmin out of her haze. She wiped her hand over her face. Micah kissed her on the forehead and then collapsed beside her. His breathing labored.

"I should get that. It might be Vicki. She and Pops are watching Destiny," Jazmin explained.

She leaned over the edge of the bed, pushing aside the braids that had fallen like a curtain over her face. She spied her phone inside one of her pumps. The other shoe's heel caught on the strap of her bra. Unfortunately, the caller was Reggie. Jazmin sent the call to voicemail.

"Is that Destiny's dad?" Micah asked.

Jazmin pulled herself upright. "Yes."

She rested the phone face up on the nightstand before scooting backward. Micah pulled her close. He placed one arm around her and she relaxed immediately. His warmth mingled with the scent of fresh soap and mint shampoo. The smell calmed her nerves.

"How can I help?"

Jazmin turned on her side to look at him. "I just want this mess to be over. I wish I could find Cicely."

"Who?"

"Destiny's mom, my cousin." His brows furrowed. "You thought—" Jazmin sighed.

Then and there, she made the decision to trust Micah. If he thought differently of her or her family, so be it. She'd picked herself up before. She could do it again. Jazmin sat up and scooted out of his embrace. He propped her bare feet on his lap and began to knead her soles. She wiggled her feet away from his reach.

"I can't focus if you do that."

Micah placed his hands in his lap. He laced his fingers together. "Okay, I'm listening."

"Reggie and I dated briefly when I first arrived at Temple. I thought he was the sun, and the moon, and the stars. I was young and naïve. He moved in on my cousin Cicely after we broke up."

Micah's face remained neutral as Jazmin talked However, she noticed him rubbing his thumb against his sports ring, winding it around his finger. Jazmin placed her hand atop his.

"Cicely got pregnant and then took off a year or so after Destiny was born."

"Wow. That's a lot."

"You're telling me. I haven't heard from her in months. Destiny will be four in June. Reggie's back and wants his daughter. But in reality, he wants my money."

"Brenda told me that part," Micah said.

Jazmin wasn't surprised. Her bestie had been close-mouthed since their heart-to-heart on Christmas Eve.

"Where's the last place your cousin lived?"

"Atlanta. But who knows where she is now? Over the summer, Brenda checked the local hotspots and recording venues. All were dead ends."

"One of my older brothers, the sports contract lawyer, works in Atlanta. Sometimes he has to hire private investigators to look into players' wives or girlfriends to make sure his clients don't end up paying child support for kids who aren't theirs. I'll call him up and see if he can help us locate your cousin."

"Really?"

"Of course. We're a team." Micah captured her lips.

She pulled back. "I just thought..." her voice trailed off. It had been a long time since she relied on someone other than Brenda, Vicki, or Pops. Her heart swelled at the realization that she could let her guard down with Micah.

"You thought, what?" he pressed. "That I would think badly of you or your cousin?" He sighed. "All families have their thing. I'm sorry I came off so holier-than-thou."

The familiar butterflies had returned and were flapping enthusiastically against Jazmin's rib cage.

"I love you," she said.

"I love you too, sweetheart." He brushed a small kiss across her lips. "I want you and Destiny to stay here. I don't like this guy making threats about snatching Destiny."

She studied his eyes. He was serious. Jazmin's heart swelled. "Me either," she said softly.

Micah's phone rang just as he opened his mouth to say more on the subject. Jazmin reached for his cell which sat beside hers on the nightstand. As she handed it to him, she saw the caller was his mom.

He tapped the phone screen. "Happy New Year," he said with moderate enthusiasm.

Jazmin took note of the worried lines under his eyes. They hadn't been there earlier. Not even as she recounted her time with Reggie. She shifted her body, hanging her legs off the edge of the bed. She attempted to get up to give Micah some privacy, but he placed a hand on her hip.

"Stay, please," he whispered.

Jazmin could hear his mother's shrill voice. "Micah, how could you embarrass us like that? I had to hear it from—"

"Mom, I'm putting you on speakerphone. There's someone I want to introduce you to," he cut her off. He pulled the phone back from his ear and placed it between him and Jazmin.

"Whhaat?" Mrs. Clarion stuttered.

"Is dad there? Ask him to pick up the upstairs phone. I want him to hear this too."

A beat later a rumbly voice joined the call. "What's this all about?" Micah's dad asked.

"Happy New Year," Micah repeated.

This time he squeezed Jazmin's hand. She rubbed the pad of her thumb over his knuckles. They were a team. Just like he'd said.

"I wanted you to hear it from me first. I met someone and I've asked her to marry me."

"Hello," Jazmin said. Her voice held a tremor of uncertainty.

She heard his mother groan in the background. Rather than respond, Micah held her hand tighter. After a few anxious beats, he continued.

"Mom, she's smart and funny, and beautiful. She makes me happy. We're the perfect match."

"He embarrassed poor Eleanor," his mother complained. Her voice sounded farther away as if she placed a hand over the mouthpiece.

"Paige Deerfield says she's as black as midnight. What was he thinking? Talk some sense into your son, George."

Jazmin's stomach dropped. She expected a little chastisement about having never met her, but she didn't think his mother would be put off by her coloring. Micah pulled Jazmin closer.

"Listen, please. I don't want to say this more than once. Jazmin Johnson is going to be my wife. She is going to be my partner through the good times and through the bad times, until I leave this earth. She will also be the mother of your grandbabies."

"Is she pregnant? Is that why you did this?" his mother asked.

Micah ignored her. "I love you both dearly, but God gave me one life to live. I'll be damned if I waste any more time putting other people's expectations and idiotic ideas ahead of mine."

"Wait just one minute," his father said, his voice rising with anger.

Jazmin sat back and nuzzled against Micah's bare chest. Although he ran his hands up and down her arm, anxiety had overtaken her calm reserve.

"I'm not finished, Pops." Micah's tone was ice cold. "I won't be starting a firm with Adam. I have no desire to continue practicing contract law."

Jazmin's eyes widened.

"My heart has never been in it," he whispered.

She understood. He needed to find his way. Returning his attention to his parents, he continued his speech.

"I'm not sure what my next move will be. I have a few interviews lined up next week."

"You're throwing all your hard work out the window. She must have the apple Eve gave Adam between her thighs because she's got you—"

"Enough!"

Jazmin jumped. She landed on his lap. Micah held her tighter.

"I won't have you, or Mom, or anyone disrespecting my wife. I'm not asking for your permission."

He took several calming breaths and then closed his eyes. Several seconds that felt like hours passed until finally Jazmin heard his heartbeat slow.

"I apologize for yelling," he said to his parents.

Maybe he said it to her. Jazmin wasn't sure. He rubbed her back, making small circles with the palms of his hands. Although neither of his parents commented, Jazmin assumed they were still on the line because she hadn't heard the telltale click followed by a dial tone. An awkward silence filled the bedroom. It probably stretched through the phone lines and traveled from Philadelphia to Chicago.

"I called to tell you *our* good news," he said.

"I look forward to meeting you both." Jazmin made her voice sound as cheery as possible to dissolve some of the tension. "I have family in Michigan, not even three hours from Chicago. I don't get home often but I'd like to remedy that."

Micah's dad grumbled. Since he hadn't outright ignored her, she held a sliver of hope that he'd come around. Micah's mom, however, didn't say anything. Micah leaned forward and kissed Jazmin's exposed collarbone. She mewled softly as his circling hands traveled to her chest. He stroked one taut nipple. It quickly came to life.

"We're going to go now," he told his parents. "I love you both."

Micah ended the phone call without saying good-bye. Ripples of pleasure traveled the length of Jazmin's spine. The pleasure intensified when the bedsheet she was still wrapped in moved against the strained points. Micah tossed his cell aside and then laid her back across the bed. He stretched out on top of her, balancing on his forearms. He was careful not to burden her with too much of his weight. Slowly, he unwrapped her from her satin cocoon.

ABOUT THE AUTHOR

C. Rose Dahl

An American storyteller, C. Rose Dahl fell in love with romance novels at an early age. Her experiences living in Philadelphia, where she worked as a high school Spanish teacher, inspired her to write her debut novel, Love, Rebooted. An enthusiastic solo traveler, she enjoys summers on the road, seeing sights like the clear blue waters of La Playa Ocean Park in San Juan, Puerto Rico. She currently lives in Delaware with her two children, a son and a daughter.